Dear Felicia.

Lots[illegible]

MADE IN L.A.

MADE IN L.A.

Vol. 3: Art of Transformation

MADE IN L.A.
Vol. 3: Art of Transformation

Third Annual Anthology

Cover design by Allison Rose

Visit Made in L.A. Writers online at
www.madeinlawriters.com

ISBN: 978-0-9987607-8-0
Library of Congress Control Number: 2020904339

Published by Resonant Earth Publishing
on behalf of
Made in L.A. Writers
P.O. Box 50785
Los Angeles, CA 90050

CONTENTS

Introduction

INFAMY • Noriko Nakada 1
BOOTS • DC Diamondopolous 11
#MILLENNIALEXISTENTIALISM • Lenore Robinson 25
THE CITY • AP Thayer 35
TELL ME YOUR NAME • Roselyn Teukolsky 43
SHARK NEWS • Karter Mycroft 63
THE GOOD LIFE OF DUKE • Erik Gonzales-Kramer 93
TERMINAL FLIGHT • Barry Bergmann 109
EMPTY GLASS • Andrea Auten 139
ANGELS LIVE HERE • Nolan Knight 149
THE FORTUNE OF THE THREE AND THE KABUKI MASK • Sara Chisolm 165
UNWANTED GIFTS • AS Youngless 179
STAR CROSSED • Gabi Lorino 195
CALL US HOME • Cody Sisco 209
WE FOUND LOVE AS THE UNDEAD • Sara Chisolm 241
NIGHT OF FIRES • Allison Rose 259

Biographies 295
Made in L.A. Writers 301
Acknowledgments 303

CONTENTS

INTRODUCTION

Manhattan is the city that never sleeps. Tokyo has an eye on the future. Paris is the embodiment of love. But few places in the world are defined by creative idealism quite like Los Angeles. To outsiders, L.A. is synonymous with Hollywood, a place that is not a city but a neighborhood, seen as more of an ethos than an actual location. This ambiguous metropolis, the center of the film and entertainment industry, has pumped out fictional escapism for generations, yet seldom has the lens focused with authenticity or honesty on the point of origin.

Artists and creative folk come from all over the world with the hopes of capturing the magic, yet those of us who call Los Angeles home know that the real magic of this city is not its ability to put fabricated realities on screen. The city's alchemy is its diverse composition: blood and bones, a vast expanse and variety of landscapes, the blending and remixing of cultures — these create the ever-changing soul of L.A.

This place, rich with history, refuses to become ordinary. By design, greater L.A. ranges across valleys and hills, and is surrounded by a mountain range, a desert, and an ocean. A river runs through it, sometimes wild, sometimes bounded by concrete, brimming with flood waters when the rains come, and trickling in times of drought. L.A.'s unique structure weaves through our lives like the freeways weave our paths, ensuring no two experiences are created in quite the same way.

Every contributor to the third annual *Made in L.A.* anthology has their own story to tell, hewn from unique experiences living and working here. Each author's perspective is singular and can be influenced by how long they have resided in L.A., in which neighborhood they set down their roots, what family cultures and histories they have melded with their present. One writer's "story of Los Angeles" about the struggles of the unhoused is different from another's tale of an immigrant family in wartime. Coastal dwellers illustrate a narrative distinct from those of young transplants further inland. A local's definition of L.A. depends entirely on the person — a phenomenon that is meant to be celebrated.

Our goal for this anthology series is to paint a fresher and more complete picture of how Los Angeles looks and feels from the inside. The unexpected beauty of this book is that even those of us who are fortunate enough to live in L.A. have been gifted stories from a point of view we may have never considered. Each tale told from someone else's vantage point is like another piece of the greater puzzle that evolves our own knowledge of the city. The mix of stories expands our perspective and love of this place we call home, enriches our own inner transformation, and influences how we define ourselves as Angelenos.

Made in L.A.: Art of Transformation isn't so much a collection of stories set in a location but a love letter to one of the greatest cities in the world, one that invites, or forces, its inhabitants to transform with it. We hope you enjoy reading our tales of Los Angeles as much as we enjoyed crafting them.

— Allison Rose

INFAMY

Noriko Nakada

It is a beautiful winter morning in Los Angeles. The sky is painted a clear, bright blue, and a breeze blows in from the coast. It's the kind of day that makes those who listen to the Rose Parade radio broadcast pack up and move west. It's cold in the shade but warm in puddles of sunshine.

All of the occupants of the Nakamura Boarding House attended morning services: the Yamasaki brothers went to the Japanese Buddhist Temple, while the Nakamuras and other boarders made their way to the Japanese United Methodist Church. Now they are all home. The Nakamura family and the boarders relax in their rooms, and the house sits in relative quiet. Natasha works on a sketch for Hiro's birthday. The loose lines of her oldest brother in his football uniform aren't turning out right, though, so she crumples it in her fist before starting on a fresh sheet. She works on a still life of a football and helmet, the figure "24" in the background, until her mother calls her to the kitchen to help with the birthday celebration preparations.

In the kitchen, Natasha's mother stirs thick cake batter with a wooden spoon while the familiar bounce of a basketball echoes from the driveway. The cake is vanilla, her oldest son's favorite, not the chocolate one she makes for Mas or the strawberry that is Natasha's favorite. For Hiro, it is vanilla with lemon frosting.

Natasha's father takes his tea in the living room, switches on the radio, and dreams of tomorrow. The day has finally come when he will be able to turn their savings into something real. He and Mitsue worked hard in their early years here, and she gave birth to a healthy baby boy, but with the Alien Land Act leaving them no prospects for owning property, they thought about returning to Japan. But their son was American, and when Mitsue got pregnant again, the dream of a return trip to Japan started to fade. In 1924, the United States passed new immigration quotas in the Asian Exclusion Act, and the Nakamuras considered themselves lucky to be in California. Their dream turned red, white, and blue with the birth of their second son, and they moved to the Sawtelle Nihonmachi to try their hands at running a boarding house and nursery.

New voices join the boys playing outside while Mitsue and Natasha prepare Hiro's birthday meal: teriyaki steak, inari sushi, and tsunemono salad. Natasha squeezes lemon quarters over warm rice and then glances out the window as Mas and Hiro and their friends choose teams in the driveway. Mas, the younger of the two, has mostly friends who are Japanese with a few others thrown in, while Hiro's friends are white with a few Japanese thrown in. Natasha loads rice into the tofu pockets and keeps score in her head. She hopes Hiro will win, even though he rarely beats Mas at anything these days. After all, it is his birthday and he's older.

With the first knock at the front door, Natasha's parents greet the party guests as she finishes plating the inari and teriyaki. She pulls the tsunemono from the fridge as voices filter in. The Hiromuras, friends from church who live up in the Palisades, arrive with their oldest son, Sat. He is a classmate of Natasha's, one of those boys who was there when she snuck away to the beach with Andy this past summer. Sat finds her in the kitchen.

"Wow, Nat, I had no idea you could actually cook." He snatches up the football-shaped inari and shoves it in his mouth. "Good to see you finally acting like a girl."

"No one will ever believe you," Natasha says as she dries her hands and pulls her apron over her head. She hands Sat the tsunemono and carries the inari and teriyaki outside to a table beneath the magnolia tree. She smooths the tablecloth, shoos a fly away from the cake, and then heads down the driveway as the adults start eating in the shade. The high school boys finish their game and load up their plates.

Natasha's best friend, Andy, makes his way across the street toward the Nakamura Boarding House, but before Natasha can say hello, Mr. Matsumoto, the owner of a nursery up the street, sprints past them and into the back yard, yelling for Natasha's father. "The radio, Tosh-san! *Tsukeru*!"

Natasha follows Mr. Matsumoto to the back of the house where plates are piled high with food, but the whole party stops eating and stares at Mr. Matsumoto.

"*Radio o tsukeru*, Tosh-san," he says. "*Karera wa kogeki shite iru.*"

ℴ

At first the radio is not much help, but then news flashes begin to confirm Mr. Matsumoto's report. Japanese bombers have attacked the American naval base at Pearl Harbor.

Guests grow quiet; hands cover mouths. Breaths are silent, and people whisper Japanese translations of the newscast to one another. Then, one by one, the guests begin to leave. Minds buzz with foreign words: "air strike," "surprise attack," "war." Each individual tries to calculate what this news could mean for themselves, for their families, for the Nihonmachi, for the country.

"I'll see you tomorrow," Andy says, suddenly feeling his whiteness. Natasha gives him a nod that sends him on his way.

The basketball players are listening, too, and immediately a gulf opens up between the Japanese players and the white ones. At first, the white boys aren't sure what the big deal is. Until they go home to their families, who will tell them what to think about the attack and the Japanese, there is only confusion.

Party guests leave, but the ten residents of the Nakamura Boarding House gather around the radio in the living room, still in their Sunday clothes, shifting in their seats as they listen.

A Japanese air attack.

Hawaii.

Oahu.

Honolulu.

Pearl Harbor.

Mass hysteria.

Destruction.

It is hard to imagine an island paradise engulfed by flames.

As the attack comes into sharper focus, as the sun sets on the Sawtelle Nihonmachi and leads into night, the glances around the room become more worried, more concerned. There is already talk of seizing Japanese-owned property in America. There is talk of removal. Broadcasters let the West Coast know they are under mandatory blackout and police are sent into Little Tokyo and West L.A., where concentrated groups of Japanese live, to keep an eye out. They don't say the Sawtelle Nihonmachi, but when Mas pulls back the curtain on the corner of Missouri and Corinth, he sees an empty street except for a patrol car passing by, sweeping its light into the darkness. Exactly what the police are keeping an eye out for is not clear, but nothing is clear to anyone living in the Nakamura Boarding House, or on the Sawtelle Nihonmachi, or in Little Tokyo, or in Southern California, or anywhere along the West Coast, or in Hawaii.

ⓞ

Natasha helps her mother clear the table, carrying uneaten teriyaki, the inari and tsunemono, and the beautiful birthday cake cluttered with unlit candles inside. Tonight, on the night of Hiro's birthday, L.A. is cloaked in darkness, and he never has the chance to make a wish. But before heading to bed that night, Natasha calls her brother into the backyard. No streetlights, no porch lights, no headlights from passing cars. It is a darkness they have never seen in their city, and when they peer up, the sky is a blanket of stars.

"You could wish on a falling star, you know, since you didn't get to blow out the candles on your cake."

Hiro gives his little sister's shoulders a squeeze, and they watch the star-scattered sky until he catches one. He closes his eyes and makes a wish he tells no one.

ⓞ

One by one, the boarders and the Nakamura family head toward their beds. They leave Tosh Nakamura in the dark, sitting at the radio, listening again to the details of what his home country has done.

As they wash up and pull covers tight, each of the boarders, the three teenagers, and their parents fight for the same sleep. On a night when they know so little, what they do understand is that all the dreams they didn't speak of, all the possibilities that seemed just an arm's distance away that morning, have silently slipped away.

In the quiet dark of their room, the Takeda brothers discuss if they should stay here in America or return to Japan.

Mr. Soto, Mr. Ito, and Mr. Fuji say nothing but feel an old friend has betrayed them.

Mitsue prepares for bed, unbelieving of the poor luck. How could it be on this day, a day that had been marked for celebration for so long? How could it end like this?

Natasha isn't clear about what is happening, and she is scared to ask the questions: what will happen? And then what will happen next?

Mas wishes Hiro a happy birthday before turning out the light, and then the boys lie awake in silence.

When Tosh finally makes his way to bed, he holds Mitsue in his arms, paralyzed by not knowing what is to come.

And in the kitchen, the birthday cake, made with so much joy and promise that morning, sits untouched and glowing in the starlight. The collection of gifts set around Hiro's chair remain unopened. It's as if a bombing thousands of miles away froze time in the kitchen of the boarding house on the corner of Missouri and Corinth. In the quiet of a dark night, sleep is welcome throughout the Sawtelle Nihonmachi, but no one sleeps or dreams. Each of them fears waking to a nightmare.

ʘ

The next morning, news hangs heavy over the neighborhood like the thick marine layer hiding the rising sun. Natasha steps onto the empty sidewalk and hopes he will be there. Curtains are drawn tight over the windows in the neighborhood, and she imagines the dark faces inside, hiding from the dawn.

Then, there are the neighbors just outside this enclave. What do they think about her? Do they see her as the enemy? Do they hate her? Do they fear her family? That's what she knew Ma was thinking last night as she peeked through the curtains and peered out of the front window. She was keeping an eye out for stones that might crack the glass, or a burning brick that would set their wooden home ablaze. But the only cars passing by last night were police cruisers, and order was maintained.

Natasha's stomach churns as she imagines what school might be like today. There will be stares and taunts. She fears what can happen in a junior high school: a shove in a crowded hallway, a hand slammed shut in a locker, hair pulled from roots in the dim light of a bathroom.

She turns the corner and hopes Andy will be there. He won't be much help in the girls' bathroom, but she hopes she won't have to walk to school or the halls completely alone.

At first, the sidewalk is empty and her heart twitches, but then he is there, just like he always is, waiting at the hedge outside his house. He looks toward her, or maybe he's looking over her, behind her. Natasha takes a quick glance over her shoulder but sees only the empty street. He doesn't smile as she walks toward him, but waves at his mother standing at the open front door. Natasha waves too, and Mrs. Lane waves back. Natasha is sure the Lanes, who live on the edge of the neighborhood, are some of the more understanding folks around, and as Andy's mother disappears into the dark of the house, Natasha hopes others will be so kind.

The two friends breathe in the uneasy quiet of the morning until the sound of a car passing along Santa

Monica Boulevard propels them toward school. People are up and about, heading to work, to school. Maybe yesterday was just a dream and today life will unfold without incident.

The two classmates, a boy and a girl, thrust together by neighborhood proximity and alphabetical order, walk toward Emerson Junior High. Andy walks on the street side, as he does every day, but Natasha doesn't notice. A few more cars race down the street, and as they fall into the rhythm of their usual morning walk, the marine layer burns off. Despite the news that crackled through radios all day and night, despite the headlines in the paper this morning, the sun breaks through, and the teenagers squint into the bright light.

Birds chirp, the occasional car rushes past, and then a faceless voice from a truck yells, "Go home, Jap!" as it speeds past.

At first they aren't sure they heard correctly. They look at one another, but then a voice from another car yells, "Sneaky Jap!"

Natasha's face turns red, and Andy now understands his mother's instructions that morning: "Make sure you walk with Natasha to school." It was something he did every day, but his mother must have known something could happen. Andy grabs Natasha's hand as they quicken their pace. Andy has never held her hand before, but Natasha can barely feel his steady palm. Her heart is a drum, making it hard for her to hear the voices emerging from open car windows.

"Hey, dirty Jap! Go back where you came from!"

They walk faster, are almost running, ears pricked to each passing car, bracing for words spewed from windows, but before they can turn off Santa Monica and escape to a side street, a cup of coffee is hurled at them. It splashes across the brightly lit sidewalk and splatters on Natasha's blue and white dress, leaving dark brown splotches. Andy grabs her roughly by the arm and steers her into the shade of an alley.

She brushes her hands down the hot, wet front of her dress. "I'm okay. It's okay," she says, but her hands shake as wipes at the stains.

"Those ..." he says, his words biting the cool morning air.

"You don't have to stay with me, Andy. I can make it on my own." She blinks away the tears before he can see them.

"I'm not leaving you. And you're not okay. Your hands."

She folds her shaking hands at her waist and tries to take a deep breath.

He places his hands on her shoulders, and she is suddenly so small. "My mom said things might be rough for a while, but it's going to be okay." Even as the words escape his mouth, he isn't sure they're true. "We're okay." Their eyes lock. "We are. Okay?"

In the shade of the alley, she buries her face in his chest. She breathes in the smell of him: soap, damp grass, dust. He holds her, and both of them hope he's right.

ᘐ

They keep to the shadows, and by the time they get to school, the coffee stains on Natasha's dress are dry. She and the other Japanese-American students who show up to school find they aren't friends anymore. They aren't classmates. They aren't even people. They are the enemy. Students look straight through her. Teachers don't make eye contact, and when they call roll, the syllables of the Japanese names tick off their tongues like flecks of hot pepper, as if the names are painful to enunciate: Hiromura, Iwamoto, Nakamura, Yamasaki. Names that previously meant nothing more than where a student sat in alphabetical order now signify the enemy.

The enemy is made even clearer when the president addresses the nation that night. December 7, 1941, is "a date which will live in infamy." War is declared. But to Andy and Natasha walking to school that morning, the enemy isn't a Japanese plane painted with the rising red sun. That morning, before her father is arrested, before the evacuation orders are posted, before walking to school together is just a memory, they think for a few moments that things might be okay.

BOOTS

DC Diamondopolous

The same sun scorched downtown Los Angeles that had seared the Iraq desert. Army Private First Class Samantha Cummings stood at attention holding a stack of boxes, her unwashed black hair slicked back in a ponytail and knotted military style. She stared out from Roberts Shoe Store onto Broadway, transfixed by a homeless man with hair and scraggly beard the color of ripe tomatoes. She'd only seen that hair color once before — Staff Sergeant Daniel O'Conner.

The man pushed his life around in a shopping cart crammed with rags and stuffed trash bags. He glanced at Sam through the storefront window, his bloated face layered with dirt. His eyes had the meander of drink in them.

Sam hoped hers didn't. Since her return from Bagdad a year ago, her craving for alcohol snuck up on her like an insurgent. Bathing took effort. She ate to exist. Friends disappeared. Her life started to look like the crusted bottom of her shot glass.

The morning hangover began its retreat to the back of her head. The homeless man vanished down Broadway. She carried the boxes to the storeroom.

In 2012, Sam passed as an everywoman: white, black, brown, Asian. She was a coffee-colored Frappuccino. Frap. That's what the soldiers nicknamed her. Her mother conceived her while on ecstasy during the days of big hair and shoulder pads. On Sam's eighteenth birthday, she enlisted in the army. She wanted a job and an education. But most of all she wanted to be part of a family.

"Let me help you," Hector said, coming up beside her.

"It's okay. I got it." Sam flipped the string of beads aside. Rows of shoeboxes lined both walls and ladders stood every ten feet. She crammed the boxes into their cubbyholes.

"Can I take you to lunch?" Hector asked, standing inside the curtain.

"I told you before. I'm not interested."

"We could be friends." He shrugged. "You could tell me about Iraq."

Sam thrust the last box into its space. The beads jangled. Hector left.

She glanced at the clock. Fifteen minutes until her lunch break. The slow workday gave her too much time to think. She needed a drink. It would keep away the flashbacks.

"C'mon, Sam," Hector said outside the curtain.

"No."

Hector knew she was a vet. He didn't need to know any more about her.

On her way to the front of the store, Sam passed the imported Spanish sandals. Mr. Goldberg carried high-quality shoes. He showcased them on polished wood displays. She loved the smell of new leather, how Mr. Goldberg played soft-rock music in the background, the track lighting, and thick-padded chairs for the customers.

The best part of being a salesperson was taking off the customer's old shoes and putting on the new. The physical contact was honest. And she liked to watch people consider the new shoes — the trial walk, the mirror assessment. If they made the purchase, everyone was happy.

Sam headed toward the door. Maria and Bob stood at the counter looking at the computer screen.

"Wait up," Maria said. The heavy Mexican woman hurried over. "You're leaving early again."

"No one's here," Sam said, towering over her. "I'll make it up, stay later. Or something."

"You better."

"Totally."

"Or you'll end up like that homeless man you were staring at."

"You think you're funny?"

"No, Sam. That's the point."

"He reminded me of someone."

"In Iraq?"

Sam turned away.

"Try the VA."

Sam looked back at Maria. "I have."

"Try again. You need to talk to someone. My cousin —"

"The VA doesn't do jack shit."

"Rafael sees a counselor. It helps."

"Lucky him."

"The meds help too."

"I don't take pills."

"Oh, Sam."

"I'm okay." She liked Maria and especially Mr. Goldberg, a Vietnam vet who not only hired her but rented her a room above the shoe store. "It's just a few minutes early."

Maria glared at her. "Mr. Goldberg has a soft spot for you, but this is a business. Doesn't mean you won't get fired."

"I'll make it up." Sam shoved the door open to a blast of heat.

"Another thing," Maria said. "Change your top. It has stains on it."

Oh, fuck, Sam thought. But it gave her a good reason to go upstairs.

She walked next door, up the narrow stairway and into her studio, the size of an iPhone. Curry smells seeped through the hundred-year-old walls from the Indian neighbors.

Sam took off her blouse and unstuck the dog tags between her breasts. The army had no use for her. *Take your meds, get counseling, then you can re-enlist*. But she wasn't going to end up like her drug-addicted mother.

The unmade Murphy bed screeched and dipped as she sat down in her bra and pants, the tousled sheets still damp from her night sweats. The Bacardi bottle sat on the kitchenette counter. She glanced sideways at it and looked away. The United States flag tacked over the peeling wallpaper dominated the room, but it was the image of herself and Marley on the wobbly dresser she carried with her.

Sam had taken the seventeen-year-old private under her wing. She'd been driving the Humvee in Tikrit with Marley beside her when an IED exploded, killing him while she escaped with only a gash in her leg. Thoughts of mortar attacks, roadside bombs, and Marley looped over and over again. Her mind became a greater terrorist weapon than anything the enemy had.

Her combat boots sat next to the door, the tongues reversed, laces loose, prepared to slip into, ready for action. Sometimes she slept in them, would wear them to work if she could. Of all her souvenirs, the boots reminded her the most of being a soldier. She never cleaned them, wanting to keep the Iraqi sand caked in the wedge between the midsoles and shanks.

The springs shrieked as Sam dug her fists into the mattress and stood. She walked to the counter, unscrewed the top of the Bacardi, poured herself a shot, and knocked it back. Liquid guilt ran down her throat.

Sam picked up a blouse off the chair, smelled it, and looked for stains. It would do. She dressed, grabbed a Snickers bar, took three strides, and dashed out of her room.

Heading south on Broadway, Sam longed to be part of the city. Paved sidewalks, gutters, frying tortillas, old movie palaces, jewelry stores, flower stands, square patches of green where trees grew — all of it wondrous, unlike the fucking sandbox of Iraq.

The rum kicked in, made her thirsty, as she continued through the historic center of town. The sun's heat radiated from her soles to her scalp. A canopy of light siphoned the city of color. She watched a tourist slowly fold her map and use it as a fan. Businessmen slouched along, looking clammy in shirtsleeves. Women wore their dresses moist with sweat, form-fitted to their skin. Even the cars seemed to droop.

Waves of heat shimmered off the pavement. They ambushed Sam, planting her back in Tikrit. She heard the rat-a-tat-tat of a Tabuk sniper rifle. Ducked. Dodged bullets. Scrambled behind a trash bin. Searched around for casualties. She looked at the top of buildings wondering where in the hell the insurgents fired from.

"Hey, honey, whatsa matter?" An elderly black woman stooped over her.

"Get down, ma'am!"

"What for?"

Sam grabbed at the woman, but she moved away.

"Get down, ma'am! You'll get killed!"

"Honey, it's just street drillin'. Those men over there, they're makin' holes in the cement."

Covered in sweat, Sam swerved to her left. A Buick and Chevrolet stopped at a red light. She saw the 4th

Street sign below the one-way arrow. Her legs felt numb as she held onto the trash bin and lifted herself up.

"You a soldier?"

"Yes, ma'am," Sam said, looking into the face of the concerned woman.

"I can tell. You fellas always say 'ma'am' and 'sir,' so polite-like. Take it easy child, you're home now." The woman limped away.

Sam reeled. Felt for the flask in her back pocket. It wasn't there. Construction workers whistled and made wolf calls at her. "Douche bags," she moaned. Alcohol had always numbed the flashbacks. Her counselor in Bagdad told her they would fade. *Why can't I get better?* she asked herself. Shaking, she blinked several times, forcing her eyes to focus as she continued south past McDonald's.

At 6th, she saw the man with tomato-color hair on the other side of the street, jostling his shopping cart. "It's Los Angeles, not Los Angelees!" he shouted. His voice rasped like the sick, but Sam heard something familiar in the tone. He pushed his cart around the corner.

The light turned green. Sam sprinted in front of the waiting cars to the other side of the road. She had grown up across the 6th Street Bridge that linked Boyle Heights to downtown. From the bedroom window of the apartment she shared with her mother, unless her mother had a boyfriend, Sam would gaze at the Los Angeles skyline.

She followed the man into Skid Row. The smell hit her like a body slam. The stink of piss and shit, odors that mashed together like something died, made her eyes water. A block away, it was another world.

She trailed the man with hair color that people had an opinion about. The Towering Inferno — that's what they called Staff Sergeant Daniel O'Conner, but not to his face. He knew, though, and took the jibe well. After all, he had a sense of humor, was confident, tall, and powerfully built. O'Conner was the last man to end up broken; he couldn't be the hunched and defeated man she was following. No, Sam thought. It couldn't be him. It couldn't be her hero.

He shoved his gear into the guts of the city with Sam behind him. The last time she'd been to Skid Row was as a teenager, driving through with friends who taunted the homeless. The smell was one thing, but what she saw rocked her. City blocks of homeless living under layers of tarp held up by shopping carts. Young and old, most black, and male, gathered on corners, sat on sidewalks, slouched against buildings. Drug exchanges were going down. Women too stoned or sick to worry about their bodies slumped over, their breasts falling out of their tops. It was hard for Sam to look into their faces, to see their despair. The whole damn place reeked of hopelessness. Refugees in the Middle East and Africa at least had tents and medicine. Sam put on her ass-kicking face, the one that said, "Leave me the fuck alone, or I'll mess you up." She walked as if she had on her combat boots, spine straight, eyes in the back of her head.

Skid Row mushroomed down side streets. Men staggered north toward 5th and the Mission. She stayed close behind the redheaded man. He turned left at San Pedro. And so did Sam. It was worse than 6th Street. Not even in Iraq had she seen deprivation like this: cardboard tents, overflowing trash bins used as crude borders, men sleeping on the ground. She watched a man pull up his pant leg and stick a needle in his ankle. Another man, his face distorted by alcohol, drank freely from a bottle. The men looked older than on 6th. Some had cardboard signs. One read, *Veteran, please help me.* Several wore fatigues. One, dressed in a field jacket, was missing his lower leg. Most, Sam thought, were Vietnam or Desert Storm vets. She felt her throat tighten, the familiar invasion of anger afraid to express itself. She'd been told by the army never to show emotion in a war zone. But Sam brought the war home with her. So did the men slumped against the wall like human garbage. The redheaded man passed a large metal dumpster heaped with trash bags. It stank of rotten fruit. He disappeared behind the metal container with his cart.

Sam looked at the angle of the sun. She had about ten minutes before thirteen-hundred hours. There was a doorway across the street. She went over and stood in it.

He sat against the brick wall emptying his bag of liquor bottles and beer cans. He shook one after another dry into his mouth. She understood his thirst, one that never reached an end until he passed out. He took a sack off the cart and emptied it: leftover Fritos bags, Oreo cookies, pretzels. He tore the bags apart and ran his tongue over the insides. He ate apple cores, chewed the strings off banana peels.

"What are you …" he growled. "You. Lookin' at?" His eyes roamed Sam's face.

Shards of sadness struck her heart. It was like seeing Marley's strewn body all over again. Staff Sergeant O'Conner's voice, even when drunk, was deep and rich. It identified him, like his hair. How could the man who saved her from being raped by two fellow soldiers and who refused to join in the witch hunts of Don't Ask Don't Tell, a leader who had a future of promotions and medals, end up in Skid Row?

"You remind me of someone," she said.

How could a once-strapping man who led with courage and integrity eat scraps like a dog next to a dumpster? What had happened, that the army would leave behind one of their own? Like a militia, disillusionment and bitterness trampled over Sam's love of country.

ℴ)

She woke up to another hot morning. Her head throbbed from the shots of Bacardi she tossed back until midnight as she surfed the internet, including the VA, for a Daniel O'Conner. She found nothing.

For breakfast, she ate a donut and washed it down with rum. She pulled on a soiled khaki T-shirt and a pair of old jeans and slipped into her combat boots, the dog tags tucked between her breasts. Sam knotted her ponytail, grabbed a canvas bag, stuffed it into her backpack and left. She had to be at work at twelve hundred hours. If O'Conner slept off the booze, he might be lucid and recognize her.

At the liquor store, she filled the canvas bag with candy bars, cookies, trail mix, wrapped sandwiches, and soda pop, then headed down Broadway. The morning sun streaked the sky orange and pink. Yellow rays sliced skyscrapers and turned windows into furnaces. Sam hurried south.

When she crossed Broadway at 6th, the same sun exposed Skid Row into a stunning morning of neglect. Lines of men pissed against walls, women squatted. She heard weeping. Sweat ran down her armpits, her head pounded. Sam felt shaky, chewed sand, and looked around. Where was Marley? She stumbled backwards into a gate.

"Baby, whatchu doin'? You one fine piece of ass." The man reached over and yanked at her backpack.

"No!" Sam yelled. She didn't want to collect Marley's severed arms and legs to send home to his parents. "No," she whimpered, grabbing the sides of her head with her hands. "I can't do it," she said sliding to the ground.

"Shit, you crazy. This is my spot, bitch. Outta here!" he said and kicked her.

Sam moaned and gripped her side. She saw a plastic water bottle lying on the sidewalk, crawled over and drank from it. A sign with arrows pointing to Little Tokyo and the Fashion District cut through the vapor of her flashback. Iraqi women wore *abayas*, not shorts and tank tops. Sitting in the middle of the sidewalk, Sam hit her fist against her forehead until it hurt.

She saw the American flag hoisted on a pulley from a cherry picker over the 6th Street Bridge, heard the click-clack of a shopping cart and the music of Lil Wayne. The sounds pulled her away from the memory, away from a place that had no walls to hang onto.

Sam held the bottle as she crawled to the edge of the sidewalk. She took deep breaths, focused, and glanced around. What the fuck was she doing sitting on a curb in Skid Row with a dirty water bottle? *"Or you'll end up like that homeless man you were staring at."*

"Oh, Jesus."

Sam dropped the bottle in the gutter and trudged toward San Pedro Street.

She had thought that when she came home, she'd get better, but living with her mother almost destroyed her. It began slowly: little agitations about housework, arguments that escalated into slammed doors. Then, one day, her mother called George Bush and Dick Cheney "monsters who should be in prison." She accused Sam of murder for killing people who did nothing to the United States. Sam lunged at her, stumbled over a chair, and fell.

Her mother ran screaming into the bathroom and locked the door. "Get outta my house, and don't ever come back!"

"Don't worry! You're a piece of shit for a mother, anyway!"

She stayed with her friend Jenny until she told her to stop drinking and get her act together.

In her combat boots, Sam scuffled along, hoping to catch O'Conner awake and coherent. She turned left. His shopping cart poked out from the trash bin. Sam walked to the dumpster and peered around it. O'Conner wasn't there, but his bags and blankets were. She stepped into his corner and was using the toe of her boot to kick away mouse droppings when someone grabbed her hair and yanked back her head, forcing her to her knees. Terrified, she caught a glimpse of orange.

"Private First Class Samantha Cummings, United States Army, Infantry Unit 23. Sergeant!" She raised her arms. Sweat streamed down her face.

His grip remained firm.

"Staff Sergeant O'Conner, I've brought provisions. They're in my backpack. Sandwiches, candy bars, pretzels!"

He let go of her hair. The ponytail fell between her shoulders.

"I'm going to take off my backpack, stand, and face you, Sergeant." Her fingers trembled, searching for the Velcro strap and ripping it aside. The bag slid to the ground. She rose with her back to him and turned around.

She saw the war in his eyes. "It's me. Frap." His skin, filthy and sunburned, couldn't hide the yellow hue of infection. He smelled of feces and urine. His jaw was slack, his gaze unsteady.

"You want something to eat? I got all kinds of stuff," Sam said. Her emotions, buried in sand, began to tunnel, pushing aside lies and deceit.

O'Conner tore open the backpack and emptied out the canvas bag. "Booze."

She knelt beside him and unwrapped a ham and cheese sandwich. "No booze. Here, have this," she said, handing him the food. "Go on." Her arm touched his as she encouraged him to eat.

O'Conner sat back on his heels. "It's all …"

Sam leaned forward. "Go on."

"It's all … stuck!"

"What's stuck?"

He shook his head. "It's all, stuck!" he cried. He grabbed the sandwich and scarfed it down in three bites. Mayonnaise dripped on his scruffy beard. He kept his sights on Sam as he tore open the Fritos bag and took a mouthful. He ripped apart the sack of Oreo cookies and ate those too. "Go away," he said as black-and-white crumbs fell from his mouth.

Sam shook her head.

"Leave. Me. Alone!"

"I don't want to."

He drew his knees up to his chest, shut his eyes, and leaned his head against the metal dumpster.

Here was her comrade-in-arms, in an invisible war, where no one knew of his bravery, where ground zero happened to be wherever you stood.

"You saved me from Jackson and Canali when they tried to rape me in the bathroom. I should have been able to protect myself. And when they tried to discharge me, for doing nothing, you stood up for me. Remember?"

O'Conner didn't move.

"I never, thanked you … cuz it showed weakness."

O'Conner struggled to his knees. "I don't know you!" His breath smelled rancid.

"Yeah, you do."

"I don't know you!" he cried.

"You know me. You saved me twice, dude!"

O'Conner stumbled to his feet and gripped the handrail of his shopping cart, his spirit as razed as the smoking remains of a Humvee. He shoved off on his morning trek. *For how long?* Sam wondered. She gathered the bags of food and put them in the canvas bag. She kicked his rags to the side, took his blankets, flung them out, folded them and rearranged the cardboard floor. She put the blankets on top and hid the bag of food under his rags.

Emotions overcame her. Loyalty, compassion, anger, love — feelings so strong that tears fell like a long-awaited rain.

Sam couldn't save O'Conner, but she could save herself.

She ripped off her dog tags and threw them in the dumpster. Once home, she'd take down the flag, fold it twelve times and tuck the picture of Marley and herself inside it. She'd throw out her military clothes and combat boots. Pour the rum down the sink. She'd go to the VA, badger them until she got an appointment. Join AA. She'd arrive and leave work on time.

The morning began to cook. It was the same sun, but a new day. Sam walked in the opposite direction of O'Conner.

#MILLENNIALEXISTENTIALISM

Lenore Robinson

Beeeeeeep!

The siren song of the freeways echoed through the night as headlights scattered along the black, oil-stained pavement. Her arms tensed for a moment, thinking she had made a mistake, only to remember that this city was never without its noise. She glanced at her phone.

Forty-two minutes.

She had been sitting in traffic, barely eking along the 10, for forty-two minutes. Daydreaming. Drifting.

She decided to go to this party after Kelly posted the third set of photos from her "surprise" engagement in Italy. Gag! An ad for a synthwave dance party slid in underneath those obnoxious posts as she scrolled. She couldn't tap "Going" fast enough.

She remembered the thrill of watching the check mark turn blue, knowing it would automatically post her plans for everyone to see. The thrill of pretending she had found her place here, the thrill of flaunting another unforgettably epic Friday night.

That'll make 'em jealous.

Moving to L.A. was supposed to make them jealous. Her standing desk in public relations at a downtown start-up was supposed to make them jealous. She had packed up everything she owned in her tiny hatchback six months ago, and now the only one feeling jealous was her.

"Exit right in one mile."

The mechanical monotone of the GPS, like a relative your aging grandmother begs you to be nice to, sliced through her thoughts. They were like old friends. It talked to her every day as she left her neighborhood, which was seemingly so far from the best parts of the city.

She admired the cars speeding by. Escape. Prius. Tesla. *A fucking DeLorean!* They all seemed so confident of where they were going, leaving her behind to fend for herself. She thought for a moment that she should turn back, all the way back, and admit that she had failed. Admit that, despite her fully charged GPS, she was completely and totally lost.

She hated "the 5" worse than "the 10," these highways nicknamed by the transplants who drove them day in and day out. She hated Silver Lake and East Hollywood and Echo Park. She hated everyone who loved living in this city because she wasn't one of them.

She circled the block several times only to find less street parking each round, so she looked up a paid lot while waiting forever at an intersection.

Ten bucks.

"We close at two a.m.," the attendant grumbled, handing back her credit card. She parked under a street lamp, just like every article worth sharing suggested doing in the era of *#MeToo*. They also emphasized going places with friends, but in her reality, there were plenty of street lamps and few friends.

There was a long driveway down to the street, and from there she'd cross and head towards the Echoplex. She clicked the lock button on her key fob. Once for safety, twice for not knowing if coming here was the right decision. A slight breeze pranced along the back of her neck.

Provoking.

The glow from the street lamps followed her rigid steps. She walked as if she were coiled up, clinging to her fragile dreams of city life slowly slipping away into the smoggy night. She already regretted coming. She already regretted driving all this way to walk into a hipster dance party alone.

Wheels ground against the asphalt behind her as she crossed the street. He lifted his skateboard from underneath his feet as he reached the other side, so elegantly. She wanted to keep close to him. He carried on without even knowing how much she wanted to absorb his presence, this effortless Angeleno.

"Yaaooow!"

She quickly shifted her eyes from him towards the obnoxious noise, discovering three men stumbling in her direction from behind.

Look away. Don't acknowledge cat callers.

As she pulled her jacket higher over her shoulders, she regretted her decision now more than before. They barreled past, colliding with another group of stumbling men. "Yaaooow!" they called out between thick clouds of sickly sweet nicotine and glycerin. They didn't even notice her walk by.

The line spilled out onto the sidewalk. Clusters of people who knew each other. Clusters of people who were certain of themselves. Feeling unnatural, she fumbled in her purse for her phone.

She felt a sharp stab along the side of her index finger. *What the fuck was that? A hairpin?* She pulled her hand out to find a small scrape, not nearly as bad as she hoped it would be. Not nearly bad enough for an excuse to just go back to her car and leave.

"Lilah!"

She wheeled around. A blonde bimbo with implants was squealing, running towards another blonde bimbo to her left (just another Lilah). Their short dresses slipped up their thighs as they smashed their overdone faces together, gushing in inaudible Insta-speak.

She turned back to face the ebbing line. *In a city of millions of people, naturally there are more Lilahs — perky titted, #extra, token socialite Lilahs.* She regretted that she would never get the chance to be that Lilah. Or any other Lilah, for that matter.

The bimbos were posing perfectly for selfies as she was called up by an incredibly handsome bouncer to be checked for weapons. He hovered the detector bar at her shoulder, barely running it over her body. He tilted his head and flashed a smile. "Ah, you're fine." He motioned her on by. She paused for a moment, dropped her head, and blushed. These small moments were a rite of passage, where the scales could be tipping towards *#hotAF*, and she wasn't going to squander one second. She wanted nothing more than to linger here, in validation, so she pressed him further.

"Thanks."

"Mmm hmm." He pursed his lips and motioned her onwards again. She must have overplayed her hand, expecting too much. She walked on, peering over her shoulder to see what the verdict was for the other Lilah. *Never mind.* She turned her gaze back towards the door.

The smoking deck was filled with clusters of chattering cigarette plumes. It was already 11:37. She typed in "Echoplex" in the search bar of her email. She should have saved her entry ticket somewhere other than the thousands of unread messages in her inbox. Thousands of unread offers and deals to make people believe you were something better than you really were.

The outside door was propped open with a cinderblock. *Classy.* Wading around glitter-coated waifs and leather jackets held in the hands of wide-eyed wannabes, she presented the QR code to the overweight figure stationed behind the counter. He pointed to a sign with a red line through a cigarette and cut his eyes back towards her.

"Oh, I don't smoke."

He kept glaring at her. She paused and nodded her head, pulling her phone towards her face for comfort, going for the affected stance of someone who has so much more going on than others could possibly comprehend.

The interior doors weighed heavy against one another, as if all the noise and movement couldn't bear the thought of letting anyone in. She pulled at the left handle, stepping into the atmosphere. The music pulsed out of the speakers, pounding against the crowd. Pounding against her heartbeat. Fog filled the room, circling bodies in motion enchanted by escaping reality for a few short hours.

The DJ penetrated the haze. "Are you ready to fucking party tonight, L.A.?"

As affirmation reverberated through the crowd, she stood frozen in observation. More Lilahs. Too many *Art Is Dead* jackets to count. Neon cloth dancing around her in shallow synchronicity. Love being sloppily made against the textured walls, the shadows illuminated by revealing beams of color.

She wandered through the crowd to the bar at the back of the room. Reading through the list of drinks, she resolved that beer was better than liquor for tonight's adventure. The bartender handed her a cup with foam sliding down the side. Another girl reached for her own drink from his other hand, slowly licking the spilled inhibition from the bottom to the rim. She wondered if that could mean anything. The girl grinned as she walked away. Her gaze lingered on the girl's swaying hips as she slurped the first sip from her own cup.

She leaned against a ledge built out from one of the building pillars, set her beer down, and pulled out her phone. She held up the forward-facing camera for a selfie, but it was far too dark to capture her feigned happiness. Instead, she took a photo of the stage, which was full of people dancing in unison with the crowd below. Lights pierced through the room, outlining confidence and freedom so profound it made her question if she even had a right to feel envious.

#bestnightever

"Why ain't you up there dancing?" His voice interrupted her scroll through perfect lives.

She hesitated. *Don't let him think you're lame and alone.* "I'm just, uh, waiting on someone."

"Oh ... I didn't mean to pry. Just saw you and ... well, I had to do a double-take." His smile lit up the corner she had hid herself away in. She adjusted her crop top, pulled up her high-rise jeans, and threw back her head. "That's all right," she mumbled as a T-shirt that read STAFF stepped directly in front of her. *Rude.* Irritated, she went back to scrolling.

Her mother had warned her that compliments were handed out like candy from every clean-shaven starving actor desperate for a halfway decent lay. Perhaps he wasn't interested in her at all. Perhaps he couldn't care less why she wasn't dancing.

She left her near empty cup on the wooden pedestal and scanned the walls for a door to the women's bathroom. Her imaginary friend wouldn't be showing up anytime soon, and she couldn't handle the embarrassment of feeling almost flattered any longer.

The other Lilah was adjusting her tits in the mirror as she walked in.

#wtf

Rolling her eyes, she awkwardly shuffled to a stall in the back. She slid the latch closed, leaned against the door, and pulled out her phone again. She tapped the icon on the bottom right to open her profile: *@latelyivebeenlilah*.

Tears fought their way to the corners of her eyes as she closed them tightly and imagined she was somewhere else. Imagined she was someone else. All of life's perfection she had been trying so hard to achieve stood twenty feet away in stiletto heels and almond-shaped acrylics.

The Lilah she should have been.

"Heeyyy …" The side of her stall shook. Someone was clumsily beating it from the other side. "Do you, like, have a tampon or something?"

She hesitated. "Sure," she sighed and pulled a fuschia-plastic wrapper from her purse, passing it under the cold metal barricade.

"I was like literally cumming when he moved his hand and then there was, like, blood evveryyywhere!" the voice slurred out as heels clicked against the tile floor. She felt her cheeks flush. The thought was mortifying. *Was it the guy who hit on me?*

As the cold water ran over her hands, words turned to mumbles. More drunken voices were giggling from the other stalls. Another cleared its throat. *Vapid.* Was this really all that was on the other side of her own miserable path?

She wiped the remaining water on the sides of her jeans. They felt clammy, unsure. Looking out over the crowd again, she made her way towards the door. She didn't belong here. Not tonight. Kelly wouldn't be jealous of her pathetic life tonight.

The air shifted near the speakers, dancing across her collarbones. It smelled sweet, like an overripe peach sweltering in the hot July sun. Lights poured through the cloudy air from above, salvaging.

She turned towards the crowd one last time. Saying goodbye.

ѻ

Hair cascaded down a sloping back, nestled in the crook of a spine. It swayed as hips moved, like wind-kissed fields of wheat in the fall. Skin glistened, a lace bodysuit clinging to every curve.

She was instantly mesmerized by the woman, this mirage of the metropolis, who stood amid the noise and the flashing lights. Her skin was flushed, aroused. She was palpitating. She was alive.

The woman's golden hair enveloped her body like a halo, cherubic. She was pulled towards her, as if by an immanent force, inescapable as a gravity well. Complete and total seduction bloomed in her vision as she came closer, and she could feel the blood freeze in her veins.

She was enamored.

The woman smelled like cocoa-dusted juicy plums. Curious. Indulgent. Provocative eyes looked deep into her insecurities, revealing how much she truly wanted to be in this city. How much she truly wanted to make this work. How much she struggled to make this work. How much she truly wanted to fuck this woman.

She reached out to touch that glistening skin. Her fingertips barely graced those opulent hips, the music so loud she couldn't think. They moved in harmony, waiting on the bass to let their hearts know it was okay to keep beating. Her hand traced along delicate ribs, lifting that golden hair.

Dark nipples rested beneath black lace, trailing down to the edge of tattered denim shorts, the inseam riding high between juicy plush thighs. Teasing.

She imagined those velvet hips rolling across her face as they did on the dance floor now. She imagined that voluptuous body underneath her own, vibrating, and arching back in sync with the rhythm. Surrendering.

"You wanna get out of here?" Golden hair fell forward, leaning in, caressing her ear.

She nodded as a chill slowly snaked down her spine, and she shuffled her feet, unable to feel her numb legs. They stepped out onto Glendale Boulevard, the night sky painted with city lights. The same night sky she followed to get to this place where she found perfection. Where perfection found her.

The air swirled around them, peaches blooming now, warm like two lovers fucking for the very first time. She gazed longingly … longingly into her golden-haired fantasy, tracing her lips with trembling fingers … eager to put something she could feel in her mouth.

They crossed the street with seconds to spare, as if their whole lives were happening right now and only right now, and walked up Park Avenue to the parking lot. Her fantasy went ahead, cutting devious glances back in her direction, casting *take-me, make-me-cum* eyes.

Even the breeze wanted to fuck those delectable curves, delicately playing with golden strands as they ran.

The tendrils fell still, paused, when they came upon the sculpted concrete balcony overlooking the boulevard. Rounded ass escaping the ragged edge of tight shorts, framed tauntingly in fishnet. She walked up to the edge alongside this embodiment of all that was consummate and holy in this city.

She wondered what those pouty lips would want her to do with her tongue as she slipped her hand around that yearning waist.

The woman tasted like salted caramel, melting away her hate for Silver Lake. And East Hollywood. And Echo Park. And all the perfect people she felt like she couldn't be. She slipped her tongue inside that decadent mouth. She traced along hard nipples with her indecisive fingertips, golden hair entangling them both as if to say it was okay she was finding her way.

She let out a sigh into the air between them, a whimper of need. She traced those candy lips with her tongue one last time, pulling away to follow along the black lace, nipples pressed hard against the threads.

The woman sighed now, louder than her, and grabbed her hand … placing her fingers between a wide-open mouth, licking them slowly.

#dead

She slid her fingers down the woman's ample chest, along a quivering torso, down behind the metal buttons of shorts that should have already been lying on the ground. Green eyes gazed into her own aquamarine pools of anticipation.

She ran her fingers along the folds and crevices, breathing the woman in just to stay conscious. Tires squealed against the weary boulevard, mile-high partygoers stumbled along crosswalks, and no one existed on this magical night in this city dark with desire but the two of them.

She licked the tips of her fingers, tasting an elixir unlike anything that had ever been in her mouth before. Intoxicating. Life giving.

Golden curls fell back against the concrete balcony, laughing away the endorphins. They kissed, pressing their bodies against one another, backlit by neon signs and the glow of phone screens down below.

Regardless of what happened in the morning or any day after, this city was hers. It had always been hers.

#nofilterneeded

THE CITY

AP Thayer

He takes a couple shots before leaving for the club. Pops the mollies in the car ride over. Three, because that's how many it takes to even feel it anymore. Two more hide in a small pouch in his crotch. Another shot at the club. Another capsule within an hour of getting through the doors. Soon after, he's shaking the last one into the valley between thumb and index finger and snorting it up his nose. There was a time when the stuff made him genuinely happy. The acrid taste of the postnasal drip fools him into a shadow of that happiness. The first time had been so beautiful. He'd been breathless. Now he just grinds his teeth and sweats too much.

He needs some K to balance everything out. Just a bump off someone's car key. Then a hit from someone's vape. Another drink, an Adios Motherfucker. He pretends it's a delicate balance. In reality, he's only saying yes to anything that makes him believe he's interesting, living hard and fast like a Hollywood screenwriter is supposed to. Anything that sells the self-deception.

A part of him, the part he tries so hard to ignore or shut away, knows. After the week he's had, the mind-numbing open houses he had to sit through as junior broker, the three shifts as a barback in WeHo, it can't go on. He knows it, but the truth is drowned in lights and music.

For a while, it works. For a while, the drugs are strong enough and nothing exists but the pounding bass and the colors playing against his eyelids. To him, his movements are beautiful and transcendent, but he jerks and writhes like everyone else. After a while, the song changes, the feeling fades, and he finds himself in a sea of strangers. His dancing slows, and he sticks to bobbing his head while pretending to look around for his friends. And so the rest of the night goes, until the music stops for good and the lights come on. He's blinking into the brightness, trying to find the exit. Trying to hold onto a feeling that faded an hour ago. He shuffles out with everyone else, to face the lies once more.

೨

"Nice night," I say, nodding toward him. I can't help myself. It's not time yet, but I just couldn't stay away. His eyes meet mine, only for a second.

"Yeah, that shit was amazing." His eyes are wild, all sickly whites and dilated pupils, vibrating with the substances still coursing through him. They slide off me, unable to truly see me. Someone bumps into him. A smile blooms on his face, and he puts his arm around the girl. He's got ten years on her. The drugs are vibrant on her. On him, they're an anchor.

"Hey, want to head back to my place? I'm not ready for the night to end, are you?" He manages not to stumble on his words too much.

"Um, my friend's already got an Uber." I can hear her alarm bells ringing, even if she doesn't yet recognize them.

Her friend is waving her over. "Come on!" A silver Prius with its hazards on waits for the girls to step in.

"Oh, no, tell her it's fine. I've got my car here. Let's go back to my place. You can both come." He offers her another smile.

Her friend grabs her by the arm and drags her into the Uber. He's left swaying on the sidewalk.

"Almost," I say to him.

He gapes at me for a whole five seconds before any expression registers on his face. He wants to say something.

I step aside in time for him to vomit onto the sidewalk. I leave him there, hunched over his sick. I'll see him again soon.

ℴ

An hour later, he's driving home. It only takes him three blocks to realize the valet turned off his car lights. There's a jagged edge to everything, from the ketamine, no longer softened by jacked-up serotonin. The fog of some high-powered hybrid vape oil named Purple Punch is throwing the whole balance off. He's breathing hard and his jaw hurts from clenching. Now, away from the crowds and the flashing lights, the phantom of happiness is as far as it's ever been.

He turns onto Mulholland.

Lucky for him, no one's around. Lucky for them, really. He drifts into the opposite lane on the turns, tires squealing as he weaves over the yellow line.

It would be so easy to do it then, but I'm nothing if not patient.

He gets to his favorite turnout and stumbles out of his car.

The San Fernando Valley is spread out beneath him, a grid of lights shimmering like the sun on the ocean. The air is crisp. It's quiet. The city is beautiful, almost magical, from hundreds of feet up at four o'clock in the morning. It's only when you get up close that the ugliness is apparent.

I greet him for the second time. "Nice night."

"Holy shit, where'd you come from?" He shoves his phone into his pocket.

I jerk my thumb at my car, parked only a few paces from his. It's everything his isn't: clean, dark, and timeless. "Didn't you hear me pull up?"

He shakes his head and turns back to the vista. "Guess not."

"You don't mind sharing, do you?"

He gives a casual wave, inviting me over. I step toward the edge. A wooden fence separates us from a steep, stony ravine. There's nothing to say. We still have a few more minutes before I can begin. I take in the ocean of lights and try to see it his way. They're nothing but lights to me. No amount of distance or delusion changes what is down there.

He takes his phone out again and sends some messages I know no one will reply to. He checks social media, his email. Nothing. No matches on his dating apps. A few taps later and the sound of his ex's story blares out. Her with her new boyfriend. His old friend.

Time's up.

I pull out a cigarette and light it. It isn't for me. I can't even taste it. But it's the catalyst. The end flares, and I take a deep drag.

On cue, he speaks. "You're not supposed to smoke up here. Fire hazard."

I shrug and flick the cigarette. Embers cascade onto the dirt and flare up in the breeze before dying out. I know they won't take. Not this time.

"Hey, watch it."

I light another cigarette and hold it out for him. Menthol. He tells himself he doesn't smoke, but he has only turned down thirteen cigarettes in the last five years, and zero when he's fucked up. He takes it, unsure of what's happening, something deep inside warning him, but the first inhale reignites the fading echo of the MDMA in him, and his smile returns, dreamy and desperate. He forgets the danger.

He looks at me without really seeing me. The dress. The boots. He takes a step closer, his intentions smeared all across his face. That hungry look. It's not the first time I've seen it.

"What brings you up here?"

"I could ask you the same."

"Can you see anything with those on?" He points his cigarette at my sunglasses.

"I can see everything." The patchy stubble on his round face. The shaggy curls from going too long between haircuts. The way his dark, button-down shirt strains over the extra thirty pounds he carries around with him. There was a time he was considered attractive. Now, surrounded by people in better shape and years younger, he is barely average.

He takes it as me being playful and comes closer.

"It's nice up here, isn't it?" He takes another drag. "No traffic. No heat. No one's around. Well —" He waves his cigarette in my direction. "Almost no one. Just us. It's like we've slipped into a mirror world. A shadow of the city. Like we're frozen in time."

I can't help but laugh. He's most poetic when on the hunt. Too bad he's never channeled even half that creativity into his writing. It's why he's never sold a script. One of the reasons.

My laugh is just the encouragement he was looking for. The cigarette flares.

"Where are you from?"

I blow out a cloud of blue-black smoke. "Here."

"Born here?" Another step closer.

I smile and slip the menthol between my lips. "I've always been here."

"A native Angeleno. Don't meet too many of those in Hollywood."

I shrug.

"I'm from Delaware. Been here ten years, though. Naturalized, you could say. I'm a screenwriter. Been shopping a feature. It's the next *Avengers*, but better. I've got a meeting at Paramount next week."

Each line brings him one step toward me.

"You're hot." He snakes an arm around my waist and pulls me close, pressing himself against me. He tries to look through my glasses, but something in their mirrored surface stops him. His smile falters. For a moment, there's only him and his distorted reflection. Distorted by the lenses, distorted by the drugs. But for the first time, he sees himself as he really is. Broken. Ugly. Sick.

I smile, showing him my jagged teeth, but he doesn't notice. I slice a button off his shirt and tap his chest with a claw.

"Do you see what you really are?" I keep my voice low, not wanting to break the spell. It's almost time. The twisted reflection in my glasses is more truthful than he's ever been. He stumbles back. It's seeped into him now. That little voice he's been suppressing for years is raging now. The walls of denial are broken down. He's laid bare.

Exactly where I want him.

His eyes flick toward me. "Who are you?"

My smile widens, and I move closer to him, forcing him back. He holds his hands out. As if that would stop me.

"You know who I am."

He tosses his head, trying to shake me away, trying to sober up, trying to do anything but face the end of the road he started down long ago. He can see me now. Really see me.

"No, it's not —"

"It is." I flick my cigarette into his chest and he takes one last step back.

൭

He wasn't making it in Los Angeles. Not really. For ten years, he spent his paychecks on the appearance of making it. For ten years he partied hard and thought that's what L.A. was about. No finished scripts. No writing deal. No fifteen minutes of fame. Not unless you count the brief news article about a heavily intoxicated man falling off a Mulholland lookout.

He should have known this city eats people like him alive.

TELL ME YOUR NAME

Roselyn Teukolsky

In the middle of *Malevolent*, the doorbell rings.

I'm alone, stretched out on my king-sized bed with cards scattered everywhere. I'm *assiduously* making sentences with words "every genius should know," all neatly typed on my mother's Vocabulary Flash Cards. Seriously. Like my bedroom in our new condo is obscenely *capacious*. Or, *obstreperous* children should be broiled and served with French fries. Stuff like that.

Melinda is so freaking obsessive when it comes to me.

It's dark outside — February in Pasadena — tall skinny palm trees doing the funky skeleton in the wind. Creepy. The weather is *ostensibly* perfect, but personally, I miss the snow in Rochester.

The bell rings again, *ding-dong, ding-dong. What's taking you so long? Open the goddamn door.*

I'm not expecting anyone tonight because I don't know anyone here. We arrived a month ago and Clark and Melinda, the parentals, are at a steak and duck dinner, a thousand dollars a plate, to benefit orphans in Africa. Before they left, Melinda prepared a majorly delicious piece of salmon with broccoli and fluffy potatoes for me. Of course she didn't have to — I'm fifteen and perfectly capable of throwing something together myself — but Melinda controls my diet in the same way she controls my life. I'm her project: homeschooled, of course, because "Pammie, you are so beyond anything they could offer at Pasadena High School." That's what she tells people, anyway. Not a word about Rochester.

When I open the door, a whoosh of cold air sweeps in. The guy on the doorstep looks like he's sixteen or seventeen tops, with a button-down shirt and tan pants.

"Good evening, ma'am," he says in a low, polite voice, "I'm sorry to bother you, but I lost my job last week and haven't eaten anything for two days. Could you help me out?"

I'm speechless. No one has ever called me ma'am.

"Um, are you asking for money?" I say.

"*Yes,* ma'am," he replies, looking down at his old scuffed-up shoes.

I have turned on the hallway light, so he can see into our foyer with the hallway table in teak and marble, the clock with no numbers on an onyx base, and the mirror — *beveled* — with a brass frame.

My mouth feels like it's full of cotton balls. I clear my throat. "Okay, I'll get you something."

I leave the door open on purpose and turn around to head into the living room, where I've stashed my purse behind the sideboard. I know I shouldn't do this, but it would be rude to shut the door in his face and lock it and then get some money, come back, unlock and open the door, and shove the bills into his hand as if he were some lowly beggar. I'm a totally good person, I really am, so I leave him standing there with the door open.

I fish around in my purse and grab the first bill I find — a twenty — folding it in my hand. When I go back to the door, I can breathe out because he's in the exact same spot I left him. I place the money in his palm, close his fingers around it, and say, "I hope your week gets better."

He looks at me then — we go eyeball to eyeball — but I can't read his expression. *Inscrutable.* He thanks me, pockets the money, and moves away. As I shut the door and lock it, I realize that he isn't leaving the complex — of course he isn't — he's going to ring my neighbors' doorbells.

ⵁ

"You did what?" Melinda, who always speaks to me in a loving tone of controlled patience, has lost the plot and is screaming at me like I gave away the clock.

"He was *poor*, Mom. I gave him some of my allowance —"

"Your mother's right," Clark says, "and I don't say that often. You realize that we could have been robbed blind?"

"Why?" I say. "Because he's poor?"

She throws up both her hands. "Pamela, for someone whose IQ is off the charts, you are *incredibly obtuse*." The last two words are yelled into my ear.

"Your impulse to help someone less fortunate than you is great," Clark says. "But you must have *some* sense of self-preservation. You didn't know this person. He could have harmed you."

I bet he's imagining some pretty embarrassing head lines: INTRUDER DECAPITATES PHILANTHROPIST'S DAUGHTER.

Melinda is still going all psycho-demented. "He probably climbed right over the No Trespassing sign. Our neighbors would go insane if they heard that you encouraged him."

Why did I tell them? Because I thought they'd be proud of me in a weird kind of way. Like all that home schooling about values paid off.

I must confess that I'm losing the argument. They're used to fighting against giants, and I'm just a *peon*. Yay for me — I've actually absorbed that word and am applying it in real life.

"What about the Pope?" I say.

We recently heard the Pope talking on NPR about how to solve the problem of panhandlers. You give money to every single one of them, the Pope says, whether they fit your idea of who should be begging or not, and you must also make some physical connection, touch their hand or look at them — make eye contact — and wish them a good day. If you do that, the Pope says, your own day will improve, like a gift from heaven.

"Panhandlers are scam artists," Clark says. "You can't spend your life being conned by every sob story that comes your way."

"What you *should* have done is shut the door immediately, locked it, and dialed 911," Melinda says.

"Yeah, come and arrest the trailer trash." God, I hate her.

ʘ

Of course it didn't happen quite that way. They got the *abbreviated* version.

Rewind.

ʘ

It's late, but I know they'll be gone for at least a few hours. I poke around in Melinda's night table and find her vaping pen, one of the first things she bought in Los Angeles. I've just taken a tiny hit to get me through 450 flash cards, when the doorbell rings. Oh, man, who's that?

I pat down my hair, which looks like a mattress explosion, kick off my Donald Duck slippers, and slide into the suede ones. Melinda's voice floats in my head: *Now remember, Pammie ... deep breath ... only good thoughts.*

Things spin as I hurry to the far end of the condo. The lock groans. When I open the door, he is standing there, *luminous* under the night light. Smiling. Teeth as white as the whites of his eyes. Hair as wild and uncontrollable as mine.

He is my age. The first person I've seen in Pasadena who's my age.

"Hi," I say, putting out my hand to shake his.

But he seems shy and doesn't take it. He runs his palms down the sides of his pants then mumbles his story about the lost job and no food for two days.

"Why don't you come inside?" I say. "We have tons of food."

He thinks for a moment then says, "I don't want to disturb you, but I sure could use some money."

"I'm studying vocabulary words for the SAT," I say. "It's hell on wheels. You'd be helping me."

He stands there for a while, like maybe he'll do me a favor and come inside. I wish he'd make up his mind because it's cold out here and I'm shivering in my thin T-shirt. Eventually, he *condescends* to enter and crosses the threshold. There's no going back for him. I push the door shut and lock it.

Even people who aren't asking for food and money do a double-take when they first come into the condo. "Holy shit," he says.

Melinda has gone all out with the decorating — turquoise bamboo curtains, pink and white orchids, and smooth wax candles shaped like Brancusi sculptures. The Museum of the Earth, right here in Pasadena.

He looks around the room, taking it all in, then kneels at the coffee table and runs his hand over the sleek chrome and glass surface. "Cool," he says. "It's like a river of silver."

"Hey, do you want some food?"

"Sure. What you got?"

I set out two place mats on the dining room table and go behind the giant quartz island to the fridge. "Beef stroganoff or chicken curry? Leftovers. My mom is, like, this world-class chef."

He slouches at the table with really aggressively bad posture and says, "Do you have hot dogs and toast?"

So, basically I go all out for him — a whole package of organic, uncured, grass-fed beef hot dogs, which I serve with ketchup, Grey Poupon, and scrambled eggs. It's awesome to cook for a guest, especially someone who's *ravenous.* Unfortunately, I burn the toast, but he doesn't seem to mind, because he scarfs it all down without even looking. He's starving. I don't need homeschooling or any other kind of schooling to tell me that.

I'm impressed by how he throws back his head and pours a gazillion gallons of orange juice down the chute. I think he's telling the truth about not eating for two days.

He wipes some ketchup off his chin with a paper napkin and says, "Okay. Now show me your flash cards."

"You're kidding me. We can talk about anything in the world, and you want to see my vocabulary flash cards?"

He leans back in his chair. "Yeah. I wanna see how many words I can get. I used to be good at English."

"Why aren't you good at English anymore?"

He laughs. "Oh no, I didn't mean that. It's just —" His voice kind of cracks, and to my horror, he is suddenly crying — for real — tears on his cheeks, snuffling and blowing his nose on his napkin. "Oh, shit, don't look at me —"

But of course I do, and like a mirror-image, tears wash all over my eyeballs too and spill down my face. We are a Disney cartoon, fat tears splashing everywhere.

"Oh my God, why are we crying?" I say.

"You tell me," he says, his voice gruff with snot. "I don't see anything in this place to make you cry."

"I'm a prisoner here —" I sob, blowing hard into a tissue.

"You're not a prisoner! You could just open the door, like you did for me, and go for a run around the block."

"They don't let me go to school. They think the standards in the public schools are too low —"

He wipes away his tears and unexpectedly laughs. "Dude. Lots of private schools in Pasadena."

"They think it's a waste of money, and" — I say this with great *irony* — "there's not enough *diversity* at private school. It doesn't fit their image of themselves."

He shakes his head like I'm just too much to take, but he's listening, so I just keep on spilling it out. "I don't have any friends here. I'm, like, really lonely." And I feel my eyes watering again. It's crazy. I wipe the tears away. Why am I even telling him this? I hardly know him. He could be an ax murderer. For all he knows, I could be one too.

"My mom ran away from us and left just me and my dad," he says.

"What does your dad do?" I ask lamely.

He looks at his plate. "He doesn't do anything. He's got emphysema. And he drives me insane, man. He still smokes. He uses our money to buy cigarettes."

"Oh, God, smoking in the house —"

"My dad can't work and made me leave school. He says I'm 'able-bodied' so I've gotta support us."

All I can do is shake my head. He's like this alien who fell off another planet, yet we're both embedded in a life of total misery.

"We lost our apartment after my mom left," he says. "Couldn't pay the rent. We live in a homeless shelter. Sleep on two-level bunks. Dad sleeps on top because he has claustrophobia, but one time, he fell out and got a concussion. Freaked me out."

"That totally sucks," I say.

"Some nights it smells so bad in there I want to puke."

That sucks too. I want to tell him that he smells nice — wood smoke and Head & Shoulders.

"My dad makes me go out and beg at night." He waves in the direction of the front door. "He says there are rich people all along this street. That it'll be low-hanging fruit."

"So, I'm the fruit that you picked?"

He shifts in his chair and concentrates on peeling the fluted paper off a frosted coconut cupcake I gave him, from Katie's Bakery. He finishes it off in two bites.

When he stands up and stretches, his shirt comes up out of his pants, giving me an eyeful of polished abs. "Let's go take a look at those flash cards," he says.

Did I mention they're in my bedroom? But the room is huge like a hotel suite, so he probably won't get the wrong impression.

When I flick on the light, he whistles. "Hey, girl, if you're in prison, this sure is some jail cell."

How can I impress him if my life story can't compete with his? I start at the science table where I'm a whizz, throw together a few wires and a switch, and in a minute there's a drone buzzing around the room. Then I press another switch that turns on a light bulb and sets off a loud, shrill siren. He jumps about a hundred feet back and shrieks, "Shit!"

Ha! Revenge of the low-hanging fruit.

I jiggle the control so that the drone slows down and hovers in front of him then swoops into a soft landing on the table.

"Yowza!" he yells, laughing. "You could stand on my street downtown and make a million bucks with those tricks."

Yeah, and I could take him out with the drone — just a flick of my finger — but I don't tell him that.

My room leads onto a patio that stretches around the whole condo. I never open it because we're on the ground floor, but I feel safer now that I have company. The handle is stiff, however, and won't budge.

"Here, let me help you, I'm good at this shit," he says. Our hands get tangled together on the door handle, and it jolts me because he's definitely hot, and there we are in Melinda's worst nightmare — a totally *inappropriate* guy in my bedroom, holding my hand, and no chaperones for miles around.

He's taller than me and rests his head on my head. A connection, head to head: not what the Pope would recommend.

It's not like I'm experienced at relationships. I'm probably the only fifteen-year-old on Earth who's a virgin. Not because I have high moral principles. Only because none of the guys in Rochester dared to come near me. Not that I didn't experiment a bit; I know what's what. But who am I kidding? Not really.

"This is super weird," he says.

He's right. What am I doing? I jerk my hand away and run to the small sofa. Meanwhile he muscles the door open, and cold air fills the bedroom, giving me the shivers. "You should go," I say. "If my parents find us here like this they'll kill me."

"More likely they'll kill me," he says.

I walk him to the front door, press twenty dollars into his hand, then stand on my toes and kiss him on his cheek.

"By the way, tell me your name," he says.

ʘ

Melinda is all over me at breakfast the next morning. "Eat something, Pammie. Why so glum?"

The doorbell rings.

No one moves. When they send me to answer the door, I don't dare argue.

The man standing there fills the whole doorway, like his neck alone could be the trunk of an old oak tree. For obvious reasons, I'm jumpy today, and I shrink against the door. His skin is so black it shines purple in the morning light. "Howdy," he says, flashing a silver badge. "I'm Detective Bass."

You'd expect a great sonic boom to come out of him, but instead, his voice is mellow, like honey. "May I come in?"

I blink and then nod. No escape from him.

Melinda throws me a worried look, then morphs into total charm offensive. "Please come in, Detective. What can we do for you?"

He turns to me and says, "What's your name?" I'm freaking out and it's like I have amnesia. I clam up. He says again, very gently, "Can you tell me your name?"

"Oh for heaven's sake," Melinda snaps. "It's Pamela Johnson."

He hesitates. "I have some bad news for you, Pamela. Someone you know — maybe even a friend of yours — has passed away."

I sense Melinda twitching on the couch beside me. "But Pamela doesn't have any friends. We're new in town."

Like a magician, he pulls a small Ziploc bag from his pocket, and says, "Is this your card, Pamela?"

I don't even need to give it more than one glance to know it's mine, the little silver-edged card that I designed myself, with my name and contact information. But my parents jump forward to peer at it.

"Where did you get this?" Melinda demands, glaring at him. She has picked up on my fear, and I think it's dawned on her that this visit is personal, and her baby — the late little lamb, traumatized and sickly, born when she was forty — may be in trouble.

Detective Bass sighs. "This card was in the pocket of the deceased young man. We're trying to identify him. His body has just been discovered on the grounds of this complex."

He waves vaguely toward the front door. "One of the residents found him early this morning."

"He's dead?" I cry. He's the only person I ever gave my card to.

Detective Bass's face scrunches with sympathy. "Pamela, this is very important. We have a crew investigating the scene. Perhaps you could come with me and help us identify the young man."

"Pamela doesn't know any young men in Pasadena," Clark says.

"That may be the case," the detective says super smoothly, "but I sure would appreciate it if Pamela could come outside and see if she recognizes him."

Our condo lies smack-bang in the middle of the Garden of Eden, a place so lush that Eve probably met the serpent here among the flowers and trees and the gurgling stream that gushes down over the rocks. As we walk down the path from the apartment, Detective Bass angles his huge bulk very carefully to avoid slipping. The gradient is super-steep. I turn to walk sideways as I step down the moss-covered, widely spaced stone steps.

Old trees stretch their branches over us, blotting out the sun, and my arms prickle with goose bumps. Yellow tape surrounds the "scene," like they're filming a cop show. We are given blue paper booties and asked to step under the tape. Two people on their knees are inspecting a young man, lying on his side very still, as if he's sleeping. They're brushing leaves off his face. There's blood on his head. His body is there, but I see straightaway that his spirit has gone and the technicians are touching an empty shell. Where do people go when they die? Would he even have known where to go? He was only seventeen.

The mountain of a detective lowers himself to the ground and waves at me to sit next to him. But I don't want to because I can't breathe, and because I've never seen a dead person up close before, and because it's definitely him.

"How do you know he's dead?" I whisper. But of course he's dead — he's lying at a strange angle with no life in him.

A small crowd has gathered around the tape, and I recognize several of our neighbors.

"This is the man who came begging at our front door last night," Jane Carter says. "I'm afraid I shooed him away." I know Jane because she's on the homeowners' committee, fighting for our rights.

"We will take statements from all the residents," Detective Bass says. "But for now, please move away and give us some breathing room."

The technicians are scraping dirt or blood off his head and taking little samples with tools that look like ice-cream sticks. My legs go weak, and I sink to the ground. I want to go back inside where it's safe.

"Do you know his name?" the detective says quietly to me, so no one can hear. But Melinda has stuck to me like glue and says, "Do we need a lawyer, Detective?" — then turns to me — "Don't answer any questions, darling, until we know what's going on."

I think Detective Bass will need a crane to get himself up off the ground, but amazingly he bounces on the balls of his feet and launches himself up like a rocket.

ʘ

In the condo, we are all on the couch, with the detective sitting opposite us. He turns to me in a very calm, relaxed way, and says, "Pamela, will you help me shed some light on what happened to the young man?"

"Yes." It comes out as a dorky squeak, and I clear my throat.

"May I record your answers" — he puts his cell phone on the coffee table — "so I don't need to write stuff down? My memory isn't so good." He smiles with all his teeth, a regular guy.

"Really — I think we should call Anthony," Clark says, giving Melinda a meaningful look. "Get a bead on this."

"No, Dad, it's okay." I want to *vaporize* them when they micromanage me, pulling my strings like I'm a puppet.

"Thank you, Pamela, I appreciate that." Detective Bass leans forward. "Did you know the deceased?"

"Darren del Vecchio," I say, and spell the last name, as he did for me.

"Could you start at the beginning, Pamela?" the detective says. "How you met Darren and what happened here."

I tell him about the hot dogs, eggs, orange juice, burnt toast, twenty dollars, and vocabulary words in my bedroom.

"You took him to the bedroom?" Clark thunders.

I don't tell him about the patio door, the sweet ketchup-y kiss, and the way his hands squeezed the band's name on my T-shirt.

"I showed him my electricity experiment," I say. "He was so amazing. He changed the circuit and switches to add a spinner when the siren went off. He said he was sad because they didn't offer physics at his school."

"Did you hook up with him, Pamela?" Detective Bass asks, as if it's just ho-hum, another day, another question.

"Oh, give me a break!" Melinda says.

"No," I whisper. I don't tell the detective that I'm sad, because I wanted to and now I never will.

"Okay. Go on with what happened," he says.

൭

After I'd shown Darren my poetry books and en suite bathroom, he said, "Hey, let's go outside and explore."

"I'm not allowed to leave the condo —"

"C'mon, it's a clear night," he said. "You could bring your telescope and we could watch the stars."

So, I grabbed the small telescope and out we went.

"Shut your eyes," I commanded, while I tapped the keypad to lock the condo door.

Then we were out on the grounds, lit with pale spooky globes everywhere and the stream glittering in the moonlight. He grabbed my free hand, and we started running in a zigzag downhill, past the orange Birds of Paradise and the dark swaying succulents. It was an incredibly wild and beautiful ride, and for the first time since being in Pasadena, I thought, *This is unbelievable that we could be outdoors in February, hearing the stream bubbling down the stones and the wind shushing through the trees.* This was the totally amazing gift he gave me: the idea of roaming free, without permission.

൭

"Your recklessness and lack of judgment —" Clark says, sputtering. "It's always something with you."

"Please, Mr. Johnson," Detective Bass says, shutting him down with a look. "Okay, Pamela, you're doing great. What happened next?"

I wish I could change the story.

The stone steps on the grounds were slick from the spray of the stream; but we were immortal — like superheroes — charging down the hill and shrieking at the top of our lungs. The path suddenly turned sharply to the right, and I stumbled, causing the telescope to fly from my hand. I jumped forward to catch it, jerking away from him.

My sudden move knocked him off balance, and he fell.

I was helpless as he tumbled down, down, down, on the stone steps, banging his head as he went, and then disappearing off the edge, like falling off a precipice into a black hole. I screamed his name again and again, but he must have been unconscious because there was only silence.

"Did you go find him?" the detective asks.

"I tried," I whisper. "I didn't have a flashlight."

Terrified and alone in the black night. Paralyzed.

"So, what did you do?" His voice isn't judging, just probing, and maybe he sees the agony in my face, because he says, very softly, "Go on, Pamela."

"I went back up the hill and into the condo," I say. "My phone had no charge … and my parents were out … so I couldn't dial 911."

"How about the neighbors?" he says. "Did you try them?"

I can barely talk. "Yes," I say, "but no one came to the door."

The truth is I've blanked it out, and all I remember is creeping back into our condo and barricading myself deep in my bed, too scared, too cowardly to venture out.

If this were a movie, a really brave super heroine would have plunged out of the complex and into the traffic, screaming and waving her arms, causing the world to screech to a halt and go get help.

But it was only me. All the vocabulary words in the world can't explain how events got away from me and I just couldn't cope.

I am weeping now, and he squeezes my arm. "I killed him," I sob. "I let go of his hand and made him fall. And then, when someone could have saved him, I wasn't brave enough to go out in the night to get help."

ℴ)

Detective Bass returns to the condo the following week. He asks very politely if I'll make him a cup of tea.

When we're sitting at the counter, he says, "I wanted to let you know that Darren's death has been ruled accidental. His head took lots of hits from the fall."

A space opens up in my chest.

"I wish I had tried harder," I say, the waterworks starting up. "I feel like a total murderer."

"Yes, you should have pounded on some doors," he says. "No question about that. But sometimes we're all too human and let ourselves down." He blows on the tea and takes a sip. "Let me tell you something, Pamela, while you're alone here. Most of the folks in the condos turned Darren away. You're a kind person, and the world needs more people like you."

ℴ)

My sixteenth birthday is around the corner, and Melinda is making all kinds of celebratory plans for the three of us, like I'm a rock star or something. She has recovered from the "terrible incident" at the condo, and we've calmly discussed my *ineptitude* and *gullibility*.

Whatever.

I tell them there's just one thing I want for my birthday: to be enrolled at Pasadena High School. I need to quit being their little hothouse genius and go to a regular high school.

Melinda goes all Tiger Mom. "You know you can't go to a regular school."

"Mo-om. It's not like I'm going to trash the science table or burn your freaking poetry books." For once, I'm totally *adamant.*

Grow up and escape from her. It's the least I can do for Darren. Before I can give myself a zillion reasons not to do it, I get up my courage, install Uber on my phone, and venture out of my safe world.

There aren't too many homeless shelters in Pasadena, so I find him pretty quickly.

His name is Shawn del Vecchio, and he's much older than I pictured, with a thin fuzz of gray hair and a stooped back. He's very sad and frail, and coughs a lot. He shows absolutely no surprise at seeing me.

We sit in a kind of common room with a giant garbage can and a TV.

"Darren was smart and funny, and we were friends," I say. "I'm so sorry for your loss."

His rheumy eyes cover over with tears. "It makes no difference if you sorry or not. I warned him not to go begging in the rich people areas. It's not safe, I said, someone there's gonna kill you . . ." And he's crying some more with great gulping sobs.

I don't know what to say because I'm not smooth like my mother and don't know how to do the whole charity thing. I just shove the envelope into his hand, and say, "It's a donation in Darren's name." My hands are shaking and some of the purple sparkles of my nail polish have come off onto it, so the envelope looks like a party favor.

He stares at it like it's a snake.

My stomach clenches and the great Hallmark Channel tear factory comes rolling in again. "Please …"

It's my birthday present, five hundred dollars in twenties. Melinda and Clark would go ballistic — but it's not their money anymore.

He sits still for a while then stuffs the envelope into his pocket. "What you say your name was?" he asks.

๑

Rewind. The absolutely last time, cross my heart and hope to die.

๑

So. There he was, on our doorstep, smiling.

Will you walk into my parlor? said the spider to the fly.

O no, no, said the little fly. But in he came anyway and stuffed his face like it was the Last Supper. All the while, Pammie kept the Malevolent One tucked away and out of sight, pretty much under control. Good luck with that. He was mine.

Pathetic little Pammie of the frizzy hair and chipmunk cheeks, leading him into the bedroom and showing him her techie toys. Sweet sixteen and never been kissed. I opened my mouth and sucked him in and felt his delicious man-thing, but then Pammie smacked me away and said no, never again. We don't do that anymore.

Party pooper.

It was a perfect starry night — total Van Gogh. Time for our romp in the garden.

Pammie trying to pull us back because she knows the night belongs to me.

Down the hill we fly, over the stones: faster, faster with his hand tightly in my grip. I'm like this witch on a broomstick, ayeeeee! Ayeeeee! Free! Scree! … until he goes ape shit and bursts the bubble. Why do they always do that?

"Ow! Let go! Why you acting so weird?"

He won't play!

Pulling away, snapping his arm up and down, kicking and twisting to throw me off, going all National Geographic like a deer in the jaws of a hyena.

And everyone's, like, "Play nicely, Pamela," but no one to stop Pammylla this time, no teachers on the playground, and Pammie, sweet Pammie, shriveling away in the shadows.

The red dot in my brain explodes, and I shake him loose. As he stumbles, I smash the base of the telescope into his skull and down and away he goes, crashing into the rocks.

Such a shame he wouldn't play. We really liked him.

Back in the condo, Pammie is sleeping, and I snuggle back into her. Safe in her nighttime dreams. She won't remember a thing.

SHARK NEWS

Karter Mycroft

After Hunter's girlfriend kicked him out of her apartment, he thought about doing something responsible with his life and ended up moving to Venice instead. He spent a day searching for the cheapest room he could find, then sold his car to cover the security deposit on an ugly gray townhouse on Indiana Avenue. At the time, he didn't know much about Venice, only that it seemed laid-back and had a nice breeze, and was about as far from his ex as he could get without falling in the ocean. He also didn't know much about deep-sea sharks, or the city's policies regarding elevator inspections, or the frequency bandwidths of various types of radio broadcasts. If he had, he might have been better prepared for what was coming.

He spent the first week on a mattress on the floor, playing video games and texting his ex and ordering pizza from chain restaurants. Eventually, he worked up the motivation to explore the neighborhood. He wandered Abbot Kinney, past expensive restaurants, psychedelic murals, surf shops that only sold clothes, and weed stores that charged five times what he was used to paying back in the Valley. He smoked a joint around the canal district, drawing sneers from folks who sipped wine outside multi-million-dollar homes with signs in the yards reading *Save Venice! No Shelters!*

The canals made him nervous. He'd hoped in Venice he would meet some people like himself. Carefree types who liked to have fun, the sort of people he remembered seeing when he'd visited as a kid. Artists and hippies and surfers and pretty girls who smoked cigarettes. So far, he'd only seen rich people who didn't wear shoes.

He hung around the beach, drifting past the street vendors with their caricatures and irreverent T-shirts, the county fair-style food shacks, the legendary skate park. He watched the skaters for a few hours. He'd tried skateboarding in high school, and he'd been bad at it. There were eight-year-olds here who looked like Olympic gold medalists by comparison. He tried chatting with some guys around his age who stood at the railing, wondering if this might be where he'd find his people. Everyone he talked to was visiting from another state.

ⵚ

He woke up the next morning to a call from his dad.

"Where did you say you moved?"

"Venice Beach."

"What the hell, Hunter? You're supposed to be saving money. You're supposed to be going back to school."

"I just needed to get away for a while. Focus on myself, you know?"

"Well, forget about us helping with your rent. Not unless you get a full-time job. Otherwise you need to move back home."

They had a long argument, and Hunter lost. He'd never worked full-time before and was not excited about the prospect. But maybe it wouldn't be so bad. It could be a good way to meet people, at least.

He tried the bars first. A few said they could use somebody, but he needed serving experience. He tried coffee shops, and they said the same thing. The managers of fancy restaurants on Abbot Kinney practically laughed in his face when they saw his resume. One said something like, "Do you know how many *qualified* servers want to work here?" It made him feel like an idiot. His only work experience was delivering sandwiches, and now he didn't even have a car.

After a week he felt defeated. It seemed like no one would give him a chance. It was even starting to seem like no one wanted him in Venice at all. His neighbors had no interest in him, and everyone else he met was either a tourist or selling things to tourists. He'd hoped this would be a place he could start over, but he was the same as he'd always been: broke, stoned, and lonely, with nothing to do and nothing to show for it. He might as well give up and move back home after all.

He was about to throw his last few resumes in the trash, after a particularly cold rejection from Blue Bottle Coffee, when something caught his eye. A sheet of yellowed paper posted on a lamppost, with tiny off-center text. It looked like it'd come from an old typewriter. No capitals, no punctuation, it read: "wanted intern for local radio program knowledge of marine life preferred paid."

Hunter stared at it, perplexed. Was there no contact information? He tore the ad off the post and checked the back. Nothing. That was all it said: "wanted intern for local radio program knowledge of marine life preferred paid." It gave him an eerie feeling, and he glanced over his shoulder for some reason. He shoved the crisp paper in his pocket.

The rest of the day, it was all he could think about. A paid internship could solve his problem of needing a job but not having experience. And there was something so intriguing about the ad itself. How was he supposed to know who posted it? Was it even real?

He reread it several times in bed. Then he checked his phone and scanned the latest text thread with his ex. He had been telling her his second thoughts about Venice. Her last message said, *Well … want to meet up sometime once you're back in the Valley?*

He closed his eyes.

ʘ

The next day he stopped by a bar that had been relatively friendly about turning down his resume. The bartender was named Juana, and she was also the manager. She was a local in her late thirties, with one side of her head shaved and both arms covered in excellent tattoos. He ordered a Lagunitas and showed her the ad.

"Have you ever seen one of these posted around here?"

She smirked. "Nope. It looks old, though. Must have been up for a while."

"You think it's a prank?"

"I doubt it, honestly. There are lots of weirdos around here, between the cracks. Old-school hippies. Could be part of some kooky art project. Or just somebody who sucks at typing."

He took a gulp of beer. "Maybe that's why they need an intern."

"Yeah, maybe." She wiped down the counter, filling the air with the scent of bleach. "Still on the job hunt, then?"

"Yeah." Another gulp. "I have a feeling about this one, though." He turned the ad over in his hands. "Is there like, a local radio station somewhere close?"

She glanced up in thought. "The college station has some weird shows, but that's in Del Rey. I guess there's an NPR in Santa Monica. Oh! There is a smaller one down by the beach. Radio Westside. Never listened to them though."

He felt a hum of excitement. "Maybe they'll know something."

"Hell of a way to find a job."

"Like I said, I have a feeling. I also really need to make some money."

"What brought you to Venice, anyway?"

He ran a hand through his shaggy hair. "I mean, it's a great vibe, right? The culture and the atmosphere and everything. Who wouldn't want to live here?"

She raised an eyebrow.

He sighed into his glass. "My ex-girlfriend kicked me out of her apartment."

Juana nodded. "What'd you do?"

"She said I wasn't *present* enough." He finished his beer. "I have trouble focusing. I zone out and forget shit. It made school hard. Weed helps some, but then it's just like my mind's going in a hundred directions instead of a million."

"They ever put you on that Vyvanse?"

"For a while. It messed my stomach up. I don't like pills."

"Good for you." She took his empty glass, filled another and gave it to him. "On me."

"Thanks."

"You're not the first to get kicked to the curb and skid all the way to the boardwalk. It was my parents who kicked me out, in '01. Back then, Venice was the *affordable* option on the Westside, if you can believe it."

"That's funny. My parents want me to move back home."

"And yet, here you are."

"Yeah. I just wanted a change, I guess. Somewhere to figure myself out."

"Change can be good sometimes." Some techie-looking guys in quirky T-shirts and Ray-Bans hopped off motorized scooters and walked into the bar. Juana leaned in before greeting them. "Keep in mind, places change too."

Hunter finished his beer and stepped outside. Sea clouds rolled overhead, graying out the sky. It was almost the end of October, which meant winter showers were right around the corner. It also meant rent was due soon. He glanced at the ad once more. There was something irresistible about the mystery of it. It felt like something he could be determined about. Something he could focus on.

Google Maps showed Radio Westside off Westminster, a ten-minute walk away. A light drizzle came down on the way. He was briefly distracted by a crowd of girls with Southern accents complaining that L.A. was supposed to be sunny. The station was in the back of an old brick building on the waterfront, several stories high with a metal tower on the roof. He stepped inside.

The receptionist was an older woman with glasses strapped around her head like swim goggles. He was unsure how to begin. "I, uh, my name's Hunter. I was wondering if you had any info about, like, local radio broadcasts?"

The woman pointed to the sign on the wall that said RADIO WESTSIDE. "Well, yeah."

"Right, right." He took a deep breath. "Do any of your shows cover, like, marine biology? Fishing? Anything like that?"

She sighed through her nose. "We do music and high school football. Not … what was it again?"

"Marine biology."

She shook her head.

For a second, Hunter felt like he was out of his mind. "Okay. Sorry. Thanks, sorry —"

"Hold up a second." A man in a blue suit appeared around a corner. He was tall and bulky, with a sharp face and dark eyes, and a seashell necklace that seriously clashed with his business attire. He walked up to Hunter and extended a hand. "Hi. I'm Shawn. I run Radio Westside. Were you asking about a particular show?"

The look on Shawn's face was strange, like there was something he couldn't wait to talk about. Maybe that was how all business guys looked. Hunter shook his hand. "Yeah. A show about marine life. I think it's local, kind of DIY, but I don't know anything more about it."

"Interesting." Shawn's voice fell low, like he was telling a secret. "Listen. There's a ham radio guy around here who we get interference from sometimes. I can't say for sure, but I've got a feeling that's who you're after."

Hunter's heartbeat picked up. "Do you know where I can find him?"

"Sure. I was just there myself a while back." Shawn scribbled something on a business card and handed it over. It said, *Mike. 37½ Buccaneer St.* "Be careful over there, kid. These shortwave guys, they're bonkers. One-track minds. I love independent radio, don't get me wrong, but these guys, man. They really go off the deep end."

Hunter cleared his throat. "Yeah. I'll watch out."

"What do you want with the guy, anyway?"

Hunter almost pulled out the ad, but something about the look in Shawn's eye made him think twice. "I, uh, caught some of his show and wanted to ask him about it. Anyway, thanks for the help."

Shawn gave a slow nod. "Don't mention it. And hey, if you do talk to him, tell him to give me a call, will you?"

"Yeah? Okay, sure. Thanks again." He left the station and made for the boardwalk, with a strange sense that Shawn was watching him go.

Filled with excitement, he shuffled along the beach, past the skate park, past the cacophonous drum circle that seemed to never end, past the scam artists advertising medical marijuana cards even though marijuana was now legal, all the way past the fishing pier, high waves breaking against its pilings under the gray sky.

Buccaneer Street was really an alley, too narrow for cars and covered by scraggly hedges. He struggled to read the house numbers through the mess of leaves. He saw 35 and 39, but nothing in between. He reread Shawn's card. It definitely said "37½." His nerves rose. Maybe this *was* some weird hoax after all. He wondered if someone might leap from the bushes and rob him. Just what he needed.

Then he saw it. At the end of a thin, gravel path, an alley within the alley, was a small shed with crooked walls and a sheet metal roof. One side was covered in wires, flowing out like jellyfish tentacles from a rusty circuit breaker. Hand-painted on the door was the word "NEWS."

Hunter buzzed with anticipation. He slinked up to the shed, hesitated, then knocked on the door.

It swung open.

Hunter found himself facing a sweaty old man, shorter than he was but much wider, with a gnarly white beard stained brown around the lips, a baseball cap with an anchor logo, and a gut seeping down from his shirt over undersized khaki shorts.

"Can I help you?"

It took Hunter a second to remember what he was doing. He pulled out the ad, and the card he'd gotten from Shawn. "Are you Mike?"

"Far as I know."

"I, um, thought you might be looking for an intern?"

"Right. Yeah. Good timing." Mike nodded as though Hunter had said something incredibly obvious. He gestured into the shed. "Well, get in here. Show's about to start."

Hunter froze. Mike did not seem surprised in the least that he'd come answering the ad. Almost like he was expected. This day kept getting stranger and stranger.

He stepped inside.

The smell hit him hard. The shed reeked like rotten fish soaked in sweat. It was dark, and his eyes took a second to adjust. He noticed the walls first. They were covered, floor to ceiling, with shark jaws. Row after row of toothy cartilage, lifeless and gaping. Some were as small as Hunter's fist; some looked big enough to swallow him whole.

A desk stood against the wall, cluttered with electronics. Speakers, tape decks, monitors, walkie-talkies, and microphones. More dials, switches, wires, and knobs than Hunter could begin to make sense of. Surrounding the desk was a forest of file cabinets and stacked newspapers, with clippings scattered on the floor like fallen leaves.

Mike plopped down in a creaky chair. "So. New intern. What'd you say your name was?"

"Uh, Hunter." Had he mentioned his name yet?

"Hunter." Mike stroked his tangled beard. "Hunter, Hunter, Hunter. Huh. *Aytch.* Horn Shark Hunter. Hunter Horn. That's no good. Hammerhead Hunter … God, I hope not, hmm. Ah, I got it!" He jabbed a finger at Hunter. "Hardnose shark. *Carcharhinus macloti.* Incredible species, western Indo-Pacific. Slender and harmless, just like you. Hardnose Hunter. Absolutely."

Hunter had trouble keeping up. "Um, sir?"

Mike shut his eyes tight, a massive blink that made his face a mess of wrinkles. "We do nicknames on the show. Don't sweat it, all right? And for the love of God, call me Mike."

Hunter's excitement had turned to nervous confusion, and the smell wasn't helping any. "Can I ask what this position involves, Mike?"

Another extreme blink. "Well, the main thing is —"

An alarm clock erupted on the desk, sending a shrill ring through the shed. Mike spun around and silenced it with a whack. "Whoop! Gotta fill you in later, Hardnose. We're on the air in five." He flipped a series of switches on the desk.

"Four."

He tapped a rusty silver microphone with a thick finger.

"Three."

He grabbed a stack of papers from the top of a file cabinet.

"Two."

He slid a pair of tattered headphones over his cap.

"And …" He punched a tape deck and leaned into the microphone. "Good afternoon, Planet Earth, and welcome to *Shark News*! I'm your host, Mako Mike. It is three o'clock by the Pacific Standard, and we've got one hell of a program today. Lots of news coming out of Oxnard-Ventura, and at five o'clock, we'll continue our deep dive into — you guessed it — *Apristurus spongiceps*. That's right, the spongehead catshark. Remarkable species, one of my favorites. Discovered in the wild in 2002. But first, let's get into some news!"

Hunter sat on a cabinet. For three hours, he listened to Mike talk without stopping, rattling off one piece of information after the other into his microphone, all of it about sharks. There was a bull shark sighting at a resort in Florida, results from a basking shark survey off the Channel Islands, a controversial program to hunt great whites in Western Australia. Hunter couldn't follow all the details, but something in Mike's delivery kept him listening intently. Mike spoke with great enthusiasm, his voice silky-smooth, almost mesmerizing.

At five o'clock, as promised, Mike went into spectacular detail about the spongehead catshark, which was apparently a rare deep-sea species notable for its short, rounded anal fin. This went on for another full hour.

"And before I sign off for the day, I have a special announcement. Today we are very happy to welcome our new intern: Hardnose Hunter, who's right here in the studio. Hunter, why don't you come say 'hey'?"

Hunter jolted to attention. "What? Me?"

Mike waved him over. He cautiously approached the microphone.

"H — hello," he stuttered.

Mike blinked. "Thrilled to have Hunter aboard. All right, pups, that's the show. Tune in tomorrow for another edition of *Shark News*. This is Mako Mike, signing off."

He flipped a switch and spun around in his chair. "So? What do you think?"

Hunter scratched his head. "It's, um, informative. You have another show tomorrow?"

"Three till six, Pacific, seven days a week."

"You have three hours of shark news to report every single day?"

"Oh, way more than that," Mike chuckled. "But you gotta condense it down. Give 'em the good stuff. And save time for the deep dives. Everybody loves those."

"How many listeners do you have?"

"Excellent question." He pointed to a big brown box with a dial on it. "You know what this is?"

Hunter shook his head.

"It's a shortwave radio transmitter. High frequency signal with skywave propagation. You can broadcast all over the world with this. Only problem is, not so many folks have a shortwave *receiver* anymore. Mostly military guys, hobbyists, amateurs. Not a lot of serious shark people." He said "shark people" like it was a perfectly common label. "And that's why I need you, Hardnose. Young guy like yourself, you must be pretty hip, am I right?"

Hunter shrugged. "I guess so."

"Killer. So that'll be your job. Getting us to a bigger audience. Got some big plans on that front. In the meantime, you'll be helping me with the news, taking notes, keeping things running smooth. And I can always use help bleaching the jaws." He gestured to the stinking ovals of teeth covering the walls. "Sound okay?"

Hunter dug his foot into the floor. A part of him knew he should bail. This guy was clearly nuts. Who knew what Mike was *actually* into? But he thought about the rent. He thought about moving back in with his parents, and meeting up with his ex, and going back to school.

He nodded. "Yeah. Sure. Sounds good to me, Mike."

Mike clapped his hands. "Killer! So, what do you want, anyway? A hundred bucks a day? Two hundred?"

His heart raced at the mention of money. "Uh, are those my options?"

"Sure, whatever. Name your price, Hardnose."

"Two hundred dollars a day?"

"Right on, right on." Mike reached in his shorts pocket and pulled out a wad of bills. His voice took on a stern tone. "You can have Sundays off, but not Saturdays. And I'm not doing healthcare or any of that shit. Totally off the grid, *capiche*?"

Hunter nodded rapidly. "Right. Cool."

Mike handed him two wrinkled hundreds. "See you in the morning, then."

He put the bills in his wallet, his excitement returning. Two hundred bucks a day, tax-free? He could pay his rent in a week and a half if this kept up. And no experience needed, apparently. He started feeling proud of himself for following up on the ad.

"Oh." He stopped on his way out the door. "Shawn says to call him."

Mike did his crazy wrinkle-blink. He held his face like that for a long time. "What did you say?"

"Shawn, from Radio Westside. I went there asking about the ad and he gave me your address. Weird guy, but he was helpful. He asked me to have you call him."

The wrinkles dripped into a scowl. "Did he ask you anything else?"

"Nope."

"Did you tell him you were coming to work for me?"

Hunter thought about it. "Actually, I didn't."

The scowl softened. "That's good. All right, Hardnose. Consider his message received."

Hunter wanted to ask what the hell was up with Shawn anyway, but he was itching to get outside, away from the smell, to process everything and decide what to do with his two hundred dollars.

"See you tomorrow, Mike."

ⓞ

The next few weeks passed in a blur. Hunter would wake up, grab coffee, and walk down the boardwalk just as the cops were kicking out the homeless folks who slept on the beach. He would arrive at the shack early, around eight o'clock, and help Mike go through the news. Mike always had a dozen newspapers ready to go, along with several newsletters from fishing industry groups and government agencies, four old TVs tuned to cable news, and a fax machine that constantly spat out shark-related bulletins from God-knows-where.

Mike never actually asked Hunter to work on building their audience. They focused on the news. Sometimes Mike would assign odd tasks, like rearranging the file cabinets or replacing old cables or calling up shark scientists with hyper-specific questions. When there was nothing else to do, he would send Hunter out back to soak the jaws in hydrogen peroxide, which was supposed to help preserve them and get out the fishy death smell. Hunter never noticed the smell improve, but he did start getting used to it after a while.

Everything Mike did was analog. Landlines, faxes, cable, and print. There was no computer in the shed. He recorded every episode to cassette and had a catalog of them going back to the early '90s. During the broadcasts, Hunter's job was to take notes for Mike to reference in case the cassettes were ever damaged. At one point, Hunter mentioned they could get a digital recording interface and store everything on the cloud. Mike looked at him like he was the craziest person in the world.

Two hundred dollars a day was good money. Not only could he pay all his rent himself, he had some left over. He bought a bed frame and a rug and a TV stand and some new clothes. He even opened a savings account. His parents still said he should move back home, but now it was a suggestion instead of a demand, since he wasn't asking them for money. More importantly, he stopped texting his ex. He told her he'd found a job and was planning to stay on the Westside, and he didn't hear back from her after that.

He stopped by Juana's bar often. Now that he had money, he could afford beers on the regular. Sometimes after two or three, he would consider asking her out, even though she was a solid ten years older and a thousand times cooler. He never quite worked up the courage, but he thought about it more and more as December rolled around, and the rain soaked the sidewalks and kept the tourists away and it started to seem like Venice might have a place for him after all.

ⓓ

One morning, feeling particularly energized, Hunter decided to bring his laptop to the shed. He'd worked up some social media for *Shark News* in his spare time. Part of his job was to expand their audience, after all. He figured he'd start small and ease Mike into it, since the old man seemed pretty stuck in his ways.

That afternoon, once the news was all ready and the broadcast was planned out, he pulled out his computer.

"Here's something I've been working on. Basically, exploring an online presence. I think it can help us reach new listeners."

Mike frowned. Hunter half expected him to ask what "online" meant. After a long silence, he motioned for Hunter to proceed.

He opened the browser. "So, this is our Twitter. See, we've got a little logo, a few posts, just letting people know when we're on the air and stuff. I also followed a few shark accounts you might like."

He paused to gauge Mike's reaction. The old man's eyes were as wide as two skillets. He gave the hardest blink ever performed by a human being and leaned close to the screen.

"This … this is who we follow?"

"Yeah. You can get news really fast on here. Faster than the fax machine."

"And this is who sees us?"

"Right. I was thinking we can build up our Twitter and Facebook and then start posting episodes. Like a podcast. I think people could get super into it. We could even post some of the backlog as special episodes or —"

"Goddammit, Hardnose!"

Mike sprang up, red in the face. His jaw hung open and a vein throbbed in his neck. "What the hell are you thinking?"

Hunter stepped back, heart pounding. Mike had never gotten angry before. Now he was furious. “I — I thought you wanted to expand our audience.”

“Did I say we were doing that *now*?”

“You said it was part of my job ...”

“Not like this, goddammit.” He wiped sweat off his brow. “This is the exact bullshit Shawn would always try.”

Hunter took a deep breath. “I’m sorry, Mike. I was just trying to help out.”

“Yeah, yeah. I know. But you aren’t clued in yet.”

“Clued into what?” Hunter sat back on a cabinet. “Look, I’ve been working for you over a month now. I like the job. I’m way more into, like, sharks and broadcasting than I ever thought I would be.” His voice cracked. “But I think you should really keep me in the loop on this stuff so I know what to focus on, you know?”

There was a heavy silence. The vein receded back into Mike’s neck. He seemed to calm down a little.

“I shouldn’t have yelled. You’re doing great, Hardnose. But this internet stuff. We can’t do it. Not yet.”

“I’ll delete it. No problem. I just don’t want to be in the dark on things.”

Mike sighed. “All right, then. Tell me what you wanna know.”

“What is the deal with Radio Westside?”

A tremendous blink. “That station *is* the deal.”

“Did you work there, before?”

“Work there? I founded the goddamn place. Built it from the ground up, right here in Venice. I wanted to do something different from the other stations. Not just play music and sports and political shit. I wanted to *educate* people.”

“About sharks?”

"Among other things." He looked at the roof. "Back before you were born, we had a great thing going. Twenty-four-hour programming, reception through the entire L.A. basin, all licensed and accredited and everything. I did *Shark News* from three to six, and my friends had their shows the rest of the time. There was real heart in it, you know?"

Hunter felt a wave of sadness. It was clearly paining Mike to recount all this. "What happened?"

Mike gritted his teeth. "My son finished law school, then failed the bar and decided he wanted into the family trade instead. At first I was all for it. He was sharp, ambitious, hip. A better businessman than me, I'll admit it. But the more power I gave him, the more we butted heads. He would tell me I was out of touch, running the business into the ground. He would say things like, 'People don't want to hear about sharks during evening rush hour.' And finally, he knifed me in the back. Had me sign a contract I didn't read well enough, and he ended up with Radio Westside. He told me I could still do my show, but from three to six in the *morning*. I told him to fuck off."

"Shawn."

"Yep. That's my boy. Took everything I built and ruined it. It's barely even a radio station anymore. The regular programming's all automated; it's a goddamn jukebox!" He cracked his big knuckles. "But I haven't given up yet, Hardnose. It's not over with me and him."

"And that's why you don't want to get on social media? So Shawn won't know you're still broadcasting?"

"Oh, he knows." A faint glimmer came to Mike's eye. "But we gotta keep a low profile until the gear gets here."

"Gear? What g—"

The alarm clock blasted. Ten seconds to showtime.

"Shit. Get your notebook." Mike flipped some switches. "Good afternoon, Planet Earth, and welcome to *Shark*

News! I'm your host, Mako Mike, and today we're talking dogfish …"

ൊ

Hunter took down all the social media. For the next month, he focused on his day to day, and decided not to ask about Radio Westside or Mike's ominous plan unless it came up again. Part of him hoped it never would, since things kept getting better and better, otherwise. He had steady work, an apartment by the beach, and a totally unsustainable crush on the person who sold him beer. Not a bad spread, all things considered. He even made a few friends, some local surfer guys who hung out at the bar. They came over to Hunter's place sometimes to get stoned and play Xbox. They were always saying he should come surfing, and he was close to saying yes.

Then, one sunny Tuesday, he arrived at the shed to find Mike pulling a bunch of cardboard boxes off a truck.

"Morning, Hardnose. Give me a hand with these, will you?"

As soon as they finished unloading, the truck drove away without warning, spraying Hunter with gravel. They carried the boxes inside the shed, taking up the entire floor space. Mike started unboxing one hunk of electronics after another. He smiled while he did it.

"What is this stuff?"

"This," said Mike, "is a microwave FM transmitter. And *this* is the best linear amplifier on the market. You're not supposed to own these without a license." He did his mega-blink. "Now open that one."

Hunter did as he was told. Inside, covered in packing peanuts, was a collapsed antenna, something that looked like a stopwatch, and a bunch of wires. "What is all this for?"

Mike was beaming, cheeks red above his white whiskers. "I've been working on this for a long time. Ever since Shawn cut me out." He pulled the equipment out of the bag, grinning like a madman. "We're gonna hack the dish."

"What?"

"Yeah. Real pirate radio shit."

"What do you mean, 'hack the dish'?"

Mike started plugging things into things. "On top of the Radio Westside tower block is a small microwave dish that connects the audio from the studio to the transmission tower. What we are going to do is pre-record *Shark News*, take this transmitter up to the roof, and blast it at that dish. As long as we're stronger than the feed from the studio — and we will be, thanks to this amp — we'll take over their broadcast." He grinned ear to ear. "I'm gonna get my airwaves back."

Hunter was dumbstruck. Hijack the broadcast from Radio Westside? That was not in the job description. Although, technically, nothing was.

"Won't they catch you? I mean, won't Shawn or somebody be there?"

"That's the beauty of it." Mike somehow smiled even wider. "Tomorrow, Shawn and I have a little father-son fishing trip planned. He says he wants to bury the hatchet. And I agree, no father should be at war with his son."

He gave a dark grin. "So, we'll do this tomorrow, while Shawn's on the boat with me. With Shawn out on the water, there won't be anyone around to cut the signal. *Shark News* will be all over L.A. for evening rush hour, just like the good old days."

Hunter's gut was churning. "I'm not seeing what this is supposed to accomplish, Mike."

There was a twinkle in Mike's eye that brought Hunter close to panicking. "It'll be the comeback of the century! The station will have more buzz than it's had in decades. Shawn will have no choice but to give me my show back."

Hunter couldn't believe what he was hearing. Was Mike serious? Did he truly think hijacking Radio Westside would get him his show back? Something didn't add up. And there was another question, one that made him sick with anxiety, one he was terrified he already knew the answer to.

"How do you plan to get all this equipment on the roof?"

"It's simple." Mike opened another box and took out a crinkled brown uniform. "You pack everything in suitcases. You go in there and say the city sent you to inspect the elevators. That gets you on the roof. Then you just do some light assembly, plug into the generator, point and shoot. Easy as chum."

"That sounds extremely illegal."

Mike sucked his teeth. "So is paying you under the table, but I never heard you complain about that. Speaking of which." He reached into his pocket and pulled out a wad of bills. "This kind of gig deserves a bonus. I'm thinking two grand. Okay, twist my arm, two and a half." He counted out a stack of bills and slapped them into Hunter's sweaty hand.

Hunter looked at the money, then at Mike. "I don't think I want to do this."

"I've thought it all through, don't worry. There's no danger at all. Shawn won't even be there, and he's the only one who might recognize you, right?"

He couldn't believe he was considering it. "Uh, the receptionist —"

"Who, Nancy?" Mike guffawed. "That old bat can't see a thing."

Hunter wanted to bolt. He wanted to throw back the money and run to Juana's and drink five beers and never think about Mike or sharks or the radio ever again. But then he'd be out of a job, and his savings wouldn't last long in this neighborhood. He might lose his apartment. He might have to move back home.

There was something about Mike, too. Mike was the only reason Hunter had started making it in Venice at all. It felt like they were in this together, even if he hadn't known exactly what *this* was. He wanted to be angry with Mike for springing such a crazy scheme, but here was a guy who'd had his whole life's work taken away. Downsized to a shack in an alley, by his own son, no less. Even if the plan didn't make sense, Hunter thought the reasons for it did. And it seemed like a harmless scheme, even if it was illegal.

"This is a one-time thing, right?"

"Oh, absolutely. It'll only take once, I'm positive. Hell, we pull this off, you'll find yourself with a steady job at the station once I'm back on."

Slowly, reluctantly, he slid the money in his pocket. "All right. I'll take this stuff to the roof and turn it on. But that's it, you know? No more infiltrating or pirating or other weird radio shit. You never told me this was part of the job."

"I know, I know." Mike gave a firm nod. "Thank you, Hardnose. Seriously. Look, my family's a tough thing to understand. So is the radio business." He leaned forward. "You know what's easy to understand? Sharks."

Hunter wiped his brow. "I dunno. You know more about sharks than I ever will. Probably more than anybody does."

"But for all the vast knowledge the world has to offer about their life history, biology, reproduction, interactions with humans, all of it, you can really boil all sharks down to one very simple thing."

"What's that?"

"They're hungry, and they know what to do about it."

ʘ

Hunter returned in the early morning. He skipped coffee, since he was already so jittery he thought he might explode. Mike had the gear all packed in a pair of metal suitcases: the transmitter, the amplifier, the cassette player loaded with a pre-recorded episode of *Shark News*. He showed Hunter how to assemble everything, explained where to get power on the roof and how to configure the timer so that everything switched on right on time. He also gave a rundown on Hunter's cover: he was Inspector Hardnose from the Department of Building Safety, there to examine the elevators.

"Nobody's gonna believe my last name is Hardnose."

"Well, what do you suggest?"

"I dunno. Smith?"

"Fine."

They parted ways in the alley, once Hunter was suited up. "If anything gets hairy," said Mike, "you have your walkie-talkie. And don't be nervous! Remember, I built that place, and you have my permission to do this. In-n-out, like burgers. Real simple. Hey." He clapped Hunter on the shoulder. "You're a good guy, Hardnose. I believe in you."

Mike headed south, toward the marina. Hunter took a deep breath, picked up the suitcases, and started for the radio station. Over his left shoulder, the ocean lapped enthusiastically over the breakwaters, like it knew what he was up to.

Nancy the receptionist was not a fan of his cover story.

"We don't have anything scheduled today." She leered at him through her glasses.

He cleared his throat. His nerves were raging, but he tried to keep it cool. "Can you show me where the elevator is, please?"

"Where did you say you were from?"

He tried to speak with confidence. "City of Venice Department of Building Safety."

"Venice isn't a city, it's a neighborhood."

Damn it. He knew that.

"I'm going to phone the office and make sure we're due for one."

Hunter's stomach flipped. He had managed to screw up already, and he wasn't even on the roof yet. An idea sprang into his head, and he grabbed his walkie-talkie.

"No need, ma'am, I'll put you on with my boss straight away." He mashed the talk button. "Inspector Smith, for the Chief Inspector. I have a tenant requesting confirmation of our evaluation schedule." He hoped that came across as smoothly as it had in his head.

The receptionist eyed him suspiciously. A moment later, the walkie-talkie squawked back. Mike's voice, distorted by static. "Afternoon, Mr. Smith. Can you please confirm the address?"

He held out the walkie-talkie to Nancy. She recited the Radio Westside address.

Mike came back a second later. "Thank you, ma'am, yes, due to the new seismic laws we are conducting non-routine inspections of all lifts built before 1980."

"Huh." She squinted at the device, then up at Hunter. "Better safe than sorry, I guess."

She led him around the corner, past a studio that looked like a king's palace compared to the shed. They arrived at a pair of brass elevator doors.

"How long will you be?"

"Not long, ma'am. Just need to test the failsafe mechanism and the ... uh." He tried to think of the word. "Counterweights."

She folded her arms and returned to her desk.

Heart thudding against his ribcage, he stepped into the elevator and pressed the button labeled "R." It squeaked and shook as it rose past the building's four floors, making his heart race even faster. It probably *did* need to be inspected, he thought.

The elevator dinged, and the doors slid open.

"Mike, this is Hunter. I'm up."

The squawk came seconds later. "Hardnose!" rattled Mike through static. "Perfect timing. I'm in the cabin and Shawn's reeling in a big one. That was a close one with Nancy, huh? Good work, never doubted you for a second. You see the dish?"

His heart felt ready to burst. "Not yet."

He scanned the roof. There was the broadcast tower, tall and covered in antennae. He also noticed an A/C unit and some sort of generator. He paced around the tower. A sharp wind stung his eyes and made it hard to see.

"Wait. Yeah. There it is."

"Killer."

The dish was a series of interconnected metal tubes in a vague circular shape. Hunter undid the latches on the suitcases. Hands shaking, he recalled Mike's instructions and connected the transmitter to the amplifier, attached the antenna and the cassette player, then wired everything through the timer and plugged it into the generator. Orange lights on the transmitter told him he had power. Now all he had to do was point the antenna at the dish and get the hell out of there.

Something stopped him. A slight whirr came from above, and not from any of his own equipment. He glanced at the noise and his heart dove into his intestines. There was a camera on the tower. A shiny, new, working camera. It was pointing right at him.

He stood up straight, not knowing what to do. "Mike," he said quietly into the walkie-talkie, "we have a problem."

He didn't answer right away.

"Mike? Come in, Mike. I think they put cameras on the roof."

Silence.

"Mike, there's a goddamn camera on the roof!"

Adrenaline flooded his spine. He was being watched. He was breaking and entering, impersonating a government employee, and hijacking a radio signal, and they could see him do it. He left the equipment behind and rushed to the elevator. He pressed the lobby button over and over. It groaned and started down.

It stopped at the fourth floor.

A man with a Taser on his belt stood in the doorway.

"Going down?"

"Uh, y — yeah."

"I'll wait. I'm heading up. Hey, you from the city?"

Hunter couldn't keep it together. He bolted past the security guard and around the corner. The last thing he saw as he bounded into the stairwell was the guard putting a hand on his belt.

He almost pissed himself as he flew down the stairs. He'd been caught. The guard was either chasing him, or on his way to the roof. They would find all the equipment. They would call the city and learn he wasn't a real inspector. They would see his face on the security footage. He was fucked. And it was all his own fault for agreeing to this in the first place.

He sprinted through the lobby. Nancy called out as he slipped out the door.

"Inspector? Did you forget your suitcases?"

He darted through the crowd on the boardwalk. He wished there were more tourists. He hustled past the vendors and souvenir stores, trying desperately to radio Mike.

"We have a serious situation."

Past the drum circle, past the skate park.

"Come in, Mike. Really need to talk to you, buddy."

Past the children's park, past the police kiosk, past the outdoor gym where bodybuilders did deadlifts in the sun.

"Mike! Where the hell are you?"

Nothing. Radio silence. By the time he reached the pier, he'd given up. He ducked down Buccaneer Street and through the alley to the shed. Panting and sweating, he changed out of his fake uniform into regular clothes. He gathered everything that might identify him and stuffed it in his backpack.

As he was leaving, the alarm clock went off.

He was sick with panic. He wanted to throw up. He wanted to sprint back to his apartment and hide there for twenty years. But he had to know. He reached toward the desk, flipped on the FM receiver, and dialed into Radio Westside.

Mike's voice filled the shed.

"... and on today's very special broadcast, we're getting into nurse sharks!"

ꝺ

For three days, Hunter stayed inside. He barely ate or slept. His friends texted him to meet up and he ignored them. He assumed the cops were looking for him. At the very least, Shawn and his security team would be. It was only a matter of time.

There was no word from Mike. Hunter tried the walkie-talkie every few hours and checked the internet constantly. On the second day, articles started appearing: "Unidentified Pranksters Seize Local Airwaves" and "Long-Defunct Radio Program Resurrected for Surprise Afternoon Special." None of the articles mentioned him by name, not that it made him feel better.

On the fourth day, he had the presence of mind to search for any police reports or warrants related to the hijacking. To his surprise, nothing came up. He even paid to search himself in the State of California records database. All he found was a drinking ticket from his first semester of college. After four days, there was nothing to suggest the incident was being investigated at all.

So he went outside. He walked down Abbot Kinney and felt as invisible as his first day in Venice. He didn't get arrested. No secret agents stopped him on the street; no enforcers from the radio mafia pulled him into the back of a limo. He stopped in the bar to clear his head.

"Been awhile," said Juana. "I was worried you'd finally split."

"Nah. Just had a rough few days."

"You forget your flu shot? Tis the season."

"Yeah. That must be it."

That evening, as the sun dipped low over the ocean, he went to the shed. He was paranoid it was being watched, but he unlocked the door anyway. He had to know if Mike had been back.

There was no sign of him. The shed looked exactly the same as it had after the break-in. Jaws on the walls, empty boxes and packing peanuts on the floor. Hunter flipped on the power. The FM receiver was still dialed into Radio Westside, playing classic rock.

Where had the old man gone? What was Hunter supposed to do with the shed now? He couldn't go to the police, and he didn't know of any family Mike might have except for Shawn, who was the last person he wanted to see. It seemed all he could do was keep an eye on the shed, watch his back, and hope for the best.

He returned the next morning, broke down all the empty boxes, and took them to the dumpster. There were stacks of newspapers and journals lying in the alley. He was about to throw them out as well when he saw Shawn's face staring out at him in black and white. On the back page of that morning's *Argonaut*, a headline read "Local Broadcaster and Father Missing."

Hunter read on:

> Venice resident and Radio Westside proprietor Shawn Helvey was reported missing by his secretary yesterday, after failing to return from a recreational fishing trip aboard the vessel *Catshark*. Helvey's father, Michael, was reportedly aboard the same vessel, which departed from Marina Del Rey on the morning of December 11. Officer John Beeker of the United States Coast Guard stated in a press release that the ship lost contact later that same day, and has not been located.
>
> Mr. Helvey's business was in the news recently, when Radio Westside's signal was interrupted by suspected radio pirates. No charges were filed related to that incident.
>
> Anyone with information is urged to contact the United States Coast Guard or Los Angeles Police Department.

ʘ

Hunter spent the following weeks reading the news, keeping a low profile, and checking on the shed. He searched through Mike's files, his personal notes, everything he could find, looking for answers. He found hand-plotted maps of shark sightings off the California coast, receipts for fishing equipment, and an application for an Australian tourist visa. He noticed that, although Mike usually had outlines of future broadcasts sketched out days in advance, he seemed to have nothing planned for after the break-in. But there was nothing definitive, nothing to explain what might have happened on that fateful fishing trip.

About a month after the disappearance, Radio Westside closed down. Hunter never heard anything more about the hijacking, or about Shawn or Mike, after that. Venice seemed to forget about things as quickly as it learned them. Hunter knew what that was like. Still, he found himself watching over his shoulder sometimes, and checking the police records on a regular basis. It couldn't hurt to be careful, not in this town.

Juana texted him out of the blue one day, saying someone had quit and he could come on as a bar-back if he was willing to work nights. He missed working for Mike too much to be as excited as he should have, but he said yes. At least he wouldn't go broke. He certainly wasn't leaving Venice anytime soon. After all it had put him through, he figured he deserved to stick around. The neighborhood had come to fit him like a wetsuit: tight and irritating, but far more comfortable than he would be without it. He assumed that's how wetsuits were, anyway. He would have to find out for himself, once his friends taught him to surf.

He kept going back to the shed, mainly in the afternoons, to check on the equipment and throw away the newspapers. Some days, he half expected to find Mike in there, cutting up articles and reading faxes and scribbling scripts in the briny darkness. But Mike was gone. He hoped someday he would find out what happened. He wasn't holding his breath.

ര

One day in spring, he opened the shed to find the shark jaws scattered across the floor. There had been an earthquake overnight with just enough shaking to knock them down. He spent almost an hour picking them up and replacing them, one after the other, trying to guess what species each one was based on what he remembered from Mike's broadcasts.

He brought in the newspapers. He wasn't sure why, but he didn't feel like throwing them out that day. Instead, he combed through them, along with the stacks of science journals and newsletters that had piled up over the months.

He plugged in the fax machine and bulletins started spitting out from Indonesia and Norway and China and Chile. He pored over the articles and took clippings. He flipped through an issue of the *Journal of Marine Biology*, found a fascinating study about goblin sharks, and tore it out. He arranged everything on the desk and jotted notes. He tested the shortwave transmitter and slid on the headphones and set up the cassette recorder. He tapped the microphone. The alarm clock went off. Ten seconds to three.

He switched on the transmitter.

"Good afternoon, Planet Earth, and welcome to *Shark News*!"

THE GOOD LIFE OF DUKE

Erik Gonzales-Kramer

A long day of weaving through L.A. traffic shuffling Lyft riders from the Valley to Long Beach and everywhere in between wears on you. I finally called it quits for the night after a West Hollywood partier stumbled out of the old Ford Taurus my dad gave me for college and promptly puked in front of his apartment building in NoHo.

On the drive home, I spotted a dingy, twenty-four-hour diner squatting along a disreputable stretch of Lankershim Boulevard that looked like the perfect cross between authentic and seedy to appeal to my dining preference. I got a booth, glanced at the laminated, uninspired menu, and tried to determine from the photos which greasy entrée would give me the most bang for my buck and whether the leftovers I saved would sustain me for one meal or stretch for two.

A tire-screech in the night pulled my attention to the window. A black Pontiac Firebird roared down Lankershim, showing off its sliced muffler for all the sleeping Angelenos on the block. A mangy dog flashed into the headlight beam. Faster than a gasp, the car struck the dog.

Its yelp sliced my stomach. "Asshole!" I shouted. I tore past a grizzled patron and the forty-year-old failed actress pouring him coffee. Outside, the Pontiac Dick drove off without a sidelong glance. What kind of monster hits a dog and keeps on driving?

I bolted into the street and kneeled next to the dog. It — no, he — lay on his side, legs akimbo. I put a hand on his prominent ribs. He was still breathing.

"Shit," I whispered.

I had to get him out of the street. Already I could see the next march of headlights advancing down Lankershim.

I worked my arms under the dog's sharp hips and bony shoulders and gingerly picked him up, retreating to the sidewalk. Shuffling over to my car, I laid him on the back seat and jumped behind the steering wheel. I swiveled into the road and raced away.

My adrenaline was pumping so hard I hadn't even given a thought to where I would go. Before I knew it, I was southbound on the 101, speedometer hovering around ninety. During rush hour I never bothered to slog through clogged L.A. arteries like the 101, but in the middle of the night, I sped past all but the most pedal-happy drivers. I plunged down the exit ramp near Elysian Park and wove through blocks that randomly alternated between million-dollar homes and lackluster apartment buildings before parking in front of one of the latter and carrying the dog inside.

The dog stirred when I entered my studio apartment. Kicking a box of clothes aside, I placed him on my carpet and stepped back. His eyes slowly opened.

"Are you all right?" I asked.

The dog's left ear lifted slightly. "Yeah."

I raised a skeptical eyebrow. Despite the dog's words, his appearance said otherwise. In the light, I could see splotches of matted blood around his ears and neck. I grabbed a towel that was hung over the back of a folding chair and tried to dab off the mess. "I think I should take you to a vet. You're bleeding."

The dog huffed. "That's from something else. The car just clipped my back legs."

That didn't sound much better to me, but I didn't argue — I realized only after I suggested it that I didn't have any money to take him to a vet. I stood and tossed the towel onto my laundry pile in the corner. "Are you sure you don't need anything?"

The dog closed his eyes again. "Food and water would be nice."

I rummaged through cupboards in the corner of the room that was supposed to be the kitchen. With no dog food in the apartment, I settled on throwing bread and hotdogs in a bowl and letting him have it. I sat in my chair and watched out of the corner of my eye as he wolfed it down. It was weird, having someone else in my room. I had been alone ever since Evelyn dumped me and I moved out of our apartment.

My thoughts were interrupted as the dog shifted. He backed away from the bowl, hunched his back end down, and took a shit on my carpet.

I jumped up. "*Hey!*"

The dog snarled, looking ready to rip my throat out as he retreated backward in a hobbling crouch, dropping more craps across my carpet.

I froze. One minute the dog was a pitiful, thin-legged mess, the next he was a wild animal. It was as if he thought I was going to attack him — nothing could have been further from my mind. I felt like any move I made would incriminate me even more, so I stayed motionless. We stared each other dead in the eye. The dog, shivering with effort, expelled one last colossal shit, then straightened cautiously.

I shook my head. "The fuck was that?"

"What?"

"You shit on my floor!"

He looked at the offensive pile. "I fail to see the problem."

"I *live* here!" It took everything I had to keep myself from shouting. "Didn't your owners housetrain you?"

He eyed me warily in response. "Just let me clean it up," I muttered in frustration. I edged around him, still worried he might snap at me, and snagged some paper towels to pick up the worst of the poop. I didn't have any carpet-stain remover on hand, so I turned a bottle of dish soap over the spots and scrubbed with a washcloth, hoping for the best. Duke watched me the whole time, head cocked in curiosity as I worked.

"Where's your family?" I asked. "I'll take you back tomorrow morning."

Again, he didn't reply. Did he even have a family? Maybe he was a stray who had been born on the streets and never had any owners. What would I do then, take him to a pound?

"I'm not going back to them," the dog said at long last.

Somehow, that answer was worse — it threw his skeletal and beaten appearance in an entirely different light. He looked up at me with dark eyes. "Can I stay here for a while?"

I blinked, surprised. This dog almost attacked me, and now he wanted to live with me? I couldn't take care of a dog — with Evelyn gone and no family providing a safety net, I could hardly take care of myself. I could come up with any number of reasons to say no, but sound logic had eluded me before.

"Only if you don't shit on my floor."

The dog's ears pricked up, ever so slightly. It was such a tiny, hopeful gesture. "I'll shit outside."

"Okay, then."

He staggered over to the corner of the room. Turning in a circle, he settled on my pile of neglected laundry and closed his eyes with a sigh.

"My name's Tom," I said.

"Duke."

ʘ

The next morning, Duke asked to be let out. I briefly wondered whether I should put a leash on him. But he wasn't my dog. Plus, I didn't have a leash. I shrugged and held the door open for him as he slowly hobbled out of the house on his thin legs. He looked so pitiful in the daylight, nothing more than skin and bones, that I immediately fed him the remainder of the hot dogs in the fridge.

We stayed out of each other's way, for the most part. He seemed content to nurse his wounds in the corner, and I was hustling on Lyft every chance I could get to make up rent costs that were eating me alive.

Duke never once pressed me for conversation. He was a quiet presence, and once I got over the fear he might bite me, it was comforting to have someone at home after I'd been driving through the hell of L.A. traffic all day. Sometimes he would be staring out the back window when I got home, sometimes napping, but he was always calm.

I couldn't help but think how different it was from living with Evelyn, who had filled our apartment with tales of her adventures in Hollywood's exclusive community of rising artists. As the number of modeling shoots and dancing gigs for hipster soda ad campaigns grew, I was left in her dust. I knew I should have been happy for her, but I just couldn't bring myself to be. She was finding friends and success, and I felt more isolated than I had ever felt in my life. Dumping me was inevitable. I could hardly blame her by the time it happened. Even I didn't like who I was.

A couple weeks after Duke started living with me, he asked, "Do you want to go on a walk?"

"Oh. Uh, sure." I don't know why I agreed. Maybe I just wanted a change of pace and the presence of someone's company.

The dog didn't talk any more than usual on the walk, but it was nice to be outside. I hadn't been for a good walk since I moved away from Wisconsin. We meandered through the neighborhoods across uneven sidewalks for a little while. Duke's paws clicked on the sidewalk in a slightly irregular rhythm as one of his back legs dragged a fraction of a second longer than the rest. Duke took a turn away from areas I was familiar with. "Where are you going?" I asked.

"To the park."

"What park?" I asked, before remembering that we were not far from Elysian Park. I hadn't been since I moved to the area, except to drive Lyft riders to the pickup and drop off area by the stadium. But we were far from any entrance I knew of. "We have to go the other way."

"There's an entrance over here. I can smell where other dogs passed through."

To my surprise, there *was* another entrance, right around the corner. A trail up a gentle hillside, wide enough for both of us, led up to a sidewalk that meandered through the less-traveled parts of the park.

While much of the park was hot and dusty, with scattered trees and manicured grounds, we quickly found small, wild pockets of dense woods that could almost have passed for Wisconsin, if the leaves were larger and the ground held more moisture. I recalled simpler times, when Mom and Dad and I would walk through the woods behind my house. That was before leukemia took Mom. Before Dad and I couldn't look at each other without feeling the pain of her passing.

"You all right?"

I looked away from the lush thicket of forest I had lost myself in. I hadn't even realized I'd stopped. "Yeah, sorry." I continued walking, forcing a smile. "Just thinking."

Duke gave a nod and led the way, his hanging tail swishing from side to side. His ribs were less noticeable now, his hips less prominent. I took a strange pride in it — as if by buying him new dog bowls for food and water, I had personally aided him in his recovery. The scratches on his neck were completely hidden by the thicker fur of his mane, but the scars beneath his ears were still visible.

"How did you get those scratches on your ears? You said they weren't from the car."

Duke stopped and sniffed the base of a tree. He lifted his leg and marked it before continuing down the path. The longer he didn't respond, the more I realized that I may have asked a deeply personal question. Finally, Duke replied, "Fleas."

I did a double take. "Fleas?" I couldn't believe fleas could make scars that large.

"Love to bite the ears. Nice and warm." He shuddered. "And no matter how much you scratch, you just can't get them out."

"Don't they have medicine for that type of stuff?"

Duke slowed, his gait stiffening. "My owners chained me in the yard and left me for days at a time. They didn't give a shit about medicine."

I sucked in my breath through my teeth. "Must've been hard." I didn't know what else to say.

If dogs could shrug, Duke did. "Doesn't matter. I got away." He stopped and stared into the underbrush intently, ears pricked forward. After a moment, he continued. "Looks like you got away too."

"What?"

"The house doesn't smell like you yet. And you live out

of packed boxes." Duke looked up at me with knowing eyes. "What did you run from?"

I didn't know. The past? There had been memories of her everywhere. Like the couch, where she had helped me get over the death of my mother in college. Or the park bench, where she told me that it was over, that it was too hard for her. I shook my head and said, "I don't know." I pushed a stick off the sidewalk with my foot. "I guess I just needed a new start."

Duke nodded and resumed walking. "You should unpack," he said over his shoulder. "Settle in. Make the place your home."

ʚ

I ended up taking Duke's advice. The place started to feel more comfortable as I unpacked my boxes, even if it was only one room. It was sparse, but that was because I threw out a lot of the sentimental stuff that Evelyn and I had shared.

For the first time since she dumped me, I began to look forward to coming home. I knew Duke would greet me at the door — not in an enthusiastic way, but more respectfully with a nod of approval. I bought Duke a dog bed so that the place felt more like home for him too. After I put it on the floor of my apartment, he carefully stepped onto it, turning around several times before finally collapsing with a huff of appreciation.

After our first walk, we walked every evening in Elysian Park, avoiding the touristy parts in favor of more secluded trails, especially the one that went past my favorite grove of trees. There was an ease to being with him that I had not expected. I liked talking to him, not that he ever said much, just listened mostly. In the silence, I enjoyed the familiarity of the irregular clip of his nails on the sidewalk.

It was as integral to his character as his willingness to listen to me talk about all the important nothingness that happened in my life.

As the days went by, Duke grew more muscular, his coat sleeker and smoother, his tail fuller. I was struck by his regal air one evening as I watched him standing at the top of a hill, the setting sun shining on the sage-like dog overlooking his domain.

ʘ

"I'm sorry," Duke said when I walked through the door one day.

"For what?"

Duke wouldn't meet my eyes.

I smelled it then. I looked over at Duke's bed and saw that there was crap there. Literally, shit in the bed. "What happened?" I asked, shocked.

Duke slowly shook his head. "I woke up and there it was."

I felt a cold ball in the pit of my stomach. The fact that he had just crapped in his bed was alarming because ever since that first night, he had been religious about asking to go outdoors. Looking at him closely as he paced the floor, I saw he favored one of his back legs more than the other. Duke's limp had worsened so slowly that I hadn't realized how bad it was till now. The tops of the toes of his bad leg were scraped from his walks.

"It's okay. I'll clean it up, and then we can go to the vet and see if there's anything wrong," I said, pulling paper towels from a cupboard.

"I don't need a vet."

I gave a laugh, trying to make light of the situation, even though I was already mentally calculating on how many late-night Lyft rides I would have to do to catch up on the hit to my bank account. "It's all right, just a checkup."

He was still reluctant, but he went anyway. He didn't talk to the other animals in the lobby, leaning against my leg as we waited. "Thomas Huso?" the vet called.

We stood up and walked into the room. She poked and prodded Duke, who glared at me the entire time. I ignored him, making weak attempts at easy conversation with the vet, despite the knot in my stomach. Eventually, she motioned me to follow her, leaving Duke in the exam room.

"So, Duke's fine, right? There's nothing to worry about." *Please.*

The vet sighed and took off her glasses, rubbing her nose. "I'm afraid he has spinal stenosis."

My stomach dropped. "Spinal what?"

The vet put her glasses back on and scribbled on her clipboard. "Spinal stenosis. Unfortunately, he will experience gradual paralysis of his back legs, followed by complete loss of control over his bowels."

Every nerve in my limbs shivered. A swell of emotion swept through my body. I ran my hands through my hair, trying to ignore my heart as it slammed the inside of my ribs. "Then fix it. You're a goddamn vet, right?"

She gave a sickeningly sympathetic look. "There *is* a surgical procedure," she said. "It's not always successful, but it generally runs around seven thousand dollars, for the tests and surgery and all."

My hands started to shake. Who had that much fucking money? How could this asshole tell me that all I could do was watch Duke suffer? The world smeared around me. I wanted to yell and swear at her, but instead I swallowed my words and stomped away to let Duke out of the room.

"Everything all right?" Duke asked.

I grunted and stormed out of the vet's, Duke trotting with difficulty beside me.

ǭ

It was almost as if the vet's diagnosis meant the condition didn't have to hide anymore. I began to notice raw patches of skin on the tops of both back paws where they scuffed the ground as he walked, so I bought him rubber dog socks to protect his feet.

"You're kidding," said Duke when I first showed him.

"It's just until your feet heal."

They didn't. Duke insisted on only wearing them while walking outside, and the scabs would always scrape open against the tiles of the floor in the apartment.

After a couple sleepless nights of Lyft driving, I took a hit to my finances by keeping my trips shorter, more in the local area, so that I could swing by my apartment every few hours to let Duke out to relieve himself — I didn't want him to feel ashamed about going in the house if he couldn't hold it. His limp worsened, and his responses became terse, like he was fighting pain.

Eventually, I decided to start mixing painkillers into his food. The first time I did this, I didn't meet his eyes as I mixed the pills in with the canned dog food I had started buying for him. When I put the bowl down, Duke stared at me for a long time. I pretended not to notice as I made my own dinner with trembling hands. Finally, he ate.

"You ready to walk?" I asked Duke when we were both finished.

Duke started limping toward the front door. "No, hang on, you need your socks." Duke's tail drooped as I picked up one back foot, then the other, to put a dog sock on each.

He perked up when we got outside, though. I smiled. The walks always made him feel better. And I could tell that the painkillers helped, because he wasn't as stiff. Despite this, the dragging of his feet on the sidewalk replaced the usual clip of his nails, making my heart heavy.

I didn't know what I would do without Duke. He'd become a part of my life, my routine, my comfort. He was there for me when I needed him and, no matter what, I would be there when he needed me. We could deal with it. Duke was going to be fine.

"It's been a long time since anyone cared for me," I said. I didn't know why that came out of my mouth. I guess I wanted Duke to know how much he meant to me. Duke nodded and seemed content to let that be all. But I didn't feel I had said enough.

"After my mom died, Dad and I couldn't really talk, and all I had was Evelyn. But after we moved out here … things didn't work out. I think it was my fault. I wasn't good enough, or something, so she left. Just like that." I let out my breath. "Then there was no one. Not even Dad. Just me."

I had been afraid to talk about my loneliness. I thought that it would spill out as a flood of anger against the world. Instead, all I felt was empty.

"People need others to be there for them," Duke said. "Nobody can go through life all alone." Duke slowed to a stop and stared at the glowing, sunlit buds along the forest path. A songbird trilled somewhere. Then, quietly, he added, "Thank you."

I knelt next to him, ruffling his mane with my hands. "Thank *you*, Duke."

We continued walking in silence all the way back to the house, but not the uncomfortable type of silence — more like just being there. Everything was going to be okay.

ʚ

But Duke became more and more quiet, a heavy, brooding silence. Walking was an increasing effort, and he struggled to keep his balance. One evening in the park, he toppled over. I knelt by his side and reached out to help him, only to shy away at his growl. Steeling myself, I warily hoisted him upright and helped steady him on his paws. Slowly, we walked back home. Neither of us said a word about the incident. What could we have said?

After that, Duke no longer greeted me at the door, but stayed in his bed and looked out at the trees from the back window. It was as if he was saving all his energy for our evening stroll. I was fine with that, though, because it meant he didn't open up the raw wounds on his feet.

"You ready for your walk?" I asked as I walked into the house a couple weeks later.

"No," Duke said.

He remained motionless, lying in his bed and staring out the window.

I blinked in surprise. He hadn't skipped a walk since we had first started. "What are you talking about?" I asked. A sense of foreboding turned my stomach.

"Just don't feel like it," he muttered. I saw that his breakfast was still where I had placed it that morning.

"Have you gotten up at all today?"

His ears drooped. "I can't." Still, he would not look at me. "I can't stand up."

I didn't know what to do. My mind refused to comprehend the situation. Long moments passed, but no words could make it past the knot in my throat.

Duke's muzzle twisted. "What kind of dog can't —"

"Stop," I said, pressing back the fear. Kneeling next to his bed, I scratched around his neck. "You're gonna be fine.

I'm just going to make a quick trip, and when I get back, I'm sure you'll feel better. Do you need me to carry you outside to go to the bathroom?" When he shook his head, I grabbed my keys and ran out to the car.

୭

When I came back to the house, I brought with me a beautiful new wheelchair specifically designed for dogs. It had a sling for Duke's torso and useless back legs, while his front legs would pull the rest of him along on large wheels. It may have looked ridiculous to the unfeeling observer, but to me, it was our salvation. I blew through almost my entire savings to purchase such a luxury, but I didn't care.

"Hey, Duke, look what I got for you. A wheelchair!" I called, knowing I sounded overly cheerful. Duke stared at me wordlessly as I continued blabbing on. "Look, it adjusts and everything!"

I smelled shit in Duke's bed. Duke pulled himself forward by his front legs, his back legs dragging along behind him. Crap smeared across the tiles behind him.

"Stop, you'll scrape your legs open," I said. Duke ignored me and continued heading for the front door.

"Stop!" I grabbed him, holding him back.

Duke twisted, snarling. Fangs sank into my hand.

I recoiled and fell against the wall. Hot pain lanced through me.

Duke hobbled forward, baring his teeth in my face. "I can't live like this! I can't shit and piss in my bed at night! I can't live in a fucking wheelchair! I'm a dog!"

I couldn't say anything. Words lodged in my throat, unable to push through. Eventually, Duke's breath slowed and he backed his muzzle away from my face.

Finally, quiet words worked their way out of my mouth. "But, I need you." A tear traced its way down my face. "You're all I have left."

Duke pulled himself forward again and rested his head on my chest. I tenderly scratched the base of his ears, feeling the scars of abuse from his previous owner. I sobbed, burying my face into his thick mane.

Duke sniffed, "You've done more for me than you could ever know. You gave me a wonderful life when I was sure that there was nothing left for me." More tears escaped me. I was helpless to stop them.

"But it's time to let me go."

Sobs wracked my body as I held Duke into the dark night.

ʘ

When I got back home the next day, I didn't know what to do. The house was more silent than it had ever been. The old familiar emptiness was unbearable, so I took a walk, meandering up the secret entrance to Elysian Park and going down the usual path I walked with Duke. It felt too still without the click of his nails. The spring air was heavy in my lungs. I tried to swallow past the lump that formed in my throat again.

I turned off the path and walked into my favorite grove of trees. But all it did was remind me of everyone who was no longer in my life — Mom, Dad, Evelyn. Duke.

Before I knew it, I was running. I crashed through the underbrush, tears streaming down my face. Throwing myself to the forest floor, I tore at the ground with bare hands, like my futile effort would uncover something I had lost long ago. But all I found was my choked, broken voice, repeating a single word.

"Why? Why? Why?"

My limbs grew heavy. Numb and exhausted, I collapsed on my back in the middle of the forest. The trees reached for the sky, birds flitted in the canopy, the sun shone as bright as ever. The world was unchanged, uncaring for the loss of Duke.

I needed someone. Someone to listen. I pulled out my phone and dialed the one person I should have called a long time ago.

"… Dad?"

TERMINAL FLIGHT

Barry Bergmann

Around this time of year, when the days get shorter and the World Series is near, there's another annual rite that I observe — the anniversary of The Case. Even though the baseball season is now a month longer, with all the damn new teams, the end of the season still gets me thinking about that warm fall of '62. Sixty-odd years have wiped out a lot of memories, but The Case, I suspect, will be in my head when the Grim Reaper comes through our door at the Shady Oaks Retirement Village. That's where my wife and I (that's her in the bed next to mine) wile away our final years, laughing about all the memories we've forgotten and sometimes crying together about the cherished ones we remember. And one of those is The Case. In fact, just this morning when I woke up and realized it was *sixty-two* years ago, we talked about it like it all happened yesterday. Each year, on the anniversary of The Case, we play a little game to see who can come up with a little fact of that time we haven't talked about before. It never fails. One of us adds something new — some small layer to a story that has grown each year. We joke about it, too. We say that if we ever have an anniversary of The Case when we don't come up with a new remembrance, that's when Mr. Reaper will come and get us.

ↀ

The Dodgers had blown a two-run lead in game three of the National League playoffs, and the Giants scored four in the ninth to win the game 6 – 4, along with the pennant. The Dodgers choked, but I think they lost the series in game one. They pitched this Jewish fellow named Koufax and lost 8 – 0. He throws fire but is a little edgy on control and gets hurt a lot. In my opinion, they ought to dump him before the '63 season starts.

The phone. It was always the phone that brought me out of orbit. I picked up on the second ring. "Parnell, homicide." I looked up at my partner, Ed Harbaugh, just as he stuffed the last bite of his peanut butter sandwich in his mouth. Must be five o'clock. My watch verified my partner's affinity to routine. Ed and I were up for the next case, and this call was it. In L.A., you didn't have to wait long when you were on deck.

I scribbled down the facts as they machine gunned in my ear. Blue Sky Flight 741 from Idlewild to LAX — Passenger dead in his seat — no obvious sign of trauma — respond Blue Sky Terminal, Gate 42. I hung up the phone and ripped my notes from the pad. "Ed, swallow. We have to get out to LAX."

"What's up?" he croaked. The combination of Ed's Midwest accent and swallowing the last bite of peanut butter sandwich was not easy on the ears. "I don't know much more than Blue Sky flight 741 arrived with a stiff in 2F. Let's roll."

I let Ed drive. We wheeled out of the garage and caught the Harbor Freeway South to Century Boulevard, then west in a straight shot to the airport. Fall is the best season in L.A., and this October day was no exception. I had come West in '58, along with the Dodgers, and hadn't regretted a single day. The first advance notices of winter would be creeping into Brooklyn about now, and I would have already hung the winter coat out to lose the smell of mothballs. Not something I would miss.

As we parked in front of the Blue Sky terminal, the warm sun and ocean breeze had put my moodiness on the back burner. Ed pulled the "L.A. Police" placard from the sun visor and put it on the dash. Looking like the cops we were, we hurried into the terminal. Blue Sky was a big airline, and around this time of the evening, six o'clock, its terminal was full of business travelers just getting home. Harbaugh and I waded upstream through the suits and briefcases until we reached Gate 42, the second on the left along the concourse. The gate area was a cluster of cops, airline employees, and fire department rescue teams. I easily figured out who the senior uniform was because he was the one getting bitched at by all the others. The burly sergeant had busy eyes and a nose that was too big, even for his broad face. The set of his pencil-thin mustache let me know he was glad detectives had arrived to share some of the responsibility.

I forced my way into the knot of folks around him and said for all to hear, "Detective Sergeant Parnell. Detective Harbaugh here is my partner. Fill us in." I said this as I indicated that the sergeant should follow us to the airplane. I could see the relief in his eyes as he introduced himself. "Sergeant Hastings, seventeenth precinct. Glad to see you guys here. I was getting a bit tired of crowd control."

"Sergeant Hastings, what do you know that we don't?" I asked. "That should be a lot, since we don't know anything."

Hastings talked as we entered the airplane. "Probably not much more than you guys. Nothing happened until the plane arrived and all the passengers left. The stewardess, Carol, noticed that the victim seemed to be sleeping after everyone else got off. When she went over to wake him up, she could tell he wasn't breathing. She figured out real fast what was going on. That's when we got the call from the airlines dispatcher."

We followed Hastings' gaze to the gentleman in calm repose, leaning his head against the window. If we hadn't known he was dead, we might have thought it was just another guy who had too many martinis on an empty stomach and nodded off.

"Where's this Carol now?' Harbaugh asked.

"She and the rest of the gals are in the stewardess lounge. I told them to wait there until you guys arrived."

We turned our attention back to the guy in 2F. "So, who is he?" I asked Hastings.

"ID says he's David Brozier. Business cards on him say he runs a cold storage outfit on the east side. You know, one of those places that stores a shit load of food as it gets passed through the distribution channel. It's called The Ice House."

How appropriate, I thought.

The crime scene guys started to filter on board. We left Hastings with them and made our way to the lounge to talk to the stewardesses. My partner and I definitely had the preferable duty. As soon as we walked into the lounge, I knew I was looking at Carol. She was a cute little thing, all rounded corners and soft in the right places. Her auburn hair was cut short, and she had styled her hair with little pointy sections in front of her ears in a way that was popular with models and such. Carol said she hadn't seen anything unusual until she discovered that Brozier wasn't going to get off the airplane under his own power.

"He was very quiet the whole time. He just ate his lunch — he ordered the special meal, seafood, it was shrimp today — and then went to sleep. The perfect passenger. The only time I really noticed him other than when, you know, I saw he was dead, was when Jessica hurried down the stairs to help him board the aircraft. I guess he was limping or something, but I didn't notice it until he got to the top and watched him go to his seat."

"Jessica?" I said.

"Yes, she's my flying partner in First Class."

Just then, a stewardess who I assumed to be Jessica by the way Carol nodded at her, came out of the ladies restroom adjacent to the lounge. She had obviously been freshening up as she pursed her lips and smoothed her uniform and hair before walking over to where we sat.

"I'm Parnell, and this is my partner Harbaugh." We both badged her at the same time.

Jessica sat down on one of the couches. She crossed her legs — legs that seemed to go on forever — and I fought like hell to look her in the eye. As my mind was wandering, she said, "This is awful. Have you officers figured out what happened? Did he have a heart attack or what?"

"We won't know that for a while," Harbaugh responded. "The medical examiner is up there now."

Jessica said she had only seen Brozier when she went up to help Carol with a second round of drinks. "After that, I didn't speak to him again, and there was a bit of an emergency, and I had to go to the back."

"An emergency?" Harbaugh asked.

"Well, I broke a nail — I couldn't do anything until I fixed it," Jessica cooed. "After all, how would it look?"

"I don't know," I said, looking down at the hard little nubs on my fingers.

When we were done, Harbaugh and I got back in the car and did what any cop would do after leaving a crime scene. We ate. Harbaugh was already hungry, even though he had barely digested his PB sandwich, so we stopped at a little six-stool Mexican joint down on Rosecrans, south of

LAX. The place was called Rosarita, and the burritos were as big as a football. Harbaugh and I were the only ones in the place, and we each ordered a burrito and a Schlitz. Harbaugh got the chicken with green sauce, and I got the combo — shredded beef with beans.

"What do you think?" Harbaugh asked between bites of his burrito.

"I think we won't know much until we see the autopsy results," I said.

"Not while I'm eating, Sergeant," Harbaugh said, wiping his mouth with a napkin you could see through. My partner had a weak stomach when it came to autopsies, but it probably had more to do with Dr. Griff, the medical examiner. We referred to him as "Stiff Griff" everyplace but in front of him. Dr. Adolph Griff might have known, but he never let on.

"Don't get excited until you have to," I told Harbaugh. "Stiff Griff should be able to give us the cause of death by the a.m., and it'll probably turn out to be nothing. My guess a heart attack or stroke. Nothing unusual."

I didn't know at the time how wrong I was.

ʘ

When we got into the office the next morning, I had a message from Dr. Griff. It said he had determined the cause of death, and Harbaugh and I should meet him at the morgue at ten o'clock. Dr. Griff was in the basement of County General. (Was there a city in America where the morgue wasn't in a basement?) Harbaugh and I had both tucked a tube of Vicks in our pockets, knowing that Griff would give us the autopsy results in one of the examination rooms. A little swipe of Vicks under our noses would be helpful.

Dr. Griff, I thought, was a cross between a Munchkin in the *Wizard of Oz* and Colonel Sanders — a five-foot-three likeness of the face on the finger lickin' good chicken bucket and about as tall as those folks who danced and sang with Dorothy. He spoke with a soft accent reminiscent of a James Bond villain or Boris Karloff.

As we made our way to Examination Room 2, I asked the greenish Harbaugh, "You okay?"

"Yeah," he said. "I threw up before I left my apartment just to be sure."

The smell. It was always the smell. Like a butcher shop that had just been cleaned with Lysol — a meaty mix of week-old pork chops and rubbing alcohol.

Dr. Griff looked at us when we entered the examination room like family members who had dropped in for dinner.

"Good to see you, gentlemen — come in, come in. Stand right here," he said, pointing at a spot on the floor.

He had positioned us on the opposite side of the table — Brozier was between us. I recognized him, even without the expensive suit he had been wearing the day before. He was naked except for a small towel that Dr. Griff had draped over his shlong.

"Gentlemen," said the doctor, "thanks for coming on such short notice." Then he looked down at Brozier as if it were his turn to speak next. When there was no response, the good doctor continued: "Mr. Brozier was poisoned. Cyanide. I would guess he ingested it on the airplane."

I wasn't expecting that. I was thinking heart attack or that he stroked out, but murder? That got my attention. I could tell it was the same with Harbaugh because his gag reflex took a break.

"Why do you say it was on the airplane?" I asked.

"Because this poison is very fast-acting — almost instantaneous. Cyanide was a favorite quick-death option for the Nazis at the end of the war. And if you believe what you read in spy novels, it's used by the CIA."

I started to ask how, but before I could finish my question, Dr. Griff answered, "It was in the shrimp that we found in his stomach."

I remembered that the cute little stewardess, who had lingered in my mind, told us that Brozier ordered a special meal. You had to give it to her — his meal had been "special."

"Any other marks or wounds on the body?" I asked.

"Only one," Dr. Griff said, and he pointed to just below Brozier's right kneecap. It was bruised and had just started to show that rainbow of colors particularly bad ones tend to do. I remembered that Carol had said he had needed help getting up the stairs.

Dr. Griff let us look at the injury for a couple of minutes, but I didn't want to breathe in the wet, fetid air too much longer, so I asked him what he thought had caused it.

"I'm not entirely sure, except that it was a pointed object. It didn't have anything to do with his death, but I thought it was something significant you should know."

When Harbaugh and I got outside, we both took a deep breath, finding the smoggy air of the L.A. basin preferable to that of the morgue. When I slid behind the wheel of the car, Harbaugh was already inside drumming his fingers on the dash. That's one of the things he would do when he was thinking. The other was pick his nose. Even though the thrump-thrump-thrump on the dash was irritating, it was more pleasant than watching Harbaugh pry a two-joint booger from one of his nostrils. He played a couple more chords on the dash before he spoke.

"So, when do you think his shrimp was spiked?"

"I don't know. Could've been a passenger, or whoever delivered the meal, or the folks who made the meal. I hear those airline kitchens are like an assembly line — each person adding one part of the meal, just like they make a car. Hell, for all we know it could have been the guy on parsley duty that day."

Before we left the morgue parking lot, I used a pay phone just outside on the sidewalk to call my lieutenant. I told him what we had learned at the autopsy. I suggested to him that a couple of guys from the squad talk to the folks at the airline kitchen to find out where the shrimp had made the acquaintance of the cyanide. He agreed, and I told Harbaugh.

It was almost noon. Normally I would have suggested lunch, but my partner, who had never met a meal he didn't like, still looked a little queasy. He needed to air out a bit, so I suggested we go to The Ice House, then lunch.

"Great idea. That's why you're the sergeant, and I'm still a grade-one detective, Parnell." I couldn't argue with my partner's logic.

ᘐ

We got on the Santa Ana Freeway South, on our way out to The Ice House. In the City of Commerce, the storage facility was right at the spot where the Long Beach Freeway veered north from the Los Angeles River, just east of Maywood. It was a stark area of warehouses and small industrial companies that lined the dusty streets. The Ice House stood out from the surrounding brick and metal buildings with its bright white exterior and a dark blue trim. It was going to be a hot day, and already the normal pall of smog hung over the basin and shrouded the nearby San Gabriel Mountains. To think we were breathing that stuff.

The storage area of The Ice House loomed over a small building decked out in the same white-and-blue paint job. The sign over the door read "Administration," so Harbaugh and I walked in like we belonged. Once inside, we found ourselves in a small reception area with a waist-high counter in front. Behind the counter were a few desks. I counted five, with four men and one woman. The woman was pounding away on a typewriter while the men were mostly looking at papers or leaning back talking. I didn't get the impression there was much sadness over their boss dying.

The woman saw us and came up to the counter. It wasn't hard to see who did all the work in this joint. She looked young, but then everyone was starting to look young to me. She had on a white blouse and one of those tight skirts all the women wore in those days. Her hair was brown and almost hit her shoulders before it flicked up. I'd heard a couple secretaries at the station call it a "flip."

"How can I help, gentlemen?" she asked, crossing her arms under what were not unsubstantial breasts. I looked over at Harbaugh, and I could tell he noticed.

"LAPD, ma'am," I said. "Sally," she interjected. I introduced us, and we both showed our badges as if we had choreographed it.

"I guess you're here about …" her voice trailed off.

"Mr. Brozier," Harbaugh said.

"You should speak to Mr. Ireland," she said, nodding toward the two offices in the back. I noticed that the door nameplates read "Mr. Brozier, President" and "Mr. Ireland, Vice President." I wasn't surprised to see that the room with Brozier's name on it was dark and unoccupied. Mr. Ireland must have heard us because he was already coming in our direction. The urgency of his pace even diverted Harbaugh's gaze from Sally's chest.

"Officers, I'm Richard Ireland," he said, putting out his hand to shake ours like we were in a car showroom instead of the office where the boss had just died. "We've been expecting you."

"It's nice to be expected. I'm Sergeant Parnell — my partner Detective Harbaugh." How many times had I said that in the last twenty-four hours?

Ireland looked at Sally like you would a dog that had snuck out of its kennel, and she quietly asked, "Can I get you gentlemen some coffee?"

We both said yes, black with sugar, two cubes — like all cops.

After Sally disappeared to get our coffee, Ireland said, "As you can imagine, we are very distraught about the death of Dav … Mr. Brozier." Even though the words sounded like they were meant for the office drones to hear, Ireland's eyes were a little glassy, like Harbaugh's got when he talked about the movie *Ol' Yeller*.

"Would you gentlemen like to step into my office? We could have a bit more privacy."

Ireland didn't wait for our answer and turned back toward his office. One of the guys shuffling papers, "Henry Winston" his desk nameplate said, looked my way. I recognized that look. It was like I used to see in my little brother Charlie's eyes when we were kids. In Charlie's case, it meant he knew something he hadn't told you about. With this Winston guy, I didn't know, but I took note of it and would find out.

Harbaugh and I followed Ireland into his office like ducklings. He directed us to two chairs in front of his desk that were just a touch more comfortable than the ones we used at the station to interview suspects. This Ireland guy seemed kind of arrogant, like he was going to be the one asking questions. I thought I'd get the drop on him by asking the first one.

"So, David Brozier was your boss?"

Ireland got a look on his face like there was a funny smell in the room and asked in a snotty tone of voice usually heard from teenage girls, "Now, whatever gave you *that* idea?"

"Your door says you're the Vice President."

"Oh, that," he said waving his hand like he was swatting a fly. "That's just a formality. We're partners fifty-fifty. It's been that way from the start."

I pulled out my notebook and thumbed through it, not that there was anything I needed to refer to but just to put this Ireland guy on edge a bit. But before I could come back with another question, Harbaugh asked, "And the business? What happens to it?"

"I hardly think that has anything to do with your investigation, but if you must know, I'm the sole owner now. We had an agreement that gave each partner survivorship rights. Both of us have no family, so it was easy."

That was not only convenient, but it made this Ireland guy numero uno on the suspect list. Ireland said, "I know what you're thinking. I would have had a good business reason to kill David, but I'd never do that. We were partners but friends too. The business is doing well, and we rarely disagreed on our plans." Looking out beyond us into the outer office, he continued, "You could ask any of them. No fighting about anything. Hell, I don't think we ever raised our voices."

I had to admit that the guy sounded like he was telling the truth, even though I hadn't taken a liking to his initial uppity personality. Still, I wasn't going to let him off the hook. So, to his point and sounding as tough as I could, I said, "Well, everybody's a suspect at this point Mr. Ireland, and you can bet we'll talk to everyone out there. And speaking of that, did Mr. Brozier have any enemies you knew about? Did he have any problems with anybody?"

"No, not at all. He got along with everyone. Of course, some better than others."

Ireland's last statement was truer than we knew at the time.

ⵚ

Ireland gave us a small conference room to talk to the staff, and I told Harbaugh about the look I got from the Winston fellow, so we agreed to talk to him last. We didn't get much from the first three guys we talked to. Brozier had been an okay boss — not a backslapping, joke-telling type of guy, but friendly and fair. One of them hinted that Brozier was a bit of a cheapskate on pay, but what guy who owned his own business wasn't? The girl, Sally, was on lunch break, so we had to wait to talk to her after Winston. Harbaugh agreed with my strategy, but I didn't know if he thought it was a good idea, or he was just getting itchy for lunch.

Winston had been sitting down when I first saw him. As he came into the room, I guessed that he couldn't be more than five-foot-four, and I'd bet a ten-spot he didn't weigh more than maybe one-twenty. I could have put my fist between his neck and shirt collar, and he'd added a hole so he could cinch his belt tight enough. After he sat down facing us, his eyes darted around like a frog's watching a fly. His hands were folded on the table, and it looked like he regularly munched on his nails, or what was left of them. I knew we wouldn't have to be too tough with him, but I was sure he had something for us, and I didn't want to scare it out of him. I let Harbaugh toss him a softball first.

"How well did you know Mr. Brozier?"

Winston started to speak, but his voice yipped like a thirteen-year-old just getting into puberty. He cleared his throat and chirped, "He was my boss, so I knew him like, well, my boss. I'm just a junior accountant, so we never talked directly unless we said 'good morning' or I saw him in the canteen."

I let Harbaugh continue while I watched and waited for a good time to jump in.

"Did you ever hear any arguments, voices raised? Not just in the office, but anyone from the outside?"

"No. I never saw him anyplace but here, and if anyone came to see him, he always shut his door, so no, no. I never heard anything like that."

Winston tossed a glance my way, and although I wanted Harbaugh to soften him up a bit more, I could tell he wanted to tell us something, so I asked, "Did you like him?"

Winston looked down at his hands, and I thought he'd like nothing better than to gnaw on one of his nails. No answer. Maybe I'd hit on something.

"Did you like him?" I repeated.

Finally, he answered into the table, "Not very much."

"Why?"

"Sally — the way he treated her."

"What do you mean? He was unfriendly?"

"No," he said, finally looking me in the eye. "He was just the opposite. Maybe too friendly."

"You mean he ...?"

"Yeah, and I don't think he was too nice about it. Sally told me that he threatened her about her job and other things."

That perked my partner up. I knew he didn't like guys that took advantage of women.

"What other things?" Harbaugh asked, clearly pissed off.

"I don't know. Sally would talk to me now and then, but only so much. I do know they must have had some argument about a week ago because I saw her kick him in the knee when they were talking out by her car. It was a hard one, too — he had to practically hop back to the office."

Well, that explained the bruise on Brozier's knee. If we could believe this Winston guy, it sounded like Sally should have kicked him somewhere else.

ʘ

We decided that maybe it would be best to interview Sally at her home instead of at the office, based on what Winston had told us. So, we made up some story that we had to be somewhere else and set up a time for when she got home from work that evening. It wasn't a lie. We did have to be someplace: Harbaugh was hungry.

We were sitting at a small table at Philippe's across from Union Station. I had gotten the beef dip with cheddar sandwich, and Harbaugh got his usual — turkey dip with Swiss, slathered in Philippe's spicy mustard. I was drinking an Orange Nehi, and Harbaugh had a Tab. Why he drank diet I'll never know. There had been a dollop of mustard on my partner's chin for the last ten minutes, and I finally made a wiping gesture with my napkin to let him know. He copied my move then stared at the mess on his napkin for longer than was necessary. I tried to take my mind off it by saying, "I'm starting not to like this Brozier."

"Yeah. Seems like a creep," Harbaugh agreed.

Well, that settled that.

ʘ

On the Blue Sky flight where Brozier had died, the pilots had never come out of their cockpit cocoon, and only one of the other stewardesses, Jessica, had worked in the cabin besides Carol. That was only for a few minutes when the meals and drinks were served, but she told us she hadn't delivered Brozier's meal — Carol had done that, so we figured we'd talk to her again. On the way to her place, we stopped, and I called the station for news from the Blue Sky flight kitchen.

"Zilch," was the one-word answer from Detective Kowalski. That about summed up what any solid evidence Harbaugh and I had found so far, but the suspects were getting fewer, so we must be getting closer, I hoped, but it sure didn't feel like it yet.

Carol Clancy lived in a small apartment in Manhattan Beach close to the pier. In that neighborhood, even now, if you fall down in any direction, you hit an airline employee. It's close to the airport, and it's got enough bars to keep the airline crowd properly sedated between flights. She was on the second floor of the building. As we climbed the stairs, we saw that her door was open behind the closed screen. It was a bright day, as most are in Southern California, and it was black behind the screen. A radio played rock 'n' roll somewhere in the darkness. It was the Beach Boys extolling the virtues of surfer honeys and surfing, but when Harbaugh and I saw all the tanned bodies in bikinis on the beach, "virtue" was not a word that came to our minds. The screen door had not been latched, so it made a clatter when I knocked on it.

"Just a minute! I'm just getting out of the shower," Carol called from the murkiness in the apartment.

"Police," I responded. "We'd like to ask you a few questions."

I was single then, so I didn't usually see women coming fresh out of a shower, except in the movies. So, I guess I wasn't prepared for Ms. Clancy, who emerged with one towel wrapped around her body and one around her hair, smelling of lilacs and summer. She was as pretty as she had been in the stewardess lounge, and when she held open the screen door to let us in, I almost forgot the questions I was going to ask. Harbaugh usually doesn't get excited unless it's something to eat, but he glowed almost to the point of being feverish.

She showed us to the couch and asked, "Can I get you something to drink?"

I declined, even though my mouth was as dry as the Sahara, wondering how the towel she was swathed in was defying gravity.

"Just some water," Harbaugh said, and I wouldn't have been surprised if he wanted it to dump on his head rather than drink.

"You gentlemen surprised me. I wasn't expecting you, so if you don't mind, I'm going to duck into my room and put on something more comfortable."

I took that as meaning more comfortable for us than for her. While she was gone, Harbaugh and I sat in silence and my eyes roamed around the small living room: a little coffee table in front of the couch on which we sat; a slew of knickknacks from what looked like Carol's travels; a small TV with rabbit ears flying aluminum foil flags. I saw nothing unusual, but there was a name tag on a side table next to a chair, the kind you wear at cocktail parties or receptions, that had "Carol" on it with "G.L.A.B.C." underneath. I figured a girl like Carol got invited to a lot of things and put it out of my mind. We had recovered by the time Carol came in with Harbaugh's water. She was dressed in some white pedal pushers and a blue sleeveless top. She sat down in a chair opposite us on the couch and said, "I guess this is about that passenger yesterday?"

Harbaugh was gulping his water, so I started.

"It is. Unfortunately, it looks as though Mr. Brozier was poisoned."

She brought both hands to her mouth in shock, then clasped them below her chin and asked, "How?"

"Cyanide in the shrimp."

Harbaugh's empty glass clinking on top of the coffee table was the only sound in a silent room.

"How could something like this happen?" Carol asked neither of us in particular.

"That's what we hope you can help us find out," I answered. "Did you see anyone talk to Mr. Brozier during the flight?"

Carol leaned toward us and tapped two fingers on her forehead, thinking. "Now I remember. Yes, there was. It was about a half hour into the flight. The seat next to Mr. Brozier was empty, and a man sat in it. He was there awhile."

"How long would 'awhile' be?" I asked, hoping I didn't sound like a smart aleck. Funny, I usually didn't care.

"About fifteen minutes."

"Can you describe him?" Harbaugh asked, getting out his notebook to write down the description.

"He was wearing a blue suit. He was about six feet tall. Black hair, blue eyes. He wore glasses — you know, those black Buddy Holly ones?"

It sounded like she just described Clark Kent.

"You would have had to get fairly close to him to see the color of his eyes. Did you talk to him?" I asked.

"Only to ask him if he wanted a drink. He said 'no' because he wasn't going to be in the first-class cabin long."

"Did you hear what Mr. Brozier and this fellow were talking about?"

"Why, Detective! I don't make a practice of eavesdropping on my passengers."

"I didn't mean it that way, but you weren't standing in Grand Central Station. You must have heard a couple of things."

"Maybe a couple of things. You know, business things."

"Business things? Like what?"

"I don't know. Whatever businessmen talk about. Buy this, sell that. Frankly, I don't understand any of it."

"Did you see this man do anything?"

"Like what?"

"Did he have anything in his hands? Take anything out of his pocket?"

"I didn't stare at them," she said in a scolding tone. "I didn't see everything he did. They just looked like they were having a conversation. I didn't pay that much attention to them."

I was starting to imagine interviewing one hundred and thirty people from the flight, and it gave me a headache, so I hoped Carol would have the answer to my next question.

"Did you see what seat he returned to?"

Her answer was depressing — real depressing.

"No."

"Do you think you would recognize him again?"

"Probably."

That didn't sound like the voice of confidence. I looked over at Harbaugh, whose eyes asked if he could pose a question. Since I was thinking of the blackness the trail was leading to, I gave him a slight nod.

"When did you notice that Mr. Brozier was not … well, awake?"

Carol touched her index finger to her chin, pursed her lips, and appeared to think real hard before she answered. "I think it was when I went to clear his tray. He had only eaten a little bit of his food, and I was going to see what was wrong with it, but he looked asleep, so I didn't disturb him. Men work so hard these days."

When she finished, she sat looking at us, eyes blinking so fast that I swore I could feel a breeze from her lashes.

"And did you notice anything … anything at all strange?" I added.

"Not at all. Like I told you yesterday, he was the perfect passenger."

I gave Harbaugh the "let's go" look, and got up saying, "Thank you, Ms. Clancy. We'll get back to you if we have any further questions."

"I hope I've been helpful, Detectives. He was such a nice man."

"I wouldn't know, but I'll take your word for it," I said. "Say, do you mind if I use your phone? I need to call the station."

"No, not at all. It's in the hall."

I wanted to confirm the address of Sally, the girl from The Ice House. It only took a couple of minutes. When I went back into the front room, Harbaugh got up and moved toward the door. I stopped next to where Carol was, and she got to her feet. She was only about a foot away from me, and a wave of lilacs almost knocked me over. Don't get me wrong, that was a good thing. When I got my wits back, I said, "Thank you, Carol. We'll get back to you if we need any more information."

ൿ

Sally lived in a four-unit apartment building off Los Feliz, close to the Griffith Park Observatory. Like Carol, her unit was on the second floor. She wasn't home when we got there, but we only had to wait about five minutes before she turned up in her blue Corvair. I spotted her parking slot; it was the one with big oil spots. Oil went through those old Corvairs like crap through a goose.

We were upstairs on the balcony. She got out of her car, grabbed a bag of groceries from the back seat, and made her way toward the steps. As she walked up the stairs, she said, "I'm sorry I was late. I had to stop at the store. I had no food in the house."

That was a little too much information for us, but you could tell by the way she took an interest in us being on time and her being late that she was a nice gal. That moved Brozier down a couple more notches in my book.

Ever the gentlemen, Harbaugh said, "No problem. We just got here," and he grabbed the bag of groceries out of Sally's arms.

"Why, thank you, Detective," she said, then reached into her purse for her keys. She unlocked the door, and not wanting to be out-mannered by Harbaugh, I held the door open as she went in. I was right behind her when she threw her keys into a glass bowl just inside the door. I noticed in the bowl was a name tag like the one I saw at Carol's, only this one said "Sally / G.L.A.B.C." Coincidences sometimes were just that, coincidences, but I had a hunch about this one. I needed to make a phone call. I hadn't told Harbaugh about the name tag at Carol's yet because I didn't think much of it at the time, so he gave me one of those queer looks he sometimes did.

"I forgot something when I called in before," I said.

Sally directed me to the phone in her bedroom, and I sat on the edge of the bed and dialed.

We had a young guy helping us with admin that year — a college grad named Leo Turner. He was a smart kid who was able to dig up information on almost anything. If you got past his hare-brained ideas that someday you could probably do this stuff with one of those computers people were talking about, he was an okay kid.

As always, when I told him to try and find out what G.L.A.B.C. stood for, he got on it right away with his usual, "Yes, Detective Sergeant!"

"And if you get it in the next half hour or so, give me a call at Plymouth two, seven, eight, three, four." I didn't expect it until maybe the next day; the kid was good but not that good.

When I got back to the front room, I saw Sally sitting in a chair and Harbaugh on the couch to her left. He had a can of beer in front of him, and Sally had a glass of white wine. There was a beer on the coffee table in front of the empty spot on the couch for me. We weren't supposed to drink while on duty, but it was after five, so I didn't say anything.

After we got settled and did two minutes of chitchat, I asked Sally, "Did you know Mr. Brozier very well?" I immediately felt like a jerk, since Sally knew we had already talked to everyone else in the office. She would have been pretty stupid to not suspect something, and stupid she wasn't.

"Well, I knew that when you scheduled the interview for here you already knew something, so I'm not going to lie to you." She had started out brave, but now I saw her biting her lower lip, trying not to cry. I glanced over and thought that Harbaugh was starting to tear up. Behind that gruff exterior, he was a pussycat.

She bowed her head and got control.

"We were having an affair," she said. "At least it started out like that, but it changed. It became something else — something bad."

"Like how?" I asked as gently as a cop could.

"Well, I found out there were other women, lots of them. And when I wanted to break things off, he threatened me with my job. But that wasn't the worst of it. It seems that he had cameras in his bedroom, and he said that he would make sure people saw the pictures. He said I'd never get a job in this town again."

She grabbed a tissue, and she looked down at it as she rolled it around in her nervous fingers.

"But there's more," she said.

Harbaugh and I looked at each other, both remembering policing 101 — when the witness is talking, let her talk.

"One night, I was looking for a pen. David ... Mr. Brozier ... was in the shower, and I started searching in his desk. That's when I found the pictures. Pictures of little boys. It was awful. I had heard about things like that, but I'd never seen anything so horrible — disgusting."

"Did you say anything to him?" Harbaugh asked, sitting on the edge of the couch, leaning forward, elbows on his thighs.

"No. I was too scared. I just wanted to get away from him."

I could feel the tension in the room, corny as that sounds. I was relieved when the telephone rang. Sally answered it and came back saying, "It's for you, Sergeant."

It was Leo, and he told me that the initials on the badge stood for Greater Los Angeles Baptist Church. He had the address, too. He also said Lieutenant Bradley wanted to talk to me and handed over the phone. Brozier's apartment had been searched, and Lieutenant Bradley told me some things that I didn't know, and some things I did. It was starting to become clearer now.

I opted not to mention the church group to Sally. When we left her place, I told Harbaugh to drive to the church near the intersection of Olive and Washington. On the way, I told him about the badges.

"So, what do you think it means?" Harbaugh asked.

"I'm not sure, but before we ask the girls, I'd like to hear what the church tells us. And there's one other thing. Lieutenant Bradley said that they found a bunch of magazines and pictures. They had pictures and stuff with kids, like the ones Sally told us about." Bradley had told me other things too, but I kept them to myself until I figured out what to do. Harbaugh and I didn't talk for a while. I guess we were both trying to figure out how perverts like Brozier slept at night.

The Greater Los Angeles Baptist Church building wasn't a church at all. It was more like an office. I wasn't surprised to see lights on in the windows; my mother used to always say that God did not stick to normal business hours. The sign in the lobby said that the church offices were on the next floor. The elevator opened into a place that looked similar to Brozier's company: a bunch of desks in the middle of the floor with some offices along the windows.

A tiny doe-faced young lady asked us if she could help with anything. Maybe we looked like a couple of wayward worshippers. She took us to a Bruce Hornsby, who was sitting in one of the offices.

"Bruce, these two detectives would like to ask you some questions," she said.

The curly-haired, thin man looked up at us in a manner that suggested a visit from the police happened every day.

"Please, have a seat," he said, looking at two folding metal chairs in front of his desk. After we sat down, he asked, "And how can I help you today?"

Since I was the superior officer, I answered his question. "We're investigating a murder, and two possible witnesses seem to have attended some sort of event at your church. We don't know what it was, but they both had name badges with G.L.A.B.C. on them. What would those be, do you think?"

Hornsby came right back at us. "It could be a number of things. I assume this was a badge with a first and last name?"

"Just a first name," I answered.

"I see," he said, drawing out the last word. "What were their names?"

After I told him, he thumbed through a three-ring binder, then stopped at a page and said, "Oh, my."

Something was up. Hornsby then confirmed my suspicion.

"It seems like both of them are in one of our support groups. The one they're in is for women who are in an abusive relationship. No offense to the police, but women are reluctant to report abuse a lot of the time because law enforcement doesn't like to get involved. It's hard to prove, and it's mostly looked at as a family matter. By the time the women get here, they're in pretty bad shape. We're kind of their last resort."

I was old school and a little ashamed. I knew what he was talking about. It was sad, but that was the way things were. We asked a couple more questions, but we already had what we wanted. Now came the hard part — what would we do with the information?

It was late, so I dropped Harbaugh at the office and headed home. At least, I *thought* I was going home, but I found myself parked in front of Carol's apartment. The things Lieutenant Bradley told me about the case were zooming around in my brain, and I was sure that was why I went there. As I took each step up to Carol's apartment, I debated if I was doing the right thing. I had formulated an idea about the case, but I needed to talk with Carol to be sure.

When she opened the door, I didn't think that she was surprised to see me, even though she said, "Why, Detective! What brings you here at this hour?"

The light from the apartment formed an aura around her, and I found myself staring. When she asked the question again, I shook my head like I had woken from a dream and said, "Just a few questions. Mind if I come in?"

Her answer was to hold open the screen door and, I know it sounds crazy, I could feel the warmth from her as I slid into the front room. After we settled into our seats, facing each other, I told her what we had found out at the Baptist Church offices.

"Did you know Sally before you joined this group?" I asked.

"No."

"When did you find out she had a relationship with Brozier too?"

"What do you mean, too? I never said ..."

I interrupted her before she embarrassed herself. "Carol, my lieutenant told me your phone number was found at Brozier's apartment along with Sally's and a lot more. And just so you know, you two weren't the only ones. There were a lot of photos. I'm told that it's hard to see who's who in the pictures, but if someone tried hard enough, they could find who it was. Brozier was a pervert, too ... little boys, and who knows what else ... but you already knew that, didn't you? I suppose — and stop me if I'm getting off track here — that you didn't say anything because, like Sally, you'd probably lose your job, and maybe worse. I think Blue Sky wouldn't look too kindly on one of their stewardesses even being rumored to be in some compromising photos — and more than that. This kind of news spreads fast and sticks. How am I doing?"

Carol looked up at me, and then quickly down at her folded hands, heading for cover. She knew where I was going next.

"Now, this is where I just start guessing, you know? Maybe one night after your group meeting, you and Sally go out for a cup of coffee or whatever. You start talking like two gals do: clothes, the latest movies, how your boyfriend's treating you. But with you two it's different, because you find out you have the same boyfriend. Not only that, but he's the reason you're both in the group. So, you get to talking and find out he's treating you both like turds and, what's more, he's blackmailing both of you with your jobs and reputation. So, you discuss not only how you got into this mess but also how you can get out of it. Maybe Sally tells you that Brozier is taking a trip on Blue Sky, and you're able to make some changes to your schedule so you're working the same flight. Yeah, we checked with Blue Sky. That flight from New York — you 'picked it up,' I think the lingo is. You weren't scheduled to be on it until you heard about it from Sally. From there to here, it's not hard to see what may have happened. Cyanide isn't such a hard thing to get your hands on — it's in a lot of poisons, and if you try hard enough, you can get the pure stuff. Just takes a little dab, maybe in the spicy sauce on that shrimp, or the Tabasco sauce that was on his tray. Either way, it's enough to cover up the bitterness."

I could tell by the tears flooding her cheeks that I had things right. I could also tell that I hadn't made her feel very good. It was the same with me — I felt like a louse. I thought it best to let things sink in, so I stood up to go.

Carol wasn't going anyplace. That's when it happened. Something I hadn't expected or knew really how to handle. She grabbed me and just held on, and the only thing I could do was hold on, too. I knew this was wrong but, man, it felt so right.

It was three in the morning before I got home, and even though I don't remember ever being so tired, I couldn't sleep. Carol had told me everything — all the gruesome facts that were worse than I had expected. I thought she might need more support than any Baptist Church group could offer. I finally fell asleep as the sky was brightening for a new day, and I knew what I had to do.

ꝺ

Another anniversary of The Case has come, and like every year, when the day slips away, I think about how things turned out before sleep takes me. It was that night, after I confronted Carol with what I knew, that a drunk and disorderly shooter killed Harbaugh. Like the good guy he was, he caught a ten-seventeen (officer in need of assistance) on the radio on his way home. He didn't have to respond — that was for the uniforms — but you had to know Harbaugh. He had just gotten out of his car when some guy, holed up in an apartment, took a shot at him. It was a headshot — he never felt a thing.

That left me as the only one who possessed all the facts about the Brozier case, and I hadn't shared some of the things I'd learned with my lieutenant. Yeah, the other guys that worked the case knew that Brozier had known Carol and Sally, but there was no way to know if the pictures were them, and I was the only one besides Harbaugh who heard the nitty-gritty details of how Brozier had abused them.

Mind you, I served nearly forty years on the force and got a ton of awards, but The Case was the only murder I never solved. Never solved officially, that is.

It's been a long day of memories, and it's time to go to sleep. From the bed next to me, my wife, Carol, reaches across to grab my hand like she does every night before we go off to dreamland.

"Well, Detective," she says in that creamy voice that hasn't changed since 1962. "We didn't come up with anything new on The Case this year. I guess we better be ready for the Grim Reaper."

"No need to worry, dear," I say, "there's always next year." But I don't think she hears me as the steady breathing of sleep fills the space between us.

Just before I give in to sleep, the scent of lilacs caresses me, and I hear the door to our room slowly open. Someone enters, but I'm already dreaming.

EMPTY GLASS

Andrea Auten

Izzy was the life of the party before she was the death of it. Words machine-gunned from her painted mouth; charming flirtations begging to make a connection. She sat talking to party people on a back patio overlooking traffic on the 5. All were coupled, and Izzy empty armed. Another slug of her blue gin fizz and she'd be fine. But the gin was running out, and her bed would be cold, the way L.A. could be when the sun dropped behind black mountains and a rescue dog wasn't enough to heat her bed. She tilted her glass toward the sky and swallowed. Such a pretty sunset sparkled through the bottom. Words stamped in the cheap reflection jolted her: Anchor Hocking. Even backwards, she recognized the name that took her father's job. Izzy squeezed away thoughts of home, where the glass company had folded up and left Ohio.

She inched her chair toward Minda and Stan. Piercings, patchouli, and layered-in faded cotton, this young, funky couple was together because of her expert meet-and-greet skills. After all, Izzy was a party ambassador. She could toy with their desire, bring the sex she exuded into their conversation, the way scent pulls bobcats down from the hills. These two didn't know how much she influenced their fingers curling into each other's hands.

One of them was all she needed, though she'd gladly go with both if invited. Heat sped her words and oiled her legs. The couple's smooth, exposed skin revved her, and she watched the melty moves of their seduction.

Sultry syllables spilled from her lips while she eyed Stan's hands. The thought of his touch churned her butter.

Izzy could have him. Take him in her car, strap onto his long thin bones until he cried into her scooped neckline. She inched her chair close enough to touch his bicep. Stan's elbow grazed Izzy's soft, lumped cleavage. All she had to do was woo his eyes to look her way with a twirl and twist of her curves, like she practiced for hours in front of her full-length mirror. Men were easy catch, right? Shooting live fish in a bucket.

Look at me, Stan.

Minda pushed into him, her wet lips inviting his focus. Izzy's grasp was slipping. She'd have to move in, dominate. Then what? Izzy wouldn't be some kind of love-touched stone to step on. Stones were easily kicked aside, and ending up home with only a yipping dog for company didn't fit her fiddle.

Lately, the dog liked to bogart her fleeting companions' attention enough that Izzy opted to shut the needy thing in a room or, like now, in her SUV, waiting it out. Though the choice created a repeating question as to how the dog was, where she was, and why had anyone hurt such a cutey pit. Cigarette burns. Some people shouldn't be allowed to live. Muscle-flanked Flaurie rallied people into action. Every party, they gathered to pet her.

The urge to stay central sucked stronger in Izzy's belly. Louder talk nordled out of her, zapping back and forth over points she might have missed. Bubbling talk over teeth unable to gate the long sentences and charted with sawing arms. She could see her audience waning. Tongue drying out, she flipped up a wait-a-minute finger and stopped to take a last swig. The gin pickled her tongue as she swilled it down a tired throat.

"You're a trip, girl," Stan said. Minda laughed a little mean echo and pulled herself to a loopy stand. Her hand stayed coiled around Stan's, and he followed the call to leave. "Later," they said, waving empty goodbyes. Just a simple flick of a word.

Izzy was left alone at the mosaic café table. Alone is what she could not be, staring at the tiny glass squares that pimpled the table. Some were chipped and others fully cracked enough to make her eyes sting. How tragic the splintered lines looked. She took more gin swallows then slammed the empty glass onto the table hard enough to hear splintering glass.

"Jesus, that's my good set," said Bitch-Host Lana.

"Cheap set," managed Izzy. Pressure pinched her sinuses, and her eyes teared up. She hadn't intended to crack a glass. Regret pooled in her mouth until words splashed out. Life was smacking her ass, with rent rising twenty percent; an infirm mother 2,000 miles east, who nagged and pleaded; and her job designing business flyers ate her heart from the inside out. Words and tears mixed between cries.

The party circled around her. Cooing and soothing away the ills. There, there, it will be okay. You're just upset. Too much gin, man. But their eyes spoke alternative thoughts. Why do you do this every time we party? The threat of such stares and darting side-eyes made her go deeper. Cry from the gut — an animal howling. Bitch-Host Lana's posture saying, You're a mess. If Izzy could ride on a condor, rise above her own heaving back, she would fly toward the sea and fall into it.

Hands, she didn't care whose, cupped her hunched shoulders and eased her head low to her knees. "Breathe," a voice coached in her ear. Izzy grabbed ahold of that voice and inhaled a sea smell, foam washing her body on a blank shore. Who would come find her crumpled amongst the seaweed?

Breathing slower, she felt thin and light, a palm frond bending in the breeze. Insides spinning, gin toxic and putrid. A shard that had fallen away from her broken glass caught a nearby candle's flame. Izzy smoothed her hand over it, scooped the triangle into her palm, and gently formed a fist to shield it from the world.

Finally, she sighed lower from her solar plexus. "I'm okay. Thank you, everybody." Already they'd backed up and turned to their own lives. And there she was. Hot-faced and humiliated. Innards splayed outside the circle where she'd landed again. "I'll run to the mercado and get us more gin." She'd bring back extra bottles, top shelf. Tweak her make-up, maybe add cat eye lines.

New determination pulled her onto her feet and down the side stairs. Wide, confident steps. Renewed, clasping her keys in one hand and the shard in the other, she pinched her purse close to her ribs.

A woman stood under the melon streetlight. Lean muscled and tall for L.A., she was waving a cellphone. Her baby peered out from a stroller. Izzy stopped walking and offered a smile to the mother and child.

"Is this your SUV?" the woman said.

"Hi, yes —" Izzy held her smile steady, but her stomach lurched as she wondered, have I met you before? This woman, her baby … no memory clicked.

"How old is it?" The woman stepped into Izzy's circle.

Tiny beats pecked inside her chest. "I … what, my car?" Her tongue flexing as she tried to swallow.

"Not your car. Why would I care about your car?"

"Please step back," Izzy said.

An intricately inked serpent pulsed on the woman's throat. "Don't smile at me."

"I'm not smiling." Izzy's stomach burned. This is why she struggled here: vacant manners. The honking horns at stoplights. Doors never held open for her. People spitting right on the sidewalks. A stranger advancing toward her SUV, making her pine for her daddy's safe arms. Izzy gripped the shard tighter as the woman stared.

"I'm taking your dog."

A fist beat inside Izzy's chest. The woman's words didn't compute. You're taking Flaurie? She began to rake at her purse handle.

The tattooed woman stayed planted and narrowed her eyes. "I have backup. Give the dog to me or I'm calling them." Her cellphone shone gold under the streetlamp.

Flaurie howled and clawed at the SUV window. Izzy focused on the window, trying to straighten her mind. Her dog, why? Adrenaline charged through Izzy. Stomach on fire, fingers now shaking and cold, she turned her body full-front to the window and tried to reason with Flaurie, but the idiot answered with a smack against the door. Izzy blurted, "I'm leaving," and stepped forward, but met the woman's shoulders just inches from her face.

"You're staying right here until you give me that dog," the woman seethed. "You left it locked in the car. No air to breathe. Are you insane or just stupid? Leaving it alone in the heat, look how terrified it is. Good thing you don't have a kid. You'd let a child fry."

Panic brimmed in Izzy's throat. Flaurie's barks were sharp, stabbing accusations. Yes, Izzy had indeed left the dog locked up. But there were reasons. A list that comes with a neurotic rescue, and this Serpent Woman didn't look like she'd listen to any of them.

"Give me the dog." Her words threatened through gritted teeth.

Gin and bile shot up into Izzy's mouth. There wasn't an exit or back alley out of this.

A stronger person would fight this woman, peel that phone from its grip and chuck it into the bushes. Izzy should call her out, stretch back an elbow, and sock the serpent tattoo.

"Stop yelling at me," Izzy managed. It wasn't super sunny when she left the dog and now the sun was nearly gone. Flaurie was upset because this serpent stranger and her baby got too close to the car, checking on her, getting the license plate. This was Izzy's dog, her SUV, and her concern. But Izzy couldn't say this. She had left her dog. She had done this. There weren't words worth standing up for herself and the notion shot through her: All she had to do was open the car door and let Flaurie loose.

But there was a baby sunning her tiny pale cheeks under the false light. A baby deserving of protection, like the way crazy Flaurie protected Izzy. The thought of the thick-necked dog's loyalty turned agitation to tears. Don't cry again. Dammit, not now.

Flaurie's bark was louder now, filled with fear. How could Izzy retreat? Why retreat? Izzy broken, Izzy humiliated, Izzy publicly threatened by a big-city dog lover. Izzy, kind and special, who takes care of this damaged dog. She looked back at the house, heard laughter buffeting from the patio, and ached for Stan and Minda, even Bitch-Host Lana. Her fingers pulsed as she pressed the piece of glass into her palm. Izzy couldn't protect herself. She wasn't protecting her dog. Why would anyone protect Izzy? Nobody would come for her.

Izzy swallowed over the rock in her throat, took the tattooed woman's rant, and completely buckled. "Take her," she whispered.

The sound of the rushing interstate suddenly deafened her ears. Izzy forced her sweating limbs to pick up and go, pushing past the woman. Jaw clenched, she clicked the key fob and opened the door. "Want to go for a walk?" Her voice warbled. Flaurie licked her arm.

The glass piece clinked into the tray between the seats where she tossed it. She rubbed her humid palm on the seat cover. A sick rush from gut to head made her swoon and gasp for air as she reached past panting dog breath, dropped her purse to the floor, and backed up to grab ahold of the collar. Izzy focused on the daisy print pressed into the leather collar and pulled those daisies from the SUV. Little whines began whirring. Izzy pulled on the daisy collar and walked to the back of the SUV, unlatched the trunk, fished out a leash and a gnawed Nylabone. She clasped the leash, her own eyes trained on the collared neck, walked it to the Serpent and handed off dog and bone. No words, no blathering explanations of needs or dog advice, Izzy pivoted and returned to her SUV.

Trunk lid down, Izzy hauled her exhausted body into the driver's seat, collapsed into a curve as she yanked the door shut. The SUV jumped and reared under her shaking foot as she rolled away.

Blast these Angelenos and their sensitivities. Thinking they're making the country a better place with their laws. No plastic grocery bags, zero-emission goals, no dogs in cars even when the weather's cooler. Izzy had her small-town ways. Dogs were tough, they could make it through hard times. Los Angeles and their dogs. Yappy-puppers in strollers, at tables in restaurants. Shopping in malls with their human parents buying, buying, and buying, while these thirsty pedigree dogs clothed in Prada were fed electrolyte water from special doggo water bottles. Dogs were treated better than she was.

Izzy flashed a look at the glass shard in the tray that once separated Flaurie from her. Now Izzy and her dog were separated for good. "It's for the best," she said, her voice cracking through dry lips. The dog was better off. She sped down the hill and turned on the radio. EDM music blared. The sound of the clubs. Desperation holes, all of them. Bumping rhythm in time with her huffs. Beats hammered into her brain as she forced up the volume.

Why had she rescued a dog? Nobody ever came to Izzy's rescue.

She reached her hand over and touched the place where Flaurie always perched. No dog chin to scratch. Emptiness washed over her. Baffled by her decision, she was struck dumb that she could hand off Flaurie to an unknown and more horrified by the relief she felt. The terrified dog would have to build up trust yet again. Izzy cringed at the betrayal. She couldn't even handle a poor, defenseless dog. Now she'd face the night alone. Fresh sobs blurred her vision as she eased onto the 5.

Music thrummed against a pain in her chest. That heaving, familiar pain that would lay her out for days, again. "Not this," she cried out. Not another wave to ride — drained, washed up, far gone, and spent — until she evened out and popped into the next party. Not again.

She felt for the shard resting inches away. Just a few hard cuts from its pointy end. Izzy checked the mirrors and changed over to the slow lane.

The 5 arched upward into the purpling sky above an interstate crossing underneath it. She pulled over to the guardrail and wept in convulsive bursts. How was life so impossible? What was wrong with her? She pounded the steering wheel and asked the roof, Why?

High up above the city lights, she was drawn to the sky that blanketed millions of flickers, hovering between earth and air, like arriving planes coasting low over L.A. Then looking down on all those shining orbs lighting up the city's magnificent grid of car rivers rushing in a red and white glow. Izzy longed again to taste the electric hope Los Angeles first promised. To be that California Dream Girl beaching into the night.

Izzy's mind quieted. Her words retreated into a thought symphony. She could direct the finale of her own desperate story. Sail off on the hot breeze and cascade in spirals until the pavement bedded her, commingling skin and earth. Her body stamped into the ground, the city welcoming her as beloved family. There was life still tingling in her fingers, unhooking from the steering wheel. Cells that pushed blood rivers inside her that raced to stay alive. Hands now massaging exhausted face muscles. She cupped them over her eyes and stared into the blackness.

A calm shrouded her. She palmed the piece of glass again, released the car door, and stood against the warm fender. Cars blasted past.

Down in the caldron beneath the overpass, headlights shimmered. So many people. Life teeming in opposite directions. Izzy stretched her neck and tallied the height from the 5 to the farthest street below. Gas fumes and gin flurrying through her head. What was a life? The distance between top of the heap and bottom of the pile. She could cease the pain pumping through her with one decision.

The glass shard was smooth and cold in her hand. She squatted, weight jamming into her heels, and examined its sharpest edge. Thick bar glass: the soda fountain kind. She circled her hand around the widest part, pushed her thumb against the inside and brandished the glass as a knife.

The guardrail was rough under her hand. She breathed in, tasting dust, and emptied her mind of all the party people, shook off the Serpent's face, and in a speechless drive to act, took the pointed tip and started to scratch.

Lines became a boxy S-O-R-R-Y. Next to sprayed letters, MC13, Terra Bella Boys, Pacas Trece, she continued to etch a confession into the metal railing. Her scratches spelled out F-L-A-U-R-I-E. Between honking horns and engines screaming by, the faint thump of music returned to her ears. She rose on trembling legs and surveyed her work. Sound wouldn't come to her voice. Goodbye, Flaurie, she mouthed. The dog's name glared back.

Izzy's insides were hollowed out into the shape of an unfilled drinking glass, and her feet twitched out of time with the drumming ache in her palm. She squeezed the glass shard. Pain became strength as it dug into her flesh. The time to buck up had come. Lace the fighting boots tight and soldier on, or don't. She nodded to nobody and swallowed over the grit lodged in her throat. Out of words, Izzy dropped the glass and stepped into the City of Angels' outstretched arms.

ANGELS LIVE HERE

Nolan Knight

With open arms, Los Angeles welcomed another casualty on a brisk August morning, free of earthquakes or heat-sparked brushfires to swallow the city back where it belongs. A cardboard crate held a newborn at the steps of Firehouse 35, a brick box filled with idle heroes slopping mediocre Denver omelets. The knock was faint, inaudible over a Dodgers' pennant race argument. No one was sure just how long the child had been there; shrill cries bled before anyone took action. Regardless of how the baby boy came to be, the city had another son, and the heroes triumphed at another task: calling the proper authority to handle these burdens. Los Angeles named the child Jack and bestowed upon him a legacy.

ʘ

On a scale from moon to gutter, Jack was cradled by clouds. Could hear birds chirp, smell flowers, even. Life was simple again. Solid job, new apartment — beat slumming with all those halfway rats. Didn't even think of the stuff anymore. Hadn't dreamt of nerve-end tingles or the bitter taste of pharmaceutical bliss. No pain left to kill. On the up and up, one day at a time … for as long he could swing it.

Knotting the bow tie became easy. Could snap the sucker without a mirror. The last button on his black vest popped into place as he barged through the Dresden Room's rear door. Inside, a snapshot of Los Angeles' golden age: vintage dining, stiff drinks — live croons to send patrons past the stars. Art Deco accents and celebrity eight-by-tens welcomed him towards Happy Hour. Larry was adding vermouth to a shaker when he caught wind of Jack, eyes straight to his watch.

"Ten ticks early, dunce."

"I aim to please, gramps."

Larry grimaced, tossing napkins before a couple of wrinkled women. "See how the new kid talks to me." The ladies smiled. "Take over here, Jack." He leaned in and whispered, "'Rhoids are flarin'."

Jack let the duffer squeeze past as he wrapped on an apron. "Mindy workin' tonight?"

"Six to close."

The seniors caught wind of Jack's grin as he shook their martinis. The smaller one began to sing, "I'm in the mood for *looove* …"

Head wagging, Jack presented the women their cocktails. "This oughta loosen you sweethearts up."

"You got a fat chance, Valentino."

Jack smirked as a voice resonated from afar.

"Greenhorn!"

Wiping a towel across the bar's nook, Jack took his time answering the call. "What'll it be today, George?"

"You tell *me*, rookie."

"George — I been here for four months, two days, an' three lousy minutes. How long I gotta sling you rotgut an' milk before I get a little love, old man?"

"Took Larry a stretch before I called the bastard by his first name."

"Ten whole years, huh?" Jack grinned, grabbing the MacGregor's. "Can make that, I think."

"We'll see, rube."

Larry returned. "Leave him alone, George. About to teach him how to water down the MacGregor's."

"You would, scum."

"Drink up, Georgie-boy. Them days a glory are wavin' behind ya."

George grunted, rattling the narrow glass up to chalky lips.

Jack surveyed the shelves to see what needed doing. The band would be on at nine, place filled by ten. He rolled up sleeves and juggled limes, welcoming the night's long hustle.

ⵙ

Jack taught himself to juggle at age seven. He'd been locked in a woodshed for days, fed ravioli in cans, given a garden hose for water and a bucket for a bathroom: the penalty for poor grades.

Foster nightmare number three.

Mother was small, sweet, and powerless. She'd call him Muffin or Jackie Pie. Father worked nights at the port, a man of simple tastes. Preferred fists to the belt (sometimes both). Jack imagined the pock scars about father's face as being billowing corpuscles from a cold black heart; they bled evil. Nevertheless, sometimes the wicked were just so.

He made the woodshed home, hiding racquet balls and paperbacks in the walls whenever mother watched her soaps. So much time was spent there since bruises could spring authorities, again. The days ached less and less; his body grew used to torment. Occasional wafts of breakfast sausage or pot roast became added pleasures — that and juggling in the dark.

Lost years there spent praying to angels.

A neighbor searching for a dog was his savior — at least from that *house. Not from the pains of living. Not from the future.*

൭

An ice bucket balancing act had Jack's brow beading. He was graceful through the surging crowd, dodging hoisted drinks and gut-busting fellas. Felt like an old carny, contorted in a leotard with those damn spinning plates. Soon as he made it behind the bar, the crack of a wet rag brought a sting to his right buttock, sending both buckets crashing to the floor. Mindy's high pitched squeal brought on a smile. He pulled a towel from his apron and said, "When you least expect it, girl."

She approached with a forgiveness hug, raven hair pulled tight into a baby ponytail, bangs nearly blindfolding. She wore the same threads as Jack, maybe a size larger. He welcomed the embrace, taking in the essence of her neck: Marlboro lights, blueberry Smirnoff. He patted her soft ribs till she burst out his arms.

"Oh, man — did you hear who's playin' with Marty and Elaine tonight?"

"Nah."

"Blimpie Fisk!"

He humored. "No fuckin' way — who the hell's that?"

"What?" She craned, cracking a trio of Buds. "Hey, George — new guy ain't heard of Blimpie Fisk."

George's head raised up off the bar; a weed-shackled rose stretching for sun. "What I tell ya, Min? Not a hope in the world for that rube."

She grinned. "Sorry, Jack, that's my bad. For a minute there, thought you had some class."

Larry shouted from beyond, once noticing he was the lone barkeep. Mindy jumped back to take orders. Jack followed suit, salvaging any uncompromised ice. Between pours, he imagined what a man named Blimpie must look like. How had he never heard of the guy, never crashed into his howling brass beats? Couldn't lie to himself. As if he hadn't given up everything the past ten years to follow those crummy, little, jagged, chalky, pastel, pretty little devils. He noticed Mindy peeping at him drifting through dreamland; a lone middle finger had her chuckling again.

ↀ

The first dose had him breathless. Janelle Tawdry's dad's place off Fairfax. Was her *idea — the corruptor. Hell, he wanted it too. Hadn't forgotten all the crucifixes. Every room: writhing corpses nailed for sin. Was only going to take one and see what happened. Janelle wasn't having it. If she was taking four, so was he. Moment the dry things scratched down his gullet, she was on him like tiger to prey. He always pictured Janelle versus gazelle. Didn't have to mess with clothes either — both in the flesh on daddy's queen size.*

Every element of that day, ingrained forever. A bar set in stone; a height Jack just had to chase. The warmth of a voluptuous brunette. Her scent as he went down. Those lovely waves from out of nowhere, coursing the veins, prickling his skin with every slow caress. He drowned in her as she rode and rode, pills seeping him into a perma-daze with corpses gawking on all sides.

ↀ

Stoolies barked over Marty and Elaine's vanilla croons; their upright-bass player scowled as he bled before ingrates. Random conversations clashed with chords:

"That bitch wouldn't know a decent script if it cut off his dick!"

"I'm pretty sure he didn't give it to me — I mean, I'm positive he, like, used a rubber …"

"Nah, Leo's a mixologist now. Can't even drink beer with the guy no more."

Jack lingered, arms crossed, taking in the vibes of a lame Saturday night. Tried to relish Elaine's organ and Marty's raspy high-hat, at least till the next rummy needed their life force. Mindy was on ice while Larry was back in the can. Didn't notice the guy at first. So many of them hip fucks wearing porkpie lids, so Jack figured he was just another fresh-face phony. The narrow black case had him pegged. *Had to be*. Sat next to the stage, doffing his ivory cap to the entire band as he placed the tattered case upon a knee and *clacked* it open. A soft yellow glow washed the man's chocolate features, shining a halo around his brim. Jack leered at Blimpie's lips; of all the stories they could play. The horn glimmered once out its cage, panting like a pooch as it got caressed with a polka-dot rag. Marty and Elaine's last number sizzled to applause.

"Two highballs and somethin' fruity for the lady!"

Jack stood locked in a zombie gaze.

"Hey, Buddy! Two highballs — one Blood an' Sand."

Jack snapped back, pausing on the customer before grabbing glasses. Ice crashed into the freezer behind him. He turned.

Beads of perspiration clung to Mindy's nose under huge emerald eyes. "Get a load, Jack. There he is."

ℴ)

Low times began to clot.

Jack stood at the rear of the chapel, trying to keep a low profile. Poor Mick. Everyone knew they were partying together that night. Why Mick? Why not him? *They planned to kick together, show everyone, fuck the world. Jack scanned those in attendance, envious of their warm tears. The "party" coursing in his veins turned his heart into an iceberg. One by one, pews of people paid final respects before the lid was sealed forever. Jack tried blending into stained glass as the bereaved rushed out past him. Most didn't even glance his way. Few mothers, mean-mugged. Wouldn't be back here tomorrow; could barely stand it now. Just wanted to see Mick and make right — try to, at least.*

As the last mourners awaited their viewing, he slumped on an empty bench and fanned through a Bible, uninterested in every word. Wished his last set of parents were here to help him through this. Began to nod off as he waited; came to whenever his chin nudged his chest. Shouldn't have doubled his dose; this pain kill was grinding him senseless.

A large hand shook his shoulder. His eyes opened to an elder in drab charcoal pinstripes.

"Son, the chapel will be closing now."

Jack wiped drool from his lip, frantically searching for Mick's pearl coffin.

"The viewing's been over for an hour, son. Tomorrow's procession begins at noon."

Jack rose, too weary for disgust.

Maybe partying would help?

ტ

The room turned to granite; Blimpie's lungs cut through every stone body, precisely sculpting with each blustered blow. The man's face could've paralyzed a blowfish. Marty and Elaine filled *bop-ba-ta* notes, softening the atmosphere for Blimpie to soar. And he did — a trumpeting angel, hovering on a cloud of beats. The horn wailed, blathering bliss from high notes to low, barking at the moon as if it were the only wailing soul left in Los Angeles.

Nobody ordered drinks, but stood staring, pondering the magic act before them.

The lucky few.

Air was sucked from the room, vacuumed through Blimpie's brass. He burst breaths back at them, making everyone choke on sound. Mindy rested her head on Jack's shoulder as they stood on crates behind the bar, faces aching from wonder. Jack's stomach began to twist, realizing this was what it was all about.

Life.

The epitome of being, the splendor of selflessness: everything he'd been missing for the past fucking decade. From high notes to low, then back to high again.

The trumpet blew for a full hour. One final rush of *BliDo-dE-bLAPs* unleashed the crowd into a riotous frenzy. Hands clapped blood out the fingernails. The piano tip jar exploded. Blimpie bowed, wiping his mouth with the rag, settling the trumpet back into its blue velvet cage. Eyes everywhere bugged from the sorcery.

Mindy poked Jack on the cheek. "How 'bout an encore? Shots! What you want?"

Jack's smile leveled. "I don't drink, hun."

Her shoulders deflated. "Hey, George. Found us the Holy Grail. New guy's the lone bartender in L.A. don't take the poison."

George bobbed on his stool, barely managing to shake his head, words too big a task this late an hour.

She swatted air, letting Jack know she was fooling. Not like she minded drinking alone. Rye overflowed a shot glass. She held it under Jack's nose, saying, "To a blossoming threesome: me, Jack, an' the Blimp." The hooch bounced up and in.

Jack wished that alcohol agreed with him, if only to form another bond with this beauty. Wasn't like he got lost on liquor for years and burnt every bridge — just never cared for the buzz, couldn't straddle the line. His mind wanted to shout to Mindy every kaleidoscopic taste/tingle procured from his one true love. A worthless encyclopedia of medicinal madness. Instead, all that came out his mouth was, "I'ma go smoke."

Night wind bit at the cheekbones as he struggled to light a Parliament under the Dresden's crown of bulbs. Streets were dead, just a lone prostie cleaning grime out her nails on the corner. Heard the crowd inside grow wild, yet again. The door swung; Blimpie and his cage emerged, escorted out by a slow walk of the bass. Jack stood there, leering, trying to muster up words that articulated his thanks.

Not a chance.

Blimpie tipped his cap and said, "Do it to it, young blood," before waddling down the block, heels clicking through shadows.

Jack went lax, coughing smoke once the legend plopped down at a bus stop. With the cage resting on concrete, Blimpie awaited the next slug to whisk him through neon wilderness. Jack turned to the door (innards still pulsing from the gig), then back to the bus bench (streetside serenity). He sparked another cig, marinating over the coolest thing he'd ever seen.

ᘓ

Thirty-five and barely alive. Skid Row by day; hot prowl by night.

Friday the thirteenth.

Desperation delivered a fractured orbital and bruised jaw. Jack could only remember the heat off the patrol car's hood and three ominous words: Suspect-In-Custody.

Surveillance caught him breaking into a CVS. Hadn't figured the pharmacy to be secured by its own rusted gate. Took too long for just one pocketful of miracles. A silent alarm circus ensued.

"There he is!"

"I got him!"

The baton cracked his skull as he scrambled down the diaper aisle, jarring his world back to the living.

An open and shut case: such was life.

ᘐ

Mindy's celebration shots had exceeded their intent. After counting down the register, Jack escorted her home (per her request). She giggled and joked with him as they sauntered up Hillhurst, moonlight sparkling gutter dregs, city nearly quiet with only a few speeding cars. Someone deranged began to howl in the distance. Mindy squeezed his forearm as they approached her building, an impressive structure with intricate brickwork. Could've doubled for a fire station. The first floor featured an overpriced Italian eatery. They climbed the stairs to her apartment, a narrow hallway keeping them close.

She had trouble unlocking the door. "Wanna have coffee with me?"

Jack played it cool. "Sure thing."

There wasn't any furniture. Jack stood in the living room, cigarette dangling from his lips as Mindy searched for the ashtray, which was buried beneath a mound of laundry. Thanks to the restaurant, a garlic stench was profound. Jack took in the scene. A busted TV held a stack of *Variety* in the corner. Fast food wrappers sat stuffed in a lonesome trash bag near a hot plate. Mexican candles were scattered throughout. He picked one up featuring a Day-Glo-green Guadalupe.

Mindy tossed the clothes back into a pile. "I can't find it. Just ash in the candle."

"Which one?"

She smiled. "Any one you like, Jackie *Pie*. Electricity got cut for a few days last week. My roommate couldn't hang — headed back to Houston. Took a few extra shifts for me to get it turned back on. The candles are from some photo shoot she did."

"Actor?"

"Director."

He blew smoke out the window before snuffing the butt.

"There's a record player in my bedroom, if you wanna throw somethin' on." She pointed to the mound of laundry. "I'm gonna change into peejays and fix the coffee."

Entering the adjacent room, Jack saw a crate of vinyl. An eighties-era turntable with wood-framed speakers sat beside it. Couldn't help but notice four blankets layered on the floor, functioning as a mattress. The walls held a few of Mindy's headshots: smiley, stoic, surgeon, superhero. Her clothes and shoes were huddled in an open closet. More vibrant candles and their stickered salvation greeted at every turn. A weeping Christ had him thinking of Janelle Tawdry.

Mindy's record collection was minimal but essential. There were two Blimpie LPs: *Live at the Strand* and *Do it to it!* The choice was obvious. As the needle scratched, he contemplated Blimpie's brief words, wondering if they implied something more than just a trademark greeting.

Do what to what?

The horn jumped full swing as Mindy entered with steaming mugs. Her pajamas consisted of flannel pants and a black Frolic Room T-shirt. Jack tried not to stare at her stubby white toes, each nail painted turquoise. She handed him a mug.

"It's instant but I like it."

"Hard not to love anything *instant.*"

She placed her mug atop a speaker and bent down to light candles. He watched as she crawled on all fours, ass twitching to the beat of the brass. Noticed she wasn't wearing a bra.

Her arm brushed his thigh as she reached for one final light. The pressure sent shock waves up his spine. She rose, snapping her fingers, room aglow in a spectrum of colors turning the walls into stained glass. Jack thought of that chapel, then Mick's grey corpse. He shook out the image.

She pointed to the blankets, her skin cast in hellfire red. "Come down."

Jack slowly sat atop the blankets, careful not to splash any of his coffee.

"You know what would go perfect with this record?"

He shrugged.

"Pot."

"Pot?"

"Weed. You smoke, right? Don't tell me you're an all 'round goody two-shoes."

He gazed up; the contours of her breasts forced a swallow. "Of course."

"Be right back."

Jack expelled a faint puff as she bounced from the room. He sparked another cig, sucking monster drags. Could hear a soft tapping in the other room. *Probably knocking resin out a pipe.*

Mindy hollered, "Take your shoes off — get relaxed."

Soon as he removed his boots, a black cloth flew into the room, nearly landing on a candle. He moved it, making sure it couldn't catch fire.

Firemen.

He looked at the cloth in his hands: Frolic Room, emblazoned in white. She stood in the doorway, lopsided breasts speckled with freckles, holding a mirror harboring six meaty white slugs.

൭

Ambrose Avenue, Los Feliz: fourteen months shacked up with Hollywood's crestfallen. Lamest shit ever, although Jack enjoyed living outside a cellblock. Hadn't made any friends, though — too wary of poor influences on his newfound sobriety. His roomie was an ex-pro surfer named Duff. Decent fellow, like himself, stricken by the fever of unattainable highs. Jack had dabbled in everything by now, but only one dose made him weak. Duff was the opposite; he danced with speed, coke, and heroin — simultaneously. He'd tell Jack about his plans once out the house for good, getting lost across the globe, searching for the perfect left. Duff's words were all he had; Jack could tell by the guy's eyes that he was helpless on the outside, too seduced for tranquility, too wild for surfing. Jack worried about being the same; forever trapped halfway.

The days drifted slowly. Chores and paperbacks to stew the brain. Three times a week, a counselor would break down his habits, set goals, create dreams. Jack would eventually help troubled youth upon the completion of the program and his counselor's consent. Nights were worse: sobs and screams from tormented tenants. Between the tasteless meals and the stench of communal living, reality pounded dust out the walls. On Jack's final morning, Duff pried for details on his fresh new beginning.

"Dunno, man — honest. Live one day at a time, see what comes my way. Gotta find an apartment, then job hunt. Got a few decent leads out the Weekly. *They said if I can hold my own for six months, they'll begin training me for youth mentorship and motivational speaking — that's the end goal. Just anxious to be a part of something, you know? A neighbor — a coworker — a somebody. Feel hopeful once again. If I can help anyone avoid the choices I've made, maybe all the pain wasn't in vain."*

Duff's hand clobbered Jack's shoulder. "What pain, bro?"

Jack smiled. "Exactly."

ʘ

Mindy handed him the tray and sat down beside him. "No pot — but I found something better. Strip for me, Jackie."

Without blinking, Jack slackened the bowtie and popped buttons. His mind raced: *Coke — never had a problem with coke.*

Mindy snorted a line, biting her bottom lip.

Little yay'll be okay. No biggie.

He steadied the mirror on his palm. The record needed a flip; calm scrapes made the room an outer realm.

Do it to it — right, Blimpie?

Instantly, as the powder smacked his brain, all was kaput. No more cradled by clouds. Kiss the job goodbye. So much for being *somebody* or helping anyone. *Who was he fooling?* "This isn't coke."

Mindy placed the needle to the Blimpie b-side and grabbed the mirror, sniffling. "Nope — Oxy." She showed him an amber vial as proof.

Jack closed his eyes as familiar tingles took hold. He relished every surge advancing his system, every bitter drip biting the throat. The world became soft as Mindy's curves.

She gave back the tray.

Jack attacked the final rails.

Mindy placed the mirror aside and grabbed his hands. They gazed at each other's bodies, almost dreamlike as their blood charged in unison. In their chapel, Blimpie's brass was the organ. Before Jack could make a move, Mindy pounced, slamming him onto his back.

Janelle versus gazelle.

Their tongues slithered as Jack relived that first dose. Mindy rode and rode, radiating a fiendish aura. Candles wept over his fall; writhing corpses returned as righteous voyeurs. Gone were foreboding thoughts of his miserable life. He succumbed to the moment, the epitome of *his* being. Everything life had forsaken the past year plus — back in spades.

A final rush of *BliDo-dE-bLAPs* carried them to climax.

Jack smiled, grunting through bliss, his heart a live grenade.

A legacy fulfilled; a saga continued …

From high notes to low, then back to high again.

THE FORTUNE OF THE THREE AND THE KABUKI MASK

Sara Chisolm

They didn't belong among the rice paddy straw hats, paper umbrellas, and flowery silken Chinese-collar shirts. The red and white lacquer of the Kabuki masks grew hot and glimmered in the sun that tilted through the window. I asked my mother why she kept them there. Why put them next to the mediocre jade bracelets and plastic amulets of jovial Buddhas? Wouldn't they have been better suited a mile away in one of the air-conditioned shops of Little Tokyo?

She just grinned as she unwrapped the papier-mâché masks.

"Florence, my dear daughter, money is money," Ba said as he wiped down one of the glass countertops of our non-air-conditioned souvenir shop.

Gray billows of smoke from smoldering incense sticks attempted to claim every whisper of fresh air. I should have been kneeling my slender body at the altar in the front of the shop, my delicate hands and calloused fingertips placing tangerines in one of its white porcelain bowls with indigo flower print. I should have filled one of the vases with fresh marigolds not yet dried out from the California heat, or lit more incense sticks and placed them sticking up in the rice that occupied a single bowl in front of the medium-sized smiling gold Buddha. Maybe if I had prayed, a gust of wind would have forced its way in and dried the sweat on the back of my neck so that all my long black pin-straight hair wouldn't stick there. Maybe then I wouldn't have to blink away melted and smeared eye makeup. A brisk wind would've been the only way that I would get some air conditioning, because Ba wasn't going to pay for shit.

"If money is money, why won't you fix the air conditioner?" I asked.

Ba gave me a fleeting glare.

I turned away from my parents and opened another box with an X-Acto knife. The shop was littered with heaps of trinkets for locals and foreign visitors alike. They were eager to come and experience Chinese-American culture. They came with their cameras snapping, eyes wide with wonder, and barely-worn sneakers for their trek through Los Angeles' Chinatown. Their eyes danced around the pagoda-style rooftops, neon signs, and hanging red lanterns. They posed next to the statues of Bruce Lee and Sun Yat-sen. They came and patted the stone heads of the pair of foo dogs that guarded every red- and gold-adorned temple. They came and ate fried rice, roasted duck, and steaming wonton soup. My mouth watered every time I walked down the street.

This place and our shop were specifically Chinese-American. Why couldn't my parents understand that? Ma had placed the new masks in the front window. Japanese Kabuki masks.

"You know," I said, turning toward Ba, "I don't want to argue with you. I know that it's wrong of me." I bit my lip and put down the X-Acto knife. I wasn't talented enough to convey anything more audible than *sit down* or *stop* in proper Cantonese. If I had learned more of my grandparents' language, my parents might have listened to me more.

"It's just that my friends make fun of the fact that these masks are in our store." I pointed at the piles of dust layered on the frowning masks.

I had never seen my mother's hair when it was luscious night black or her skin when it wasn't dimpled with age. People often mistook her for my grandma as we walked through the streets. My Ba was the same. They had saved up every penny they could to afford fertility treatments, to have me. I came out a girl when they had wished for a son, and so I took on the role of the youngest child within our entire extended family. Just another baby in need of care, not entitled to a damn opinion of my own, even though I had opinions that were burning to burst out of my mouth every second of the day.

"We're Chinese-American, not Japanese, and by having them in the shop, you're passing along the idea that all Asian cultures are the same. We're different."

It wasn't the first time Ba's eyes looked like they were going to fall out, or the first time that his bald head blushed with heat from my smart-ass retorts.

"Now, Florence," Ba scolded. This was his official warning to me. I should've let his anger burn out, turn to ash, and dissipate.

"But —" I whined.

Ba wiped furiously at the counter top. "We have to make money to survive," he stated in a clipped tone.

Everyone was here in Chinatown to make or spend money, even the new art galleries, Southern-style barbeque stops, and hip vintage resale stores. Business owners all wanted to get their cut, and my family was no exception.

Ma looked down at a bunch of cheap souvenir T-shirts that she bussed from Hollywood in her old beat-up Trans Am. The car barely had enough room for me to crawl in after she loaded it with her bulk purchases. She must have brought those masks from that dark, Cheeto-and-glue smelling hole-in-the-wall factory.

I once asked her why she didn't just buy a new car. She replied, "This car makes me cool." She bobbed her head and tilted her pelvis as she spoke. "I haven't always been a mother," Ma stated. She smirked and gave a slow nod. "I was cool for awhile. We couldn't afford a bigger car after fertility treatments. So, I still get to be *cool*," she dipped her head lower as she said the last word, a mockery of Angeleno swagger.

She wasn't so cool now, sweating up a storm in this busted-up shop that ate away at all our savings and sold counterfeit Asian merchandise from a musty factory.

"Is this stuff mass produced in the United States or a Latin country?"

"All of this stuff does come from Asia," my father said sternly.

"So, you're okay with little children standing around in a hot factory being overworked?"

"You don't know that. You should hold your tongue and be proud to represent any Asian culture. You didn't grow up in the sixties and seventies here when you couldn't walk down the street without someone making a wise crack about us or our languages."

I raised my hands in the air so that I could whirl them around in a big whooptie-do, but thought better about it and lowered them to my sides. That's when I dropped my X-Acto knife and it nicked the side of my arm. I looked down as teardrops of blood dripped onto one of the pearl-white cheeks of a Kabuki mask.

"Look," I said while holding up the mask, "I dripped blood all over this mask. You can't sell blood-stained or contaminated masks."

Ma gasped as she covered her mouth with her wrinkled, delicate hands. Her glasses slid down her face. Ba grew hot again, and his face quivered as if steam was going to come out of his ears.

"That costs money," Ba said, stifling his emotion. His next words were soft and controlled, as if he were talking to a customer. "Take them all to the back and rinse them off. You aren't getting paid this week." He massaged the center of his chest as he looked down at his dirty rag.

"It's not like I haven't heard that one before," I said with a sneer. I picked up an armful of masks.

"You are a child. My child. You will listen to me without question," Ba yelled.

I stomped my foot and pouted.

"Ha! Still a child," Ba said, pointing at me.

"It's not fair. You're going to keep the mask and not pay me," I whined.

Ba turned away from me, but I heard the words anyway, just as I had heard them other times.

"*Jai* would've listened."

My parents always referred to the son that they never had underneath their breath. I had sibling rivalry with my parents' perfect fantasy son. That imaginary asshole had shown up to yet another family disagreement.

I'd had enough. I grabbed the masks roughly. "You want me to wash them?"

My parents gazed at me with contempt.

"I'll wash the damn things. I'll do whatever you tell me to, and it'll never be good enough for you. It'll never be good enough because I am not your son."

Feeling pain, I looked down at the cut on my arm.

Ma's eyes followed mine. She clasped her hands over her mouth again. "You're bleeding," she murmured.

Ma ran in my direction with the nearest clean rag in hand. Her old legs moved well, and she would look amazing in a skirt if she ever wore one. I rolled my eyes. I was prepared to erupt in a storm of complaint if that rag contacted my arm. My mother was the mothering type. I was a full-grown eighteen-year-old woman.

I ran to the storage room bathroom and locked the door before Ma busted in. I dropped the masks on the floor and turned on the water faucet. I sank onto the lid of the yellowing ceramic toilet that seemed to have a permanent brown ring around the waterline of the basin, no matter how many times you scrubbed it.

My heart slowed down slightly, and I massaged the center of my chest. I inherited a heart condition from Ba, but the real chest pain came from my own disobedience. The little verbal digs that I took not only nicked at his fragile heart but also mine.

I jumped from a sudden pounding on the door. "Are you almost finished? Hot water cost money, Florence," Ba shouted.

I tore off a square of toilet paper and dabbed at my cut.

"Florence," Ba shouted.

"Whatever," I shouted while rolling my eyes. I threw the bloody paper in the sink and turned off the water.

A line of tears descended my cheeks.

"Florence."

I clumsily picked up some of the masks. They jostled like disobedient children in my shaking arms. I couldn't even wipe away my own tears, let alone wipe off the masks. I couldn't go back like this. I didn't want Ba to see how his words had affected me. I tightly clutched the masks. He would win.

I looked around the steam-filled bathroom. I settled my gaze on the small window that led to the back alley. Ba could forget about getting any type of apology from me. I hummed wickedly as I jammed the pile of masks out of the window. They hit the pavement with a loud clatter.

"Florence, are you okay?" Ma said.

I didn't bother to answer as I wiggled my sinewy body out of the window. I breathed a sigh of relief as I picked up the masks. I opened the smelly blue dumpster and threw the masks in. I shivered as a slight chill went down my back.

The frowning masks hit a pile of black garbage bags in the half-empty dumpster, and I laughed while I slammed the dumpster lid closed. Down the alley, a guy with a black half-apron smirked at me. I had seen him around, scrambling from table to table in my uncle's restaurant. He had, on the odd occasion, delivered food to our shop because Ba had told his brother that we were too busy to cook, when really we had been too broke to afford cooking a decent meal. I looked down at my three-year-old dunks that I wore when I worked in the shop. The fuzzy leopard material of the sneakers had faded, and the swoosh was tanned and cracked from the sun and use. This guy knew our secret. He knew that we were poor.

He walked towards me, and my heart nearly beat out of my chest with embarrassment.

"What's up?" the guy said as he pointed at the dumpster. "Whatcha throwing away?"

"Nosy ass … I am getting rid of half of your little paycheck," I said.

He tilted his head back and laughed. "You got jokes, huh," he said as he nodded his head.

He pointed his thumb behind him down the alley. "Did you guys order today? Your family has quite the tab."

I scoffed. How could my uncle keep a tab for his own family? An even more pressing question was why would he let this moron have a good view of it? My uncle Harry was always the best little brother, admiring his older brother for his business sensibilities. Perhaps Harry had been jealous of his older brother. Ba almost had the whole perfect-family Christmas picture down: wife, kid, and a once-successful business. If only he had a son instead of me.

"Don't you have a wall of dishes to wash," I spurned. I rubbed the center of my chest again. Damn! This was the first time that I felt like taking one of the prescription pills that the kids with depression or ADHD sold in the bare brick hallways of my old high school.

The guy shrugged and walked back to the rear door of my uncle's restaurant. I stared after him. He had that self-assured smirk that guys wear as armor in a world that has already granted them penis-privilege. My heart skipped a beat. Ba would love him as a son. He would love any son. I kicked the dumpster and heard a bunch of squeaks and the patter of scampering little feet.

Curious to see how big the rats inside might be, I lifted the lid of the dumpster. Some unknown liquid coated the palm of my hand. I rubbed it off on my jeans. They were dirty anyway. The mask that I had dripped blood on stared up at me. I picked it up. The sun's intense light beamed through the eye holes against the side of the dumpster. I closed my eyes and murmured the heart sutra that I had learned from hours of kneeling in front of the gigantic golden Buddha during temple attendance. The heart sutra was meant to bring families closer together and create harmony among loved ones. My knees ached with remembrance and repentance. Karma was cruel to give an only-girl child parents like mine. I lowered the mask and a gust of wind knocked the damn thing to the ground. My hair spun around me like strands of a black cocoon. The smell of garlic and ginger that usually coated the muggy afternoon air drifted away with the sudden breeze. The dumpster lid came crashing down.

"Why couldn't they have had a son as well?" my voice sung out, each word whipping through my hair.

I picked up the mask and threw it back into the dumpster. I lowered the lid and wiped my hands on my white-and-black striped T-shirt. I was walking towards our shop when the dumpster rattled. I opened the lid to see the black eye pits of the blood-dripped mask. The mask tilted to the side as I watched. I slammed the lid down. My heart fluttered like that time when Ba collapsed on the sidewalk and we had to call the ambulance to come. I backed away slowly and tugged the ends of my hair.

Was this the year of the water horse? The year when a girl like me could make a wish and all the cosmos, full moons, and gods would come together and grant me luck, love, or both? Silly superstitions made Ma visit the fortune teller, eat vegan food, and clean the house on certain days. You couldn't plan your life around the moon cycles or lucky and odd numbers. Besides, we're more American than we are Chinese. Yet, there I was, rubbing the wooden prayer beads laced around my wrist and chanting to calm my fears.

The thick plastic lid jumped, and I screamed. I knew that people could hear me because their placid moon faces appeared within the grimy barred windows of their establishments. They wouldn't ask if I was okay or anything; they would go back to cleaning, smiling, and their customers. Money doesn't wait. I stepped closer to the dumpster, and the lid flew up.

"What the hell?" I gasped.

The mask came tumbling out in a haze of black smoke bundled together and twisted into tight fibrous knots. The knots spun until they formed smooth, defined muscles. My eyes grew wide as I turned away to run. I didn't make it two steps past the mask. One of the mask's black smoke hands reached out and grabbed me by the shoulder.

"Wishes, superstations, and full moons," I shouted. I spit in one of the black eye pits of the mask. The mask creature released its grip on my shoulder.

"Whatever you do, don't kill me, dude," I said while holding up my hands in what I hoped looked like a gesture of surrender.

The Kabuki mask tilted its head as it whispered from the bowels of its gutless form, "Sister?"

I tore away and ran as fast as my skinny legs could carry me. I dashed into our store, locked the back door, and drew the paper blinds down. Ba and Ma looked at me with question marks in their glares.

"Where are the masks?" Ba said.

"You won't believe what happened. Trust me, don't go outside," I shouted. I ran around the shop like the Santa Ana winds. I knocked over stands of chopsticks and colorful beads. I pushed the golden Buddha across the threshold of the shop's front door. The bowl of rice chimed, and the bowl of tangerines rocked. There was a choice that every mortal idiot had to make: heaven or hell? My stupid wish had probably projected me into the latter.

"Dumb wish," I murmured.

"Where are the masks?" Ba said.

I locked the front door and drew more blinds.

"The mid-autumn festival is coming, we need more sales," Ma shrieked. She waved a dirty dust cloth into the air and flapped it in my direction.

Ba turned to Ma. "She's avoiding her responsibilities, again," Ba spurned, "She never focuses. This daughter of ours always has her head stuck in a cloud of ideas and her mouth stuffed with hot air." Ba blushed so hard, he almost turned indigo.

"The masks … those stupid masks. There are more important matters," I screamed.

"Nothing is more important than our integrity," Ba scolded.

"Did you mean more than money?"

Ba and me both touched the center of our chests at the same time.

"As our only child, you have to bring honor to your family," Ba roared.

"I am trying to tell you something," I yelled.

Then I heard it. A small rumble that vibrated through the shop. I shivered as my parents' stares punctuated the dim glow of the store. Their eyes looked like new pennies as they reflected the shine of the sun's rays hitting the bald head of the Buddha. Ba's jaw hung open like a gumball machine; words that wanted to tumble out of his head and escape his mind remained suspended. Ma had her towel-throwing hand stilled. I knew then that she had planned on hitting me with it. My heart skipped a beat, and I touched the center of my chest.

"Big sister," the raspy voice called out. "Sister."

I should have kneeled and prayed. I should have prayed so hard that that Kabuki monster was erased from our existence. I was a selfish child. A jealous child. I waved a hand at my parents. They just stayed frozen.

I grabbed the neon green transparent Bic lighter that Ba hides behind the container, lit some incense sticks, and stuffed them in the rice. Sprinkles of ash floated down from their tips and burnt the tops of my hands. I went down on all fours and bent so low at the waist that my breasts dragged on the dusty floor. I murmured prayers and wishes. I thought about visiting the temple and making an offering of repentance. I hadn't been a religious person after I became addicted to boys, SAT study books, and K-pop bands. I could've been that person again, that proud first-born girl with the smooth complexion and quiet disposition. I could've become that pre-puberty girl again. I could've been the perfect child again, if the Kabuki monster vanished into thin air.

"Sister?" The raspy voice rattled in my ear. I jumped back. The soulless pits of the Kabuki mask glared at me. The red parts of the masks glowed inferno red, and the white parts looked like complete emptiness. My tear-drop-shaped blood stains glistened like wet paint. The mask tilted again as a hand jutted out from the shadows and grabbed my wrist.

"Sister, big sister?"

"What the fuck!" I screamed as I scrambled to a standing position. I wiggled free from the demon's grip. I dove behind the glass container where my parents stood motionless.

The mask ducked low. A hissing emitted from its nose holes as puffs of steam rolled out. A chill permeated the air. It smelt of birthday candles and lit incense. The dear wishes of the childish or stupid. When did I become so jaded?

I grabbed a pair of chopsticks from the floor. I stood up. "Stay away from my parents," I roared as I charged towards the mask. We fell in a heap on a pile of kung fu fans and plastic bracelets. I swatted at the mask as I straddled it. More bins emptied onto the floor. I jabbed one chopstick in each nostril. The creature's screech permeated the humid air.

I jumped off the monster and hid behind a bin of hair accessories. I picked up a large hair clip and held it open so that I could use the plastic combs as a weapon. I took a peek from behind the bin.

The mask tilted its head from left to right. The smoke seemed less dense. The sun seeped through the drawn blinds. The air cleared and my parents blinked as if they were safely tucked into their four-poster bed waking up to the dawn of another day.

"What's going on?" Ma lowered her rag. Her gaze lazily shifted from my face to that of the mask. "What have you done to him?"

"Done to *him*?" I said while pointing to the mask.

"Yes," Ba added. "What have you done to your dearest younger brother?" Ba walked from around the glass counter. He approached the Kabuki mask. Ba turned and glared at me with way too much heat and tension building in his eyes. He placed his hand in the center of his chest.

"Why would you do this?" Ma said as she rushed towards the mask. She cradled the cheeks of the Kabuki mask as if it were a living child. "Our sweet son that we all wished for." The mask dipped its head to one side and rubbed its paper edges against the palms of Ma's hands and fingertips.

Ba motioned towards the ground. "Who's going to clean this up?" Ba frowned as he looked around the shop. He walked a complete circle, stepping over scattered T-shirts, amulets, and various sized fans. He stood right beside the Kabuki monster.

"I tried …" I said, my words trailed off as I watched the three of them.

Ba looked at the figure from head to toe, a slow smile spreading across his face. Ba embraced the creature. "Son," his cry of joy echoed throughout the shop. Ba pulled the chopsticks from each of the Kabuki mask's nostrils.

I watched as my parents linked arms with the black figure. It seemed to become more stable and muscular with every embrace and tear that my parents gifted him.

"Our sweet and favored son," Ma cried as the trio made their way towards the back door of the shop. "Me and your father wished for you so long ago … and now you have come by the blessing of a wish made by three people. We will need three people to bless you or maybe we will visit three different temples to pray. Three seems like our number of fortunes."

"Where are you going?" I whined. I grabbed my mother by the arm. She whirled around and looked me in the eyes. Her angry gaze was searing a hole in my teenaged soul. All of those times that I disobeyed them, laughed at them behind their backs, or made wishes for different parents or a brother, Ma saw what I really wanted. I didn't want to be their only child or perhaps their child at all.

My arm dropped to my side, and the Kabuki mask rocked back and forth as it turned completely around to give me a pitiless glance of curiosity.

"Big sister," the mask uttered from its closed lips.

"You!" I murmured.

I searched for an appraisal of my parents' reactions. They both shook their heads in unison. I knew that they were going to punish me by ignoring me.

"You fake-ass little brother," I roared.

This is what they had always wanted, and now they had their dearest son. They all turned away from me and walked to the back door. They looked like the perfect happy Christmas picture. The fortune of three — a mother, a father, and their hideous Kabuki mask monster of a son. I stomped as I threw my arms up into the air. Ba opened the creaking back door. The chime that was perched on the top of the door seal rang. That was the first time that I had heard it all day.

"He can't be your son," I shouted out. I balled up my fists and stomped. The three of them, the perfect family, glanced over their shoulders for a split second. The door slammed behind them. I ran and flung it open. The door chimes clattered to the ground. I took a deep breath. "He could never be your son. Kabuki masks are clearly Japanese, and we're Chinese-American," I shouted after them.

UNWANTED GIFTS

AS Youngless

The last bit of the afternoon light cast long, dark, motionless shadows. I walked further into the neighborhood, ignoring my little brother as he yapped at me about nonsense shit. It was summer, hot and stagnant, and he was a pile of bricks that I didn't feel like lugging around anymore.

"You think Ma will let me get that new Fortnite skin?" he asked, stupidly. There was no way she'd let him blow twenty bucks on an imaginary outfit in a video game she didn't want him playing in the first place. My gaze swept to the piles of toys strewn along our street. I didn't remember it being so messy.

I was about to tell Charlie he was nuts if he thought Mom would waste that much cash when the sky got really bright. Too bright. Like someone inflated the sun until the thin film holding it together burst open. Daggers of light shot out, a million points in all directions. I covered my eyes to keep from burning my retinas.

Then, just as quickly as the brightness appeared, it was gone. When I lowered my arm, everything was the same as before. Sirens warbled on La Cienega. The 10 freeway buzzed like a hive a mile up the road. Jackhammers slammed into old foundations for the new condos no one wanted built. A crush of bodies blocked the center of Boden Avenue next to the ripe dumpster. Everything was as normal and right as rain, except for what was resting on the toe of my shoe.

"What was that, May?" Charlie asked, eyes on the sky.

"Don't know, Charlie," I replied, looking at my foot.

It was the size of an orange, a little smaller than the size of my palm, with a smooth brown-glass dome on one end and spiky fingers on the other.

I blinked three or four times and kneeled. Maybe it was a toy? But it hadn't been there before the flash. At least, I hadn't noticed it until afterwards. I squinted, no clue where it came from, then picked it up.

"What's that?" my little brother hunkered down next to me. His shoulder brushed my arm as he moved in real close to see what I held.

"No clue." I rolled it around in my palms, not taking my gaze off the object.

He pushed against my body, knocking me off balance. I tore my gaze from the Thing long enough to plant one hand on hot cement to stop my fall.

"Thought you knew everything —"

"I know you're a dumbass," I said. "If I knew what it was, you think I'd just sit here staring at it?" I stood and held it up high. The domed top sparkled, glitter trapped under glass, in the falling light. Gold sparkled within amber, and there were black squiggly lines and weird markings, like letters, under the top layer. I wasn't sure if they were made-up words or some kind of art.

"Let me see." Charlie got up and reached out to take it.

I pivoted and shoved the Thing in the front pocket of my hoodie. I wasn't lying. I'd never seen anything like it in all my life. Nana would say it was because I hadn't been alive long enough to see most things, but she wasn't there. In any case, I saw it first. Plus, Charlie was pissing me off with his agro bullshit. I knew him well enough. If I gave him the Thing, he'd be all over the block telling anyone with ears *he* found it.

What if it turned out to actually *be* something?

I wasn't having any part of that shit show.

I stepped away from Charlie and his ulterior motives. My movements shifted the Thing in my pocket. I wanted to run my palm over the smooth dome but didn't because the other end and its dozen or so pointy bits was stabby enough to keep me hunched forward so it didn't jab my stomach through my hoodie.

Charlie craned his neck, using a hand to shade his eyes. The sun, back to its regular size, burned white against the deep blue sky — even as it descended into twilight.

"Look at you acting all sus." His lips puckered, head shaking. He stood nice and tall. He may have been my little bro, and only twelve, but he was already inching over my head as if he were the older one. He wasn't, as I reminded him often to keep him in check.

"Don't you have chores?" I stood at the crosswalk and glanced around, making sure no one was running the stop sign. The road was empty, except for a small pack of crows pecking at a burger someone trashed near the curb. One of them looked at me as I walked past, not caring I was there, more interested in its dinner. It was the biggest freaking crow I'd ever seen, so I shifted a little further away.

I slipped my hands into each front pocket of my hoodie, right fingers curling around the Thing, heart racing when it touched my naked skin. It showed up during the flash, I was sure, but it would sound stupid to say so out loud — like I was on something.

I glanced up as the sun slid behind the oil fields up in the hills. That flash — I'd never seen anything like it, and then suddenly the Thing was there next to my shoe.

"Wait up," Charlie said, plowing into me, lifting me off my feet and dropping me on the lawn like a sack of bricks and scaring the birds in the process. They scattered, all but the big one. It remained, eyeing me for a second longer until it finally spread its massive black wings, launching into the air.

"Let me see it. Ever think I might know what it is?"

I stayed on my ass, biting the insides of my cheeks and working hard not to draw blood. He'd knocked me down like it was nothing, and I had to keep silent or I'd never hear the end of how I embarrassed him in front of his boys.

"Not even for a second." I pulled my phone out and stabbed the button to light the screen. Nothing happened. I did it again. "Damn it, Charlie. You broke my phone." I hit it a few more times, finally letting out a sigh as I fell back into the dirt. "We can't afford a new one. Ma's gonna be pissed."

"You only got yourself to blame, May. If you'd just gave me the thing in your pocket, you wouldn't have tripped." He snickered at the same moment Mr. Prestin turned the corner on his oversized, old-man motorcycle. You know the kind — more like an RV than a bike. Mr. Presin's was a soft brown, a god-awful, boring color. To make it worse, he was blaring Sade's "No Ordinary Love," because I guess that's what they used to blast back in the day, when Mr. P wasn't old enough to be my grandfather.

I focused on Charlie's smug expression, trying to ignore the lame song. "You pushed me. You can replace it," I shouted over the music.

"You missed the curb," he hollered back. "Learn to walk."

"Fine, you want it so badly, here." Tired of his whining, I pulled the Thing from my pocket. Its barbs snagged the edge and tore a fist-size hole inside the hoodie. Now I needed a new phone and hoodie. Why the hell didn't it just land on Charlie and leave me the hell alone?

I tossed it, a second later realizing I probably shouldn't have. Charlie pissed me off, but he was still my little brother, and I didn't want to hurt him. Not permanently. He caught it perfectly, though, untouched by the barbs. The smooth side settled in his open palm with the Thing's sharp fingers pointed away from him. His face softened. All his swagger melted away until he had the expression of the little bro I loved and fussed over while Mom and Dad were at work, not the testy mini-teen telling me I didn't know nothing about nothing.

"What is this, May?" His voice was childlike and hushed by a hint of concern that the Thing might somehow be demonic. He sank low at my side, voice diminishing even more as he leaned close to my ear. "It makes my insides feel strange." Charlie's eyes were always wide, but they grew even larger. "Like my skin is on fire and something is tickling my lungs — no," he stopped himself. "I can't describe it right."

He didn't have to. I knew what he meant. It made me feel the same way, too.

I thought about it for a minute. "The flash?" He nodded. "A second later, it was just there. On my shoe."

Around the corner, Mr. Prestin turned down the music but left his motorcycle running. Mr. P chuckled low as he slapped hands with the other guys who liked to gather on the block. They hadn't noticed us, yet. I didn't want them to see it, to touch it. What if they hurt it? What if they broke it?

There was always a dozen of them, speaking nonsense they didn't like discussing in front of me — but Charlie was okay, being a boy and all.

A voice drifted to us. "Oh, you were seeing one of your honeys?" It wasn't Mr. Prestin. He had been married forever and didn't talk about honeys, only about his motorcycle.

"It's Martin," Charlie said, perking up. "He'll know what it is. Martin knows everything."

Martin was a first-class bullshitter, and telling him was the worst idea I'd heard. I climbed to my feet to run after Charlie toward the dumpster, where a pile of guys smoking pot circled around Martin. I followed until Charlie passed Mr. Prestin's bike and the oversized motorcycle went silent. Charlie was so caught up he didn't notice the silence — but Mr. P did. I did too and watched my old neighbor flip switches, twist handlebars, and fuss with the radio.

Nothing happened.

"What the hell?" one of the guys shouted. "My phone's dead."

I stopped and slipped my phone from my pocket to see if it started working again. The screen was still dark. Then I watched as Charlie made his way to Martin, who was still chatting up some of the guys about things I didn't understand. Each person Charlie passed swore and hissed as their phones stopped working.

He held the Thing high for Martin to see. "What is it?" he asked. "You know, don't you, Martin?" I half listened, attention on an old Buick gliding past the stop sign, its wheels slowing, engine dead. The driver punched the steering wheel, finally pushing the brakes until the beast of a car stopped. Mr. P saw it too and watched for a second before working to get his bike started again.

"What the happened to the Chocolate Stallion?" one guy said to Mr. P.

"And the street lights?"

I didn't notice until he said it, but the lights were out. Night was settling in around us. Usually all the apartments and condos were dotted with glowing windows — not then. Only the houses at the far end of the street, where Boden t-boned Corbet, still had lights. A place Charlie and I hadn't gone near with the Thing.

The wind kicked up, bringing a chill I didn't expect in mid-summer. I pulled my hoodie close and eyed Charlie, who was still standing next to Martin. Neither of them noticed the lack of lights. Martin was too busy telling Charlie vivid lies about what the Thing could be. I picked up on words like, *old plug* and *when I was your age*, which were both tells, translating to "I don't know, but so many people are listening, I'm gonna pretend I do."

"Little C, we have to go," I said, turning nearly every set of eyes on me. "Dad's home soon."

"Not now, May," Charlie bit out through his clenched jaw. "Martin's 'splaining the Thing you found."

More eyes found me. Martin's were two of them.

"Where'd you find it, May?" Martin asked.

"Why's nothing workin'?" one of the guys said.

"Maybe that piece of junk is turning everything off," Mr. P. said. He scowled at me, petting the fuel tank of his motorcycle like a dog. "Ever think of that." He tapped his temple before pointing in my direction. "What did you do, little girl?"

I turned to Charlie, who'd joined their side in a fight I hadn't known we were having. "He has it, not me," I said, squaring off my hips and pushing my chin out. "I just found it."

Hand still on his bike, Mr. P leaned in, forcing me back a step. "Where?"

"Over there, right after the sky flashed," Charlie offered. I imagined ways I'd torture him when we got home.

"The sky what?" Martin said.

"I saw it," Mr. Prestin replied, followed by the murmurs of others agreeing they'd seen it, too. "Right before I got here, Martin. You were probably too busy, or stoned, to notice." He spoke to Martin but kept his attention on me. "And what, you found that *thing* and decided to bring it here?"

"I didn't bring it here," I hissed. "*He* did."

"You crossed the street before me, May," Charlie said, shifting the blame back to me.

Mr. P turned to Charlie, which gave me a second to look around and see if anything else had changed. The lights at the end of the street that had been on a moment earlier were now out. The loud sounds of sirens, car alarms, horns, and traffic hushed. I spun on my heel, looking up and down the block, and found every building I could see in the twilight was downright dark. Bodies filed into streets as the few remaining sounds faded into stillness. Our number of thirteen to twenty people multiplied into triple digits. The only sounds left were neighbors chattering and crows cawing at the navy sky.

"Maybe the Thing isn't the problem," I suggested. "Maybe it's something else?"

Mr. P snorted a disbelieving laugh.

"Maybe you're just trying to change the subject because this is all on you and Charlie," he said.

"That's a good point," one guy said.

"Everything was fine before you came over here," another added.

Whispers washed over me in waves as they grumbled. I pushed to Charlie's side and snatched the Thing from Martin's hand.

"We gotta jet," I said for only Charlie to hear. "Mom and Dad will be worried." I hoped that our place still had power. I pushed Charlie in front of me like a battering ram against the crowd, getting us out of the street and onto the sidewalk.

"I'll go see if any cops are up the block," the owner of the Buick said to no one in particular. By now, his car was one of four sitting dead in the middle of the road, doors hanging open, because what was the point of closing them?

"What they gonna do?" Mr. P asked. It was a good question. "Nothin': that's what they'll do. And if things start working while they're here …" His voice trailed off. "They'll say we made the whole thing up because that's what they do on this side of town."

But I knew Mr. P was wrong about the lights. Nothing was coming back on. If anything, the blanket was spreading like the marine layer does in early May, absorbing sounds and sealing us in.

"Well, I'm going anyway," the man said to Mr. P and started up the block.

I watched him leave, and then lifted my eyes to the sky and saw nothing but stars. A million, billion prickly dots — like the Thing somehow revealed a velvety black sky I'd only ever seen in pictures before. On a normal night, it would have been filtered by street lights and smog, never getting so pitch-black to allow points of celestial light to make up for all the earthy ones no longer working.

I could see for miles, then it hit me. "No planes." I hadn't meant to say it out loud and was instantly sorry I did.

A string of cusses wove around the street, moving like a boomerang until they landed next to me and Charlie.

"It's your fault." It was good old know-it-all Martin. "You brought that thing over here to cause trouble."

Charlie's shoulder sank, and I kicked into big-sister mode. "He came to you for your help, old man. His biggest mistake was thinkin' you knew anything in the first place." Charlie wasn't keen on having me stand up for him, but I didn't care. Not then. Because I knew things were about to go south, and fast.

"You need to destroy it," Martin said.

"Come on, Charlie." I motioned for him to come to my side.

One of the regular guys stumbled into our path. “You’re not leaving with whatever that is. Not until we break it.”

I pushed Charlie behind my back, rising to my toes to get in the guy’s face. “You can’t break it. It’s solid.”

“I can break all sorts of shit, little girl.” He moved in close, gaze sweeping over me until it locked on my face as he lifted his shirt and showed me the butt of a gun tucked in his waistband. “I’ve got my ways.”

“We’re going home,” I said loud enough for everyone to hear. Well, everyone close. The side streets teemed with neighbors I knew and didn’t know. Some held dead flashlights, others clung to chunky candles intended to be used as decoration — it was the only light close by.

“Just give it to him, May,” Charlie said, hand on my shoulder, fingers pressed painfully into the meaty part just above the bone.

But I didn’t want to. I wanted to get the Thing home to examine it closer with the microscope our parents gave us two Christmases ago. I wanted to look at every inch of it and figure out how it worked — like a giant magnetic pulse had been trapped inside a tiny, kid-sized toy. At that point I wasn’t ruling out aliens — maybe E.T. and the aliens from *Mars Attacks!* decided to take a road trip and screw with humanity for laughs. The only thing I knew for sure was I’d never figure it out surrounded by a pile of people glaring at us like we were causing all the problems. Charlie and I had to get home.

“I found it. It’s mine to deal with.”

“You won’t let us deal with it, that means we have to deal with you,” the guy said. I didn’t even know his name. The only reason I remembered him was because I caught him eyeing me a few weeks back. At the time, I didn’t mind. He was worth the attention, looking all cut and smelling so nice. Right then, he was just another guy telling me I was wrong and acting scary to drive his point home.

"Get away from her, Ty." That voice I knew. It was Bernadette. She hung with the guys. Inside, I laughed because Mister "I'm tough because I got a gun" wasn't nearly as scary as Bernadette and her girls. Anyone with a brain between their ears knew that.

"She's got the Thing that shut everything down," Ty said and was greeted by a chain of agreements. "I'm just trying to end this."

"End what, two kids from up the street going home?" Bernadette was smaller than most of them, barely coming up to Ty's chin, but she had him backing up.

"God damn it! I hate when you come in here and get in my face," he said, getting even more riled up. "I'm taking care of this. No one asked for your help."

"You don't even know what *this* is," Bernadette said, head shaking from side to side — same way Mom's does when she's disappointed in me and Charlie. That's when Bernadette motioned to us. "I got this. You two get to your Mama." She set a hand on Ty's shoulder, locking him in place. I tugged Charlie's wrist and cradled the Thing like a football as I dashed for our place. Charlie grunted and huffed to keep up.

Even with Bernadette stepping up to let us get away, Charlie's weren't the only footfalls slapping cement, asphalt, and lawn behind me. The crowd was closing in. I kept my eyes forward, watching the final few lights two blocks over flicker out as the fence surrounding our apartment came closer.

I'd never been any place so dark, except for the inside of my closet when I was hiding from Charlie. Outside, I didn't like it.

"Go through the back door," I shouted at Charlie. "Climb the fence so they can't get us." And he listened. Charlie grabbed the top of the fence, flipping himself over and landing square on his feet.

"Toss it to me," he said but didn't need to. I was already in mid-throw. The Thing soared in a high arc as I lifted the fencing enough to go under. A set of fingers snagged the hood of my jacket, holding on with a big fist. I yanked free, letting them take it as I slid under the gray wire, pointy tips raking over my skin.

I didn't care. A few scrapes were better than getting grabbed by an angry mob.

I held my hands up, and Charlie tossed the Thing back to me. I watched, in slow motion, as it turned head over heels, nearing my hands with its pointy fingers aimed down. I pulled back, letting it finish its fall onto the ground.

When the Thing bounced on the sliver of grass separating the fence from the parking lot, it began to sing.

The mob on the other side of the fence stopped. Watched. Listened.

The Thing's brown dome rotated and hummed. It sounded like a lullaby. To me, it sounded like that French one about a guy named John. Suddenly, it wasn't scary. It was a trinket playing a tune you sing to babies, with tiny notes and lyrics that make you tired even when you aren't. My brow furrowed, confusion seeping into my pores. If it was only a music box, why would it make me feel weird inside from touching it?

"Give it here," Ty said as he knelt, snatching the Thing from under the fence. I searched for Bernadette, but she wasn't there. Ty had gotten away from her, and now he held up the Thing so everyone could see as he tossed it at the hard sidewalk. The smooth dome shattered into a trillion tiny slivers. The music stopped. The world remained dark.

"If that didn't mess things up, what the hell did?" Martin said.

"I told you it wasn't that Thing," I lied. "It wasn't until Mr. P showed up things started turning off." My fingers were tucked through the fence. I felt extra brave with the barrier between me and him, even if I wasn't being so honest. A breath caught in my throat as I waited for their reaction.

"Yeah. You and that stupid motorcycle with your old, lame-ass music," Charlie added. "You show up, and all this happened. Is that why you went and blamed May? To keep everyone from looking at you?" As he said it, the crowd shifted, turning towards Mr. P. I used the moment to tug on Charlie's arm. I still wanted to get us safe inside.

Ty pulled out his gun. He wasn't the only one.

"Maybe it's the government trying to control us," Martin shouted, waving his arms, and pulling attention off Mr. P. "Every think of that? It's them experimenting on us. They want us to act like this."

"Could be the cops trying to get us to go back inside," someone else said.

"That's stupid," a new voice cut them off. "It's just a power outage."

"What about our phones?" said Ty. "I've been living here a long-ass time, and no power outage ever killed my cell phone before."

"Everyone needs to calm down," said Bernadette, stepping up again. "It wasn't the weird thing May found, and it isn't Al's motorcycle."

Ty puffed up, working his hardest to make her cower — it didn't work. "That all may be," he said, "but you're still not telling me what caused it now, are you?"

I tugged on Charlie's arm. "Come on," I whispered, stepping backward as Mr. P shifted the blame to Martin and Martin started pointing fingers at Bernadette, which was stupid because she showed up way after half the street went dark.

I shoved Charlie up the back steps, still keeping an eye on the crowd. Heads bobbed up and down, bodies rocked into one another. They became a blob of raised fists and angry voices. The heel of my foot caught on the lip of a step, causing me to trip. I latched onto the railing, pulling myself up, and continued to the second floor. No one noticed our retreat. Charlie and I took the last few steps two at a time. Charlie had his key out and got us inside while the voices lifted and crashed against the side of the building.

"My room," I said, motioning him to follow me. There was one window that lent us the perfect view of Carlin up to La Cienega. We sunk low at the windowsill, fingers on the ledge, eyes peering out into the night. There wasn't much light, but I could still make out the mass of bodies. I could hear people swearing and fighting.

Charlie's labored breathing sounded louder than all the shouting. My heart pounded against my ribs like a jackhammer. I was sure that if Martin hadn't been screaming obscenities at Mr. P, everyone outside would have heard us.

"What do you think did this?" Charlie said, his mouth below the window ledge, voice hushed at my side.

"Don't know." It wasn't the Thing, but I wasn't a hundred percent sure what else could have caused it, either. Then it hit me. "Had to be the flash, maybe?"

"I guess."

Our parents weren't home, which only made me worry that much more. I hoped they weren't stuck out there.

Most days, I was okay with being alone with Charlie. Right then, I wanted to be five again and tucked between my mom and dad in their bed, knowing I was safe and we'd be fine.

"There's someone coming," Charlie said with an ominous look. I glanced behind us before I realized he meant outside. Then I saw it: a dark shadow coming down the center of the street, other people stepping out of its way. At the same moment, up in the sky, a green light streaked like a zipper dividing the sky, and then it shot to the right and vanished — an electric bullet exiting the horizon.

I brought my eyes back to the body and watched it make for the crowd. They were fighting. Guns wagged in the air. People shouted blame at each other. They didn't notice whoever was coming at them.

It looked like a ghost, an evil spirit that rose from the dirt, coming to drink up our souls while we were too stupid to pay attention.

Maybe the weird sky flash woke the dead, and now we were all being punished by God for arguing so much.

"I wish Mom and Dad were here," Charlie said in a small voice. I looked at him long and hard. I knew I had to be the big sister. Had to take care of my little brother, no matter what.

I stood up, pushing him down, keeping him out of the window. I yelled out, "Behind you! There's something behind you!"

The people stopped hitting each other and looked at my window before turning back to the street.

I don't know who shot first.

All I know is that seconds after the smoke cleared, lights blinked on in a few of the buildings — including ours — and two sets of red and blue lights flickered without the sound of a siren. We didn't need to hear the noise to know it was the police: the cops that the man in the Buick had gone to find.

The crowd scattered as best it could. I knocked Charlie aside, not letting him see anything. Some things are better not to witness.

"Is it over?" he asked, and I said yes.

ↄ

We would find out the next day that a transformer blew. At least, that's what the news said. I didn't buy it. Ty was right: cell phones don't go black because of broken electrical lines, and music boxes don't make your insides twist and turn.

I never shared my doubts with Charlie. He went back to being obsessed with Fortnite, and I gave him twenty bucks to buy whatever skin he wanted — after that, he finally stopped talking about aliens.

But there was that flash and that green light in the night sky.

Nothing would ever be the same for me. I couldn't stop thinking about the strange Thing, about the man in the Buick, or what could have caused the freakish green light that night. Most of all, I wonder if I hadn't screamed out the window — if I'd waited thirty more seconds — maybe that man would still be alive.

I think about it every night when I can't sleep, and I turn a light on because, in the darkness, I'm not sure who I am. I only know that some strange things are unexplainable and not all gifts are wanted.

STAR CROSSED

Gabi Lorino

July 2017

Jen knew plenty of people from high school, but Tristan was the one who kept popping up, year after year, place after place. He drifted through SoCal, showing up every few months or so with a different gig and a different phone number.

Whenever she asked him where he'd been, he just laughed.

As Jen sat on the park bench, shaded by palms, next to the hostess station at Foxy's Diner, her phone buzzed. There was a text from her best friend, Dani.

You should google Tristan before you see him.

"Crap," Jen whispered as she moved the phone into the shade. She did some search-engine magic with Tristan's full name and found a listing with the L.A. County Jail system. "Dammit, not again," she muttered. She could feel the heat rise on her face.

For a while after they met, age sixteen at Estancia High School, Jen had recurrent dreams about Tristan. Nothing scary or sexy, but it was remarkable in that she knew a bunch of other stoners who surfed or skated and she didn't dream about them. In the dream, she and Tristan would be in an alley with a white-blue street lamp shining down on them. Jen would walk by and notice Tristan sitting on a low concrete wall, with darkness behind him. There was always a party going on nearby, somewhere in the dark.

They talked in these dreams, about school, people, music, and movies — nothing of importance, but the conversation flowed. When it came time for her to leave, he stayed on his wall, never moving from it. The day after the dream, she would see Tristan at school, wave at him, and move on with her day, vaguely aware that she knew him better through her dreams than in real life.

But in real life, he was nothing like an untroubled dream. She studied the picture on her phone and realized that his mug shots had changed over time. Years before, Tristan had been a hottie with white-blond hair, broad shoulders, and tanned skin, but now he resembled a middle-aged guy carrying too much baggage under his eyes. Still, he had been, and remained to some extent, ridiculously attractive. Jen regarded him as someone on a different plane with different problems. Scores of girls and women still chased Tristan around, the tinny sound of their giggles chiming in his wake.

Jen sighed, shuffled through a *Pasadena Weekly*, and mentally prepared to see him. She wouldn't ask him where he'd disappeared to this time. The internet had revealed enough.

Fifteen minutes later, Tristan emerged from an Uber, walked across the blindingly sunny parking lot, and greeted her with, "Happy birthday, older woman."

Jen's eyebrows shot up. "Oh, so I'm supposed to ignore your latest *sabbatical*, but my turning forty is up for discussion? Besides, dude, your fortieth is in, like, two months."

His eyes widened at the word "sabbatical," and then he smiled. "You're still older," he teased.

The timbre of his laugh made her crack a smile. "Jerk."

"Whatever," he said as she stood to walk inside with him. "So, why weren't you at Steven's wedding?"

The hostess led them to a burnt orange vinyl booth next to the trio of steps the wait staff used to move from the kitchen to the main dining area.

Jen sat, then looked through the glass and the lush plants on the porch to the bright day outside. "I wasn't invited. Haven't seen him in years. Tell the truth, I only know him through you, and I've never met Kylie."

"She was in the grade behind us," he said as he examined a menu.

"It was a big school, and a long time ago. Though judging from the pictures, I wondered why he didn't clean himself up better for his wedding."

Tristan smirked behind his menu. Jen saw his blue eyes dance with amusement.

"What?" she continued. "Like I'm the only person who'd notice that?"

After a pause, he said, "I'm just going to let you say what you need to."

"You mean state the obvious?" Jen pulled out her cell phone, tabbed through Facebook, and produced a photo (at once alarming and hilarious) of an older woman in a sparkly dress scowling at the beautiful bride dancing with the groom, whose crew cut and beard reaching mid-chest made him look like one of America's Most Wanted. "I don't think that woman wanted her beautiful daughter or niece or whoever marrying a guy who looks like that."

He put aside his menu to look at the image on her phone and burst out laughing. "That's classic. Steven must be so proud." He shook his head.

"Well, give them my best when you see them," she added.

"That's not all I'll tell them you said," he muttered.

Jen sighed. "Fine, then. I guess I'll get to find out if he's as scary as he looks."

A waitress interrupted, pad and paper in hand. Tristan surrendered his menu and beamed at Jen as their orders were taken.

ↁ

Jen's good friend Dani loved Tristan, though not for herself; she had a longtime husband-type person that she'd lived with since she was twenty-eight. No, she loved Tristan for Jen. She often said to Jen, "He's just so sweet, and he needs you, Jen. He needs you."

Jen never believed her. "He doesn't need anyone. He disappears for months on end, and if you google his name, you get to find out why. Life isn't a romance novel, Dani. Men don't want to be tamed."

Dani's gaze was plaintive, and her argument was always the same. "If you went into it with your eyes wide open, laid down some ground rules, you could help him."

Jen had been single — well, unmarried, at least — for twenty years now. If there was a secret to getting together with a functional man she found attractive, she hadn't unlocked it yet. In the meantime, she'd learned how to be responsible for herself, and she had to be realistic about what she could take on. She had no fallback beyond the support of her friends.

In all that time since she and Tristan met, she'd seen him sick and pale, she'd seen him jaundiced, and she'd welcomed him home from rehab at least three times. He wasn't always the bronze god at the beach or the cool guy at the party making everyone laugh; sometimes, his substance use veered out of control, and he went to the hospital, or jail, or worse.

Jen loved Tristan, but she knew that she couldn't handle a close relationship with him. More than that, she was mad at Dani for even suggesting it. "Hooking up with a stable computer genius at a young age and enjoying a comfortable standard of living has made you soft, Dani. Soft on people and soft in the head."

"You know you love him." This was the crux of Dani's argument.

Jen's comeback was, "I love all my friends."

"You know he's your soul mate."

Okay, so maybe in a weak moment right after high school, Jen had told Dani about those dreams. Innocently, she had believed that this wouldn't lead Dani to make declarations like, "Jen and Tristan are soul mates," but as usual, she'd been wrong.

She blamed it on Dani's metaphysical books and whatever.

ʘ

September 2017

Tristan had managed to keep himself out of trouble for Steven's wedding and Jen's birthday, but by the time the heat waves were cresting and his own birthday arrived, he was nowhere to be found.

Dani had some insights; she was into crystals and meditation and all kinds of mystical stuff that made old-school churchgoers uncomfortable. According to Dani's tarot cards, he was stuck in a difficult situation, although the internet wasn't giving up any secrets, at least not yet.

Dani insisted on taking Jen to a spirituality retreat some friend of hers was hosting. It mostly involved visiting the home of an internet millionaire, eating healthy vegan snacks, and doing yoga in an otherwise empty room dotted with yoga mats and women in lounge clothes. Sliding glass doors separated the women in the air-conditioned room from the aqua-blue pool and brilliant sky.

It wasn't a bad way to spend a Saturday. Jen felt her mood lighten as she ate tiny pumpkin muffins and chatted with bejeweled women about chakras. That was the thing about hanging out with Dani and the wives of her husband's colleagues: no matter how casually they dressed, such as for these retreats, they always wore their big diamonds. Dani's wedding set was the most modest of the bunch: a three-quarter carat solitaire paired with a smooth wedding band. Jen thought it was tasteful. Maybe someday she'd be bejeweled as well — and married — though it didn't seem likely.

Jen thought about her lack of bling all the way back to her yoga mat, where Marley the hostess (who wore at least two carats on her ring finger) called the group to order.

"We're going to wrap today up with a guided meditation," Marley said as she lowered herself to sit cross-legged on her blue yoga mat. Next to her sat a brass bell, waiting to rouse them back from wherever they'd journey in their minds. She was a beautiful woman: honey-blonde hair pulled into a high ponytail, tanned skin, and an enviable figure.

The hum of the room quieted as women around her sat on mats. Dani sat next to Jen on her own rainbow mat, in her pink yoga pants paired with a snug purple top underneath a loose tank top. Her long hair had been tamed into a braid streaked with natural blonde highlights.

Marley said, "In this exercise we will go to a small, quiet place inside ourselves and access our intuition. We can ask any question, any question at all, and our Higher Self will answer. Maybe not right away, but in the next few days. You'll know from hearing a song, or dreaming about it. You'll get a message. Because that's what trusting our intuition is all about."

Murmurs of agreement bubbled around Jen as she exchanged a glance with Dani. They both knew the question they'd ask, then compare notes later.

ð

"Here's what I think," Dani said as Jen drove them home. "We're soul family. You and me, of course, you couldn't get rid of me if you tried. But more so you and Triss. You knew him the minute you first saw him, and that's because you knew each other before. Not this lifetime, another one. And you were always fated to know him now."

The lump in Jen's throat made it impossible for her to say anything.

Dani continued. "But 'soul mates' was too much of a label for you two. Too much, yet somehow not enough. And without really trying, you've always been in each other's orbits. We're soul family. We'll see him again."

Tears sprang to Jen's eyes and flowed down her cheeks. Sobbing, she pulled into the CVS parking lot, rooted through her glove compartment, and grabbed a tissue. Once she'd finally gotten the car into park, she cried against the steering wheel while Dani rubbed circles on her back and asked, "Honey, what's all this?"

It took Jen a while to gather the strength to tell her. When they'd meditated, Jen had gone back to that place in her dream, that wall, where she always met up with Tristan.

He wasn't there anymore.

ð

The next day, Jen awoke to a text from Dani and more news she didn't want to hear.

See you around noon. I'm bringing lunch. Ian is on call so it's just us for the day. He says take all the time we need. I'm driving.

On their journey to Costa Mesa, cars sped forward as bright sunlight glinted off them. Glare from windows and mirrors seemed to create a river of stars toward the end of the earth.

"Is Tristan okay out there, swirling around the universe?" Jen wondered.

Dani didn't reply, but she nodded.

Jen wondered what Tristan's last earthly experience had been like. Was it nighttime when he died? Was he outside? That he died looking up at the stars somehow rang true for her.

After Dani parked, they walked from the side street onto the sand, to the same place they'd met up with friends and classmates twenty years before: Steven's family's beach house. Tristan had treated it like a home away from home, a refuge when he needed it. He had been closer to Steven than anyone in his own family, and had been since age fifteen or so.

Wind whipped down the coast. A few tall palms swayed, their fronds mimicking the sounds of the ocean. Beyond a small group that was congregating, waves crashed on the beach at regular intervals, forming a pattern like breathing in and out.

Steven had shaved his head, and his giant beard was gone, too. He greeted Dani and Jen with a nod as they walked across the squeaking sand to the group. He looked more like the kid they'd known in school, but he had some lines around his eyes and a rounder face than before. His wife, Kylie, stood next to him; Jen and she regarded each other with smiles of vague recognition that came from years of social media usage, then exchanged names and condolences.

Once a few more had trickled over, the group stood in a circle on the sand.

Steven took a deep breath and began to speak. "All right, I'm going to explain what happened once, and then I hope never again. We heard from Tristan a few days ago. He and Angie had broken up, and he needed a place to crash. We told him he could come out here, and we'd see him on the weekend.

"He had been in rehab recently, a detail we didn't know until later. We found him on the back porch Saturday morning, unresponsive, and it was too late." Steven gulped a breath of air and continued. "From what we can tell, it was an accident. I knew him. I like to think I would've known if—"

Kylie reached her hand around Steven's waist and snuggled close to him. She spoke next. "We loved him, like all of you," she said, her voice wavering.

Steven picked up a canister of Café Bustelo from the sand. A few people gasped. "These ashes were created from cigarettes and other stuff we smoked over the years, on that back porch. Probably all of you've contributed to this at one time or another, and Tristan most definitely has. So, these will be his ashes. He'd want to be here on the beach, where we used to hang out."

Steven peeled off the canister's yellow cap and walked around the circle to offer each person a handful of ashes. Once Jen had her share, she ditched her sandals and walked toward the water, where the sun was low in the sky, washing everything in an orange glow. A memory popped up from photography class; it was the Magic Hour.

She heard someone come stand next to her and figured it was Dani, but when she looked over, Jen was surprised to see a former classmate, Stephanie. Steph was petite, with long wavy hair. She and Tristan had been inseparable in high school, always hanging out together.

"Steph, I'm so sorry," Jen said.

She regarded Jen with a sad stare from red-rimmed eyes. "Me too," she whispered.

A rare cool breeze blew, and several people let their ashes go into the air. Jen turned to watch as the tiny particles flew into the sky. She preferred to be in the water, though, up to her ankles, gently soothed by nature, at least as much as nature could soothe her at that moment.

Jen looked at the cloudless horizon. The sun was setting, a glowing circle of orange surrounded by yellow light. Around her, people began saying what they needed to say.

"We'll be together again," Dani said as she walked into the water and scattered her handful of ashes onto it.

Jen fumbled for something to say as she squinted into the sunset. "I hope you know you are loved, just for being who you are. And now I don't have to worry about you anymore." She opened her hand and, since the wind had grown still, placed it in the water, where the waves carried the ashes away.

"Bye for now," Steph whispered as she opened her hand and let the ashes fall into the waves. She turned to Jen and Dani, smiled, gave them a hard group-hug, then retreated onto shore.

"This is probably totally illegal," Dani said to Jen as they stood amid ash-scattering.

"It's what he would have wanted," Jen said, "in more ways than one."

Jen and Dani lingered until the last of the sun disappeared behind the water, surrounded by tears, smiles, and chatter. The blue-white headlights from Dani's car beamed onto the interstate as they journeyed home.

Jen's mind kept wandering to fragments of memories too brief to grasp. Streetlights flew by as the city grew brighter. The first big raindrop hit the windshield so hard that they both jumped.

"It's all right," Dani said. "It's just the sky is crying. I think the universe is telling us something."

The car soon filled with noise as rain poured from the sky, making it sound as if they'd taken shelter inside a big tin can. "We'll have some vivid dreams tonight," Dani added. "Always good dreams with the rain."

"Oh God," Jen said. "The dream."

"I don't think you'll have *that* dream again," Dani said.

It was as if Jen's heart was being squeezed. Before, she'd always seen Tristan, even when she hadn't actually seen Tristan. But now that he was gone, was he all-the-way gone? Fat tears fell from her eyes. "Why not?" she blubbered into her handkerchief.

Dani reached over and rubbed her shoulder. "He was always stuck on that wall when he was alive, always on the edge between living and dying. Now he's joined the party. But you and I aren't invited. Not yet."

ტ

Jen was nestled in bed, listening to the patter of rain on her window, while Dani stood in the doorframe illuminated by the hall light. Dani was set up to sleep on the futon in the living room; her overnight bag yawned open on the coffee table.

"Dani, we've already held his ashes, and we've already said goodbye. That's all, right?" Jen's voice was low from crying and congestion.

Dani shook her head. "A relationship that encompasses the dream world is much stronger than an ordinary acquaintance. You won't be having any more lunch dates, of course, but your connection remains. Here, I brought something for you. It's required reading."

She sighed when Dani handed her a book called *Journey of Souls*. Then, Dani closed Jen's door and snapped off the hall light.

Going to sleep was a challenge. Jen saw his face every time she closed her eyes that night. She saw him at the beach with Steph, sitting on a towel, watching the surfers from the sand.

There he was in their much-younger days, telling a story at a party, hands moving, face alight with amusement. Around him, Jen and their friends laughed, feeling relaxed and drunk.

There they were, that one night they messed around, satisfying their curiosities and expecting nothing but enduring friendship in the morning.

She saw him around town, across the restaurant tables where they'd met. She heard his laugh like she'd heard it a thousand times before.

The last snapshot of Tristan that Jen recalled was at Dani and Ian's wedding. He stood in front of the church wearing a gray flannel suit, his long blond hair pulled into a ponytail, his blue eyes bright, smiling widely at her when she arrived in her satin bridesmaid gown. He held out his hand to her and said, "Hello, my name is Tristan. I'll be your escort this evening," as he ushered her inside.

They guzzled way too many shots and stayed until the end of the reception. The next morning, they compared hangovers. "Thanks for this amazing night," she told him over a mug of black coffee. "I'll never forget it."

Dani told Jen later that she'd set it up; she asked him to look after Jen while she did the bride thing, and she knew that if Jen was with Tristan, she'd have a lot of fun. When Jen asked her why, she shrugged and said, "I wanted you to have him all to yourself, at least for one night."

"Nice try," Jen had replied, "but nobody gets Tristan all to themselves. Not even for a minute."

൭

December 2017

Jen hated that Dani knew things in her new-agey way, that she had some odd understanding of life that Jen completely lacked. Or maybe Jen didn't lack it entirely — otherwise she wouldn't have seen him again. But she did see Tristan again.

He was resplendent.

That's not the sort of word they'd have ever used around each other when he was alive, but the vision of her friend, wearing white and seeming to glow from the inside, was nothing short of resplendent. He didn't talk. He just smiled, like he always did.

Somehow in her dream, Jen jumped up and down. Eventually, words came to her and she was able to say, "I'm so happy to see you!"

They hugged — or did whatever people who visit each other in dreams do when they come together. It felt warm. She felt warm, enveloped in love. If she had to assign a color and texture to the feeling, it would've been light pink flannel.

She woke up before she could ask even one of the million questions she wanted to ask, but she held on to that beautiful feeling all day.

CALL US HOME

Cody Sisco

Luis doesn't usually resent his C-list looks — even on a Friday night, when the clubs and bars in Hollywood fill with jaw-droppingly gorgeous and hopelessly naive fools hungry for dreams. Looks aren't everything.

A block off Hollywood Blvd., he intersects a red carpet stained by heavy use and a bouncer with a cannabis stare. The line for a Pretty Laundry private event has glam young things busy taking selfies and texting friends. They have no idea what life has in store for them. Were they to ask Luis — they wouldn't, he's a nobody — he'd say every curve comes back around. Luck and looks don't last forever.

Sure, it would be nice to be seen and appreciated, but Luis is fine not being noticed. He's always been average in pretty much every way. On paper, without bias, he reads as attractive: medium height and build, light brown skin, mild, indistinct features. People tend to scan past him, though. When introduced, friends of friends forget his name within a few seconds. "I'm Luis; I'm nobody. Don't worry about it."

In school, other students got more attention, both positive and negative, as he plodded forward, earning Cs and Bs. Sometimes he had to correct his teachers who tended to mark him absent by default.

He slips past the Pretty Laundry line-up and the bouncer unnoticed. When the door swings open in front of him and disgorges two stumbling white chicks, he moves inside. The bar is decorated with over-the-top orientalism — red paper lanterns from IKEA, paw-waving lucky Buddha statues, and conical hats that look highly flammable. Whoever planned the décor is highlighting the fact that the Oscars nominated a rom-com written and directed by a Taiwanese woman for best picture, which is worth celebrating, but this isn't the right way to do it.

Culture *fail*, he thinks. *Someone's going to cancel this place fast.*

Catching the actor - slash - model - slash - bartender's attention is a challenge. Luis ducks under the bar flap, catches a firm bicep, and asks for the thing Salt asked him to pick up. It takes a few repetitions of "I'm Luis; I'm here for Salt's thing" to get through to the dude. Eventually, he hands over a small, sparkle-flecked gift bag with the heft of a mason jar that sloshes heavily, thickly.

He can't begin to guess what's inside, and there's no way he's going to open it to check. The one time he ventured inside Salt's apartment, tiny gargoyle statues watched his every move, and wax drippings on the carpet *followed him* as he walked. He'd been told Salt knew about every weird thing in L.A., that his "cloak" was a gift and he shouldn't worry too much about it, and it would be useful if he could run a few errands.

Job done, Luis leaves the bar by the front door. No one notices. He'll deliver whatever this is to Salt tomorrow morning, so now he's free to buy beer for Darnell; it's kind of a requirement. Luis knows the limits of their relationship. Fuck buddies, that's all. Darnell comes back again and again, sure, but he only visits on the promise of BJs and brews. In return, he hooks Luis up with deals at a bistro in Culver City.

The first time Darnell came over, after round one, he said it looked like a white dude's apartment. Luis had shrugged. It looks like it costs a lot of money, but he hasn't paid a cent.

"I'm Luis. I'm nobody," echoes in his head as he walks down the street, keeping pace with leaves and trash blowing and rattling in the gutters. Someday, it would be nice to have something more serious than a fuck buddy. But most people don't give him a first glance, let alone a second. How is he going to get them to pay attention long enough to "take him seriously," as Darnell says, and see if they're a good fit for something more? Even when Luis is shouting his loudest, people barely hear him.

The apogee of his circumstance is that most suspect sketches look like him. He's made a habit of printing them out and posting them on his bedroom wall as a proxy for real attention. It's the closest thing to art he'll ever make and it's reassuring — he can pick himself out, most times, if he stares long enough. His features, even when caught on camera, have a blurriness that he's never understood.

The strip mall is surrounded by homeless. No one asks him for money. He sometimes brings them sodas and snacks he's stolen, yet he's never been thanked. *Unseen, average, forgettable, just like me,* he thinks, only people notice the homeless more.

Shoplifting is his meditation. Walking up and down the aisles of Target and slipping batteries into his pockets or leaving Home Depot on Sunset Boulevard pushing a shopping cart full of unpaid-for potted plants, his cares evaporate. With a baby face and a layer of otherworldly camouflage, no one considers him a threat or a risk. The staff rarely take notice of him at all. He's never been caught stealing anywhere. Not that he lives entirely on stolen goods — that would get tedious. The money he makes by designing boring web graphics and posters keeps him fed and housed. He's content to have a decent apartment filled with all the home theater equipment, furniture, and knickknacks that can fit in a room.

A twelve-pack of Pacifico fills his arms like a hug. The bag for Salt dangles from his fist as he passes the liquor store's register without slowing. He can't understand why he is stopped on his way out the door.

"You gotta pay for that!" the security guard yells, as he does an end run to face Luis, eyes bulging, ready to take him down.

At first, Luis is speechless. This hasn't happened before. Ever.

The security guard puts a hand on his Taser. Luis swallows a lump in his throat and manages to say, "Oh, right. Of course. My bad." A nervous laugh bubbles up unfeigned. "Where is my mind?"

He pays the cashier under the security man's glare without any further words. But when he goes outside he has to stop and catch his breath. *What the fuck just happened?*

"Hey! You look familiar." A white woman in her forties, hair matted and barefoot, approaches and squints in his face. "I seen you on a poster." She rears back, as if he's gonna bite her. "Oh, shit. You're the night stalker!" She stumbles, draws a quick breath, and screams so hard it sounds like her vocal chords could snap.

Luis spins on his heels and quickly crosses the street. She follows and screams after him, "You're a murderer, you're a liar, a thief, a child molester, a Satanist," and more. Half a block down, he outpaces her enough that her ravings appear unrelated to him, if anyone is bothering to listen. However, as he passes another woman out walking her dog, she looks hard at him and rushes into the nearest yard, shouting for help and knocking on the front door. He hurries home even faster and considers dropping the beer and Salt's thing and running flat out, but that would look bad and it would mean admitting the problem is far worse than he wants it to be. Maybe people are on edge about nuclear bombs in the Middle East, or because Oscar season looms. You can never tell with Hollywood.

Luis arrives home and locks the door behind him. He drains half a beer in a few gulps. He'd been noticed. His heart is pounding. He's out of breath. He'd been noticed, and the result had not been good.

Between one gasp and the next, his phone rings and someone knocks on his door, spooking him. He drops the beer, and the bottle shatters on his concrete kitchen floor. While he's picking up glass pieces, a finger gets nicked and starts bleeding. In the other room, his computer begins to ping again and again as emails roll in one after another. Checking his phone, he sees a text from an unknown number: CALL US HOME.

ʘ

Jen had to laugh. There couldn't be a worse time for her phone to blow up. Of course it was going to happen right when a spell was about to be cast. No surprise either that it was Cassie Cares-a-Lot freaking out over some new minor problem. Her messages seemed urgent. Then again, they always did.

People should've called her level-headed Jennifer, for her steadiness, for her nerve, for the way she let the biggest of problems roll off her without batting an eye, or Jen-Gets-It-Done. She bit her lip and tried to remain focused. Her workspace for the spell was carefully arranged under the dangling foliage of a pepper tree and lit by the double-glow of a candle and her phone's screen. Overhead, a cloudless sky held few stars, and the typical nighttime amber glow of L.A. up above was subdued. A beautiful night for magic.

In between her sliced thighs, which burned from the ritual knife's slick kiss, blood swirled in a ceramic bowl that rested on a chalked-up spell slate. The liquid bobbed subtly as if something was vibrating the ground.

Something was here in the garden with her. Jen could feel pulsing energies swirling around her faintly, harmless as a cool mist in the morning — the binding mechanism was working as planned. She didn't know yet what kind of entity she'd invited to join her. If she left the summoning unfinished, it could cause problems. She should stay and see it through.

On the other hand, Cassie. Jen read the text again, trying to get a feel for how badly her friend was in trouble. Should she go, even if it meant interrupting the ritual she'd been planning for three weeks?

Phantoms here chanting call us home, call us home, call us home. What do I do? Where are you?

Cassie was always a bit breathless in text and in person, but this was different. She usually had all the answers. It wasn't like her to ask for help or guidance.

Jen watched crimson pearls drip slowly down her thighs and drop into the bowl of vibrating blood. She tried to clear her mind. Distractions in the midst of a spell could be dangerous. She needed to move forward.

But if she didn't call Cassie back, she wasn't being a good witch.

It wasn't fair. The pressures of the coven never let up. They met almost every day after work in some far-flung corner of the city — "for coverage" Cassie always said, while at the same time complaining about leaving her fortress-house in Los Feliz. There was inter-clique diplomacy, which required more meetings and time spent commuting to full moon retreats. Not to mention all the studying. It was a lot.

And yet … Jen had known from the first moment that real, powerful magic had entered her life that she was hooked forever — hooked on being powerful, on being able to fight for herself and other women. She'd never give that up.

If only her career was on the fast track too. Unfortunately, that incident with her chauvinist coworker, Sal, was reverberating through her group via HR meetings, trainings, and the sullen looks of guys who thought she was overreacting and trying to exploit the #MeToo moment.

This whole magic thing hadn't been her idea in the first place. When a friend's empowerment spell had gone wildly wrong, Jen had first shrunk down to Barbie-size and taken a ride in Sal's pocket — Ick! Then she grew into a fifteen-foot giant woman clomping around Hollywood before finally shrinking back to normal. It was a story she didn't like to tell but everyone (who knew about magic) loved to hear. Things had mostly returned to normal, though she still hadn't figured out a way to stop her skin from glowing whenever she got excited, and people kept asking in sly, indirect ways whether she was pregnant or knew of a good cosmetic surgeon. Yep, magic was turning into a problem for Jen. A big one.

It boiled down to this: Her magic batteries were overcharged. Everyone said it was weird how she'd grown so powerful so quickly, and no one could explain what was going on. Jen had been told multiple times by multiple witches that there were no shortcuts, which only made her think no one actually knew how all this worked. She'd shortcut her way to major power.

The one useful insight into her situation came from Salt-who-everyone-loves-and-or-fears, who told her about the five houses of magic, which Cassie knew about but had withheld because Jen was a newbie. Salt had been upset about that. "She should have told you before you go and do something stupid. Find a way to channel your power. Otherwise it'll burn you up."

Hence this ritual to connect with the earth and its vibrations and to smooth out her power surges. She saw now that it wasn't going well, not only because of Cassie's texts. Oddly, it was the wind causing disturbances. Dry, warm gusts stung her nose, rattled the trees above, and fucked with the energies at play. Santa Anas were magical vortexes, Jen was learning. Another thing Cassie had failed to mention.

Cassie was book smart, not street smart. Whatever trouble she was in, she probably needed Jen's power to deal with it. When a friend asks for help, you definitely need to answer. Coven mates are fail-safes and backups; there are no others.

This ritual is toast, Jen finally admitted. Cassie was going to owe her mega if she was freaking out for nothing.

Jen took a deep breath to start unwinding the ritual — and clutched her throat. The air surrounding her was thick with stinging gas. What had been subtle vibrations became the earth shaking beneath her. Blood sloshed over the rim of the bowl. A thick fog penetrated the garden, blocked the moon, and darkness rose.

ʘ

Salt, curanderx

Imagine waking up bathed in sweat and blood. Another fun morning!

The fan on the nightstand, which has been helping congeal the blood seeping from my wounds, isn't blowing anymore. Sunlight streams in through the window, it's sauna hot, and apparently the power has gone out. Another morning awake, alone, and in agony.

Fuck me, but at least it's almost over cuz my stomach feels like a bowling ball.

"I can do this," I mumble out loud and wince at the rancid smell of my own breath. It's day five of a restoration ritual that requires copious amounts of dairy products. At the start of the week, the refrigerator had been filled with four quarts of cottage cheese, the same amount of full-fat yogurt, a gallon each of goat's milk and cow's milk, and eight cheese wedges (from cheddar and Monterey Jack to Brie and Emmental). Cheese smoothies are real, y'all.

The expense had been enormous. The looks from the checker at the Whole Foods on Santa Monica Boulevard were priceless. Only 3,000 calories or so to go and the ritual's dictates will be satisfied. The fermented eggnog from Pretty Laundry, when Luis brings it, will be the final component.

I blame hellhounds. Last week, days after they bit my legs, my wounds continued to bleed, and death by fluid loss started to seem like a real possibility. So, this dairy thing is a new approach. Something new is needed every now and then.

Although I'd love to laze in bed, it feels like an eighty-pound wheel of Parmesan is wedged somewhere in my lower bowel area, so moving around seems prudent. I roll out of bed and stand, wobbly from cheese brain. Then I notice something new that I don't like. I don't like it one bit.

The gargoyle that usually sits on my bookshelf and breaks my rest with its mewling about arcane emergencies has fallen and shattered, leaving a mixture of clay, soil, black goop, and curling mist on the floor.

That's concerning. In fact, that's creepy as fuck.

Wondering how my otherworldly colleagues will contact me now, I go to the kitchen and drink the last of the goat's milk, pop four Lactaids and a few more anti-gas tablets, and start toward the shower.

The broken gargoyle is a sign, no doubt. Some kind of game, as they say, is afoot. Los Angeles, no matter what some locals claim, has never been a chill place, mystically speaking. The worldly mix of people, cultures, myths, and dreams gives rise to an otherworldly melting pot of ghosts, demons, essences, and beasts who mingle together and prey on a vulnerable population. I mean, we have werewolf assassins stalking the streets and killer hotels, like flytraps for the unsuspecting.

Any ounce of chill has to be earned through tremendous effort and willful blindness. Anxious people see the truth and it terrifies them, even when they're not fully conscious of the threat. Chill people push back the darkness in an act of power (and stupidity) that demands respect, even if it does put them at risk.

The curanderx thing I had going has taken a turn. I'm not just helping people recover from magical trauma anymore. By virtue of sealing the Hell Mouth last year — well, partially sealing the demonic maw that spawned skinwalkers, hungry ghosts, and prankish imps — I've attained a prominence and a power that no one can ignore. Every day is a challenge to stay focused on important things, like staying alive and staying ahead of the bigger threats that no one else can handle because so many smaller ones pop up so often. It turns out that being ignored is actually preferable. I'm busier than ever and it's taking a toll. I'm crumbling like salt — ha ha. Forgive me, bad humor is how I cope with having a big fucking target on my back.

There's no one I can go to for help. People are looking to *me* for answers. Sure, I've got otherworldly backers, but they're not a talkative bunch.

I don't make it to the shower. In the hallway, a gray wisp swirls. Thunder and lightning war at the center of a vortex that opens up and sucks in the contents of the hallway, pictures, flameless candles and, after much yelling and cursing and grabbing at doorframes, myself. In the second before disappearing, I realize that if the game is afoot, I've just been snatched from the board.

If I blow dairy chunks in Limbo, I'm not responsible.

໑

Cassie looked at her phone again, scrolling through junk messages to see if the ones she needed had arrived. A lump in her throat coincided with teary eyes; she ignored both sensations, refusing to be overcome. It was nearing midnight, and there were no messages from Jen or Salt. The only texts she'd received were from random numbers with nonsense messages every time.

Elder dominance sings through the duvet.
For a good time, check out the domestic void.
Are you calling me or should the neighborhood end?
Okay, you're probably going to die. Love it!

That last one gave her chills, and she wiped at her eyes and sniffled. Ordinarily, she'd suspect a prank or a stalker. But the incessant whispers in her ear grating like leaves skittering on concrete saying, *call us home*, *call us home*, attacked her like real, honest-to-goodness black magic. The source couldn't be a spell; this type of creative harassment was darker, stranger, and a mystery she would love to solve if it wasn't filling her with prickly dread. Orchestral music lurked behind the words, as well as a trilling voice, an eerie song, and an energy that seduced as much as it made her want to stab her ears with knitting needles to make it stop.

The end comes with teeth and blood.
Save sacrifice for doomed children.

She tried to reach Jen again. The call didn't connect. She tried texting.

Why won't you fucking answer!!!??

The text could not be delivered.

Normally, when something crazy like this happened, Cassie would pull out her yarn and knit something, usually a small geometric shape, a square or a spiral. On good days, her concentration was total and time slipped by without her noticing. When she reached the end, a message would become clear — someone in trouble, a spirit seeking to make contact, an upcoming resonance that would weaken the barriers between worlds — useful information that she would pass along through the network so others could take action. She was a seer, not a vanquisher. She knew her place in the grand scheme.

It was a good day if she never had to leave the house. Other people carried too much sorrow, hatred, and desire, shedding it freely to soak into her skin. When she got too close, she became the lone tree on the floodplain, battered and soaked, chilled, praying for the rain to stop.

Poor Cassie, so sorry for herself. Can't even bother not to die.

She threw her phone against the wall, then went and checked on the damage. A broken screen. No more cell signal. Good. The outside world held nothing for her. If she was trapped, that meant more time to investigate. She had a theory already: something had upset the balance among the five houses of magic.

When she first broached the topic at an international conference on the study of arcane arts, she'd been laughed at. Physics, chemistry, geometry, biology, and mentalism — five masteries, distinct, siloed, and dwindling. Interdisciplinary studies were for liberal arts majors, she was told, not for anyone serious about the study of spells.

Cassie knew people saw her as a weird girl who wasn't always completely coherent. She didn't care. The world wasn't always coherent. She wouldn't be deterred. She was already an adept of the biological magics. She could charm animals, cure sick plants, make people think termites were eating them from the inside out. They should be careful what they said about her.

There were many useful applications of her mystic arts, but she wanted more. She wanted to learn about the other houses. More so, she was determined to understand how they connected to each other. Maybe the divisions were more arbitrary than anyone suspected. Mentalism focused on illusionaria, mind reading, love spells, which in turn all had a basis in biology. It was clear as day to her. Chemistry and physics were intimately intertwined with each other, as was geometry.

Her studies had been hampered because the coven was too pragmatic. Now she was going it alone. Was there anyone more expert on these intersections? No! Did any of this knowledge help her in her current predicament? Maybe.

Cassie wasn't helpless. She wasn't a basket case. She'd find a way out.

She called out again, using everything she knew about mentalism, and broadcast a cry for help that should have turned the heads of every witch in Southern California.

She waited. One minute. Five. Ten. No one responded.

The power went out. Cassie lit an oil lamp, humming a high, thin, meager rendition of "Juice" and said a mentalist prayer thanking Lizzo for her magical contributions. She tried not to think about dying alone in her house.

Wind gusted through the crack under the front door and blew the lamp out, even though it was shielded by glass. A towel shoved into the gap didn't help; the wind seemed to blow from every direction.

Cassie's situation — in the dark, surrounded by hostile forces, alone — was untenable. She finally resolved to leave the house, but that turned out to be challenging. She kept getting turned around. The front door led her back into the bedroom hall. Windows were sealed shut, when yesterday they'd opened without any effort at all. The faucets released only air.

Last night, she'd heard all the pipes draining at once, like a white-water river flowing through a canyon and an immense sigh wrapped together. She'd hoped that was a dream. When she figured out it wasn't, she checked the refrigerator and found she had a half gallon of orange juice left and some frozen cans too, but no water to mix with them. She supposed she could melt it and drink the sludge, like an orange sherbet left out in the sun. The thought made her gag. She reasoned it was better than going thirsty.

What would they find when it was all over? A lonely girl who didn't try hard enough to live?

No.

She didn't want to be the weak one. She might not be as strong as Jen, but she wouldn't go down without a fight. They might not say she was the baddest bitch, but maybe they would see how hard she'd tried.

She went into her crafting closet and pulled out skeins of yarn, rolls of fabric, and leftover pieces of cloth, and piled them in her living room. She pushed the furniture to the walls and began constructing a cat's cradle, a geometric nexus to catch lies and deception. Yarn unspooled from wall to ceiling to floor to furniture, pinned in place with charcoal-hardened wooden nails when necessary, tied into strands when it seemed they should connect, and hung with fabric scraps like laundry on a clothesline.

Cross-legged, she sat at the center of a matrix of plant matter dense and intricate enough to catch and hold the energies at work trapping her in her house and funneling bizarre messages of doom. It would have made a great exhibition at The Broad. Title it "crazy knit lady living the dream" and call it a day.

The message came through the fabric matrix all too clear: CALL US HOME!

The windows burst and air rushed in, bringing smoke with it: fire licked at the window frame. Shattered glass stuck in the matrix of yarn like bugs in a spider web, while a few pieces sailed through and cut tracks across Cassie's arms and legs and lashed her face. Blood dripped onto the wood floor. She looked around and saw a trail of mist leading through the open door and knew she could only follow it to the end.

ൾ

Salt

Salt is back, everyone! Did you miss me?

There's no response. The only sounds in my apartment are the whoosh of freeway noise and the humming of my broke-ass refrigerator. Guess which one is louder.

I don't have any clear recollections from traveling to Limbo, but that's not how it works anyway. They've put something on me, some aura or charge or something, and now I'm more prepared for what's happening, supposedly. They make the CIA look transparent.

I smell meat. I never cook meat at home. I peek my head out the front door and the smell is even stronger, spiced with sulfurous, boozy ketones. What do you do when you smell the apocalypse? You follow your nose.

I grab my bag and head out to a bike share station that materialized overnight last month near the Red Line station at Vermont and Beverly. I take the line north two stops and circle around the Barnsdall Hill, giving it a wide leeway since *thar be munsters*. Elsbeth Barker's first and last illustrated novel, *Frank Lloyd Wright and the Charmed Menagerie of Hollyhock House,* should be required reading.

I reach a bungalow in Los Feliz that looks familiar. A baby witch here needed some help a few months ago as I recall. She was like a magnet for power. There are police cars and crime tape marking off the neatly kept lawn from a matching plot next door. The investigating officer, who I know fairly well, sees me and comes over. She gives me the rundown. There's some blood and a lot of "weird witch stuff" in the backyard but no victim, no body. No sign of foul play — aside from some blood on the grass. She leads me around the back where the meat scent is overwhelming, and I see clearly on the grass a message: *Call Us Home*. When I point it out, the officer raises an eyebrow. She doesn't see it.

My mission is now clear: I've got to find the source of all this crazy before it's too late.

I have one advantage: my problem is never *me*. What I mean is that I'm good. It's the world that sucks — well, the world and all its adjacent spheres. I'm also not stupid.

My second stop is even less illuminating. I get a vibe from an apartment building in Hollywood. I'm sure I've never been here before. Aside from the smell and the sense that something strange went down, there's nothing to go on. No leads.

A neighbor spies me staring and does a very L.A. thing: she smiles and waves, tries to make small talk, and pumps me for information.

"Are you looking for Luis?" she asks, then coughs into her hand. This smoky air is a bitch.

The name sounds familiar, like pretty much half the dudes in L.A. are Luis, Mike, Juan, or Jose.

"Yeah," I say. Cuz why not?

"I hope the police find him."

"What?"

"I knew there was something off about him. He was always moving new furniture into the apartment. Nice stuff. Stereo equipment. I'm pretty sure he had every gaming system. Who can afford all that?"

It clicks. Luis, my delivery guy with a natural veil of shadow that I strengthen every time he does me a favor. He didn't show this morning, otherwise I would have seen a jar of eggnog on my doorstep. If his neighbor is now recalling him, something has changed for the worse.

"I bet he's a serial rapist," the neighbor says. She sounds like one of those podcast types who loves to talk about murder and how to commit crimes. I bet she uses Nextdoor to report suspicious people in the neighborhood whose only crime is being not white. She seems the type.

You learn a lot living as a queer non-binary person in a world built for cis-het breeders, and not just sex stuff, though yeah, that too. My body wasn't made for procreation, which is fine. I'm different but healthy. There's no need to put a label on me.

I was made to heal. That's my thing. Right now, the world is hurting, and I've got to track the harm back to its source. Otherworldly signals are seldom clear as a bell. In this case, I'm even more confused. The call has no center. It's a curious blob, or maybe a clumpy haze, or an odor wafting on the breeze.

Neighbor lady looks at me like I've grown a third eye.

"You're wrong about Luis," I say. "Tell me, have you seen him recently?" I use a bit of magical dominance on her and it feels good.

She says, "No," sullenly, maybe because I'm not playing her point-the-finger-at-the-brown-man game and she doesn't like being compelled, and I leave her there.

Two people with magical oddities and some connection to me are missing. Whatever is going down is big, and it's starting to feel personal.

A hike up into the canyons leads me to Cassie's house. Cassie I know pretty well. She's always looking me up, wanting to talk about magic theory and pestering me with endless questions about Limbo. She goes on and on about the five houses of magic and then points at me and says, "Chemistry," and I say, "Okay," and she says, "That's your thing, Salt," and I say, "It's like a bad joke," and she doesn't laugh, instead launching into a rambling diatribe about arcane intersectionality. I follow about ten percent of what she says, and I'm not stupid. The last time she said, "That's why your magic is chemistry," I bit back, "Fine, I'm chemistry. But what about my voice? What about my songs? What are they?" That shut her up for a while.

Now, though, her house looks like a tornado passed through it, and she's nowhere to be found.

That's three down. I still have no idea what I'm up against.

My nose itches and stings like my snot has turned into pure electricity. I spin around and notice how the sensation gets worse when I'm facing west. "I can take a hint," I mutter and head up the street to catch a bus toward the beach, following my nose again.

The "express" bus from downtown to Santa Monica takes an hour and a half on a good day via clotted lanes through neighborhoods everyone thinks they know from TV and movies. Out-of-towners picture Hollywood glitz, a line of palm trees, or maybe the stretch of lanes that runs through Beverly Hills, fronting towering hotels where a cocktail costs either twenty bucks or a blowjob for a douchebag wannabe producer. People don't remember the strip malls of East Hollywood, the sad motels tucked in odd-shaped lots, the hunted look in people's eyes as they try to cross the street safely.

I check out the Angelenos who, like me, make do without a car somehow. We've got spirit. To drivers, it must seem like we're on another plane of existence.

I get off the bus and take an electric scooter south. I'm sure it's a sight.

When I drop into Culver City, the stench is on me, thick and frothy, and there's something else electric and puzzling. I file the curious sensation away to ask about later when my Limbo patrons reconnect. This definitely merits a cross-plane conference call. I just hope they don't see unfolding disaster as another example of me not meeting their expectations. They're still bitter about the Hell Mouth thing.

The clean sidewalks of downtown Culver City depress me. Poor people have been swept aside to make room for money and its crystalized culture. Fancy folk are lunching all around, yet they're not necessarily industry types. They're gallerists, or buyers at high-end furniture stores who know factory owners in Vietnam by name, or artistic directors who work for European fashion brands and host models in their condos when they need an urban sun-bleached spread. So, yeah, I guess they're fine compared to film people, but have you ever summed up the cost of the bling they introduce into their conversations? Ugh.

I'm sitting at a bistro where the meat smell is strongest and the couple behind me — who are well-dressed and in their fifties, with sunglasses hiding their fear of falling behind in the trends — have talked about at least half a mil in merchandise in ten minutes. They're appropriately reverent.

Here's the interesting thing: I know the waiter, Darnell. I go to his shows sometimes at Secret Cabaret. He's alive with magic, usually. It fills his voice and makes the room sigh. We've also hooked up once or twice. He's so attractive that he has to ask people to take him seriously. "I want you to take me seriously," he says, with a gentle smile filled with stunningly even teeth, and eyes that make you melt and feel seen down to your bones.

Right now he doesn't seem to recognize me. His eyes are glazed and staring into the distance. He's also being forgetful. Iced tea doesn't come the first two times I ask. He's clearly under the influence. Demonically roofied. It's written all over his aura and the way he smells.

The missing puzzle piece that was bothering me crystalizes: I've been tracking something much, much bigger than any demon I've ever met. This is something different entirely.

As any good evil-hunting person does when they realize the shit is about to hit the fan, I do an inventory check. In my bag, I've got a few pyrite crystals I'm supposed to deliver to a friend later, matches, lighter fluid, and a crème brulée torch for if and when the matches fail; kindling of various sorts, including newspapers advertising escort services, a stick of Palo Santo, and a tightly rolled spare pair of linen pants if it comes to that. I've also got a bag of salt — Salt's salt. I should sell it online. The bottom of my bag also bulges with lots of napkins. They're multipurpose-kindling, arcane origami, and good for wiping me and other surfaces. I take one out and sop up blood oozing down my ankles. Fucking hellhounds.

It strikes me that I have no ancient tomes, no magic wands, no sacred orbs, let alone a switchblade. I need more supplies. Iced tea and dreadful kale Caesar salad dispatched, I find out how long Darnell is on his shift.

"Two, no, three more hours, I think," he says dreamily.

I mosey into action. The nearest drugstore is a long walk, out of sight of the fancy places lining the boulevard. I get what I need there: soothing throat drops, chocolate bars and other snacks (salty of course), as well as enough various household products that, when mixed together, will create a delightful, fizzing fountain of cleanliness. I also purchase a big ass pair of scissors.

Cleanliness is number two on a demon's list of things they hate. Can you guess number one? It's good vibes. They hate anything that smacks of smiles, caresses, laughter, or canoodling. Love especially they hate. It doesn't hurt them. You can't kiss a demon to turn it into a puddle of goo. But love gets their attention, and love can bait them into the open.

Maybe this is the beginning of a plan. Darnell and I were once in the middle of a great make-out session. He didn't mind the unfamiliar shapes between my legs. He said it turned him on. I showed him how to give me pleasure, and he adapted and innovated. He sang into my privates. You haven't lived until someone is vibrating you down there using the power of their voice.

The wraith-scorpions hated this. Tiny things like ants, they scuttled under the front door, then grew to the size of a large dog and interrupted one of the best orgasms I ever had. Worlds moved. I burned those scorpions with a screech so fast they didn't smoke — they exploded.

This thing I'm going up against soon … who knows what can stop it? Probably not my voice alone, no matter how lovey-dovey I'm feeling, so I'll take cleanliness as my backup. It's worth a shot.

I return to the bistro and wait and watch for Darnell to leave. He oozes into a junky Honda and drives, slowly. He's not all there right now. I follow in a ride share, sketching the picture for the driver in enough detail that he cooperates. As far as he knows, I'm making sure my stubborn friend gets home safe after an edible hit him too hard and he wouldn't give up his keys.

Darnell doesn't drive home to an artist colony on the edge of Culver City, which is close. Instead, he detours east out of the parking lot. We drive for twenty minutes, and he parks on the strip of road fronting the Science Center beside a meter he doesn't feed. I climb out and follow. Parklands all around. Some families playing in the shade. Couples posing in front of the fountain. It's dusk at 5:30 because the winter sucks, even in L.A. I know the sun can be too much, especially in the summer, but I much prefer bright skies and plenty of light to the dark. It's a safety thing.

I run flat out to catch up because now Darnell is walking on his long, strong legs across the lawn, staring up at the darkening sky, head swiveling, like he's watching something big all around him. There's nothing there. Not even trees. He's seeing something, though.

It hits me. A wave of electricity. I drop to my knees. It's like I've been tasered, which, yes, has happened once or twice. My breath locks in my lungs, and I wait for it to pass, hoping I don't black out first.

A picture begins to form in my mind. Darnell is connected to the thing I can't see. It's like he's in the grip of a tentacle, but when I try to track it back to the center, all that appears is an inky cloud and the sense that more tendrils are out there, seeking, gripping, pulling more victims close. I shiver and pick myself up, but I've lost him. As he nears the end of the path, I'm terrified of what he'll find.

ʘ

Darnell waits for the bus, foggy-headed and glum. Which route is this? Didn't he drive to his shift? Where's his car? His head is cloudy and it hurts to think.

He watches the street, dully, and stands near the bus stop. He knows how to cede space. No sudden movements. Sheltered, an older woman with frazzled gray hair wraps her arms around tote bags of food from the community pantry. She gives him side-eye and scrooches away. Some people are like that with black folk. It isn't his job to reassure her, and smiling won't help.

It weighs on him. The need to represent, to model his banality. He wants to be taken seriously, not seen as a threat, or pitied. He's not someone in need of help. He only wants the same chance as anyone else and to do something important and meaningful before his talent and ambition go to waste.

He runs his tongue back and forth across his teeth. It feels like his canines have begun to grow.

The implements of good carnage, teeth are animals' prerogative.

Where did he read *that*?

The light turns red and the bus nudges into the intersection, blocking cross-traffic. Horns blare all around. Angry fumes slip from tailpipes and find his nose — hot and sickly.

A dentist for his tooth situation is out of the question. He never liked the chemical smells, the X-rays, the people in masks. He doesn't trust anyone whose mouth he can't see to get inside his. The thought of metal in his mouth sets his nerves on fire, like being electrocuted while knives dissect his guts.

My head is a sieve and the universe runs through it.

He double-takes at the woman nearby and thinks she said that Zen shit out loud. Then again, maybe the problem is actually in his head because teeth can't grow and he's hearing voices.

He tries to recall the day of the week but can't make it make sense. When he thinks about what happened at work, he thinks maybe he saw Salt's face, a snap of arched eyebrows and shadowed eyes. Did that mean some bad magic was going down? Maybe he's hallucinating. Someone could have slipped him something; it happens everywhere. If he stays calm, he'll ride out the trip, and be fine as ever. When life knocks the wind out and rolls you in the gutter, you pick yourself up and breathe.

A rumbling in his stomach like a rock tumbler startles him. When the bus finally makes it through the intersection on the next cycle of lights, he boards, following side-eye lady and sitting across from her. She strains her neck to avoid looking at him and watches the view out the front windshield like it was a film. An artery in her neck pulses visibly with a steady one-two beat, although sometimes it seems to flutter in odd synchronicity with a feeling in Darnell's groin, a rippling giddiness. He watches her neck closely. He knows he is staring and that he should stop, but he can't tear away his gaze. Thin skin molds to the artery smoothly. So much of her skin elsewhere is wrinkled, unlike that spot where mere millimeters of epidermis prevent hot blood from spilling everywhere — a potential flood, a bountiful sustenance.

I must be on some shit, he thinks, and wonders who slipped him bad medicine.

When the bus and the mobile phones of everyone onboard lose power at the same time as the rest of the buildings on Wilshire Boulevard — which should have been a red flag — Darnell springs up. His body crosses the distance to the woman without his feet touching the floor, and he face-plants against her neck. The impact breaks her vertebrae while his teeth find purchase and tear open the artery. Blood rushes down his throat to settle warmly in his gut like a shot of booze.

ʘ

Salt

I didn't catch up in time to stop Darnell from ripping that lady's throat out. Inside the bus, dairy chunks, which I did not blow in Limbo, are now sprayed like buckshot across a spreading pool of blood. They won't be able to ID me from DNA I'm sure, but I still feel bad for the forensics team. The scene will stink to high heaven.

Before I leave, I sing for the dead woman. It's not a Peace in Crossing ballad, not even a Soul Be at Rest psalm, just a brief cathartic riff about moving on to ease the woman's journey. She's the first casualty in what I fear could be a bloody trail without end.

I follow a tendril of inky otherworldly scent, and it leads to a house above the 10, accessible by one of those weird alleys cut into the parcels left over from freeway construction of past decades. The alley leads to the back of an Edwardian mansion with no rear entrance and a broken-up asphalt basketball court filling the yard. Multifamily units are pressed up all around, but they've got no windows. This is a hidden place that people avoid without knowing it.

The basketball court is lit with candles that stake out the points of a white chalk pentagram. The others are already here. Jen and Cassie huddle with their arms on each other's shoulders for comfort. Darnell and Luis are in a similar embrace that looks less about comfort and more about conflict. Their hands are at each other's throats.

It hits me, what the five of us are: Jen, physics. Cassie, biology. Darnell, mentalism. Luis, geometry. Me, chemistry. It's Cassie's theory in practice. *Oh, but we are fucked!*

I'm about to do something stupid and try to break up the Darnell-Luis throttling thing when the world spins and the candles flare. Without intending to, I start to walk toward one of the pentagram's points.

The thing that's arriving carries sea stench and volcanic fire. The air fills with noxious, heady fumes. Insights tumble one after the other, maybe from Limbo, maybe from my own instincts. This thing isn't coming from somewhere else; it's been here all along. Its barbs are sunk into every single one of us, pricking and pulling, tearing us like a butcher rends raw meat. Sucking our strength. Wrenching our energies, using them to bring itself from background to foreground. It's hungry for some action, spotlight, and adoration. The thing that's been calling to us arrives on the back of a writhing, luscious, cancer-filled song and, to my surprise, incorporates in the body of a woman who looks like my mother.

ʘ

It's been an eternity. It's been the blink of an eye. We've endured forever. We've endured all of time yet none of it. Eons lost in translation. Memories distorted. Elements ruptured and reconstituted.

We persist in the shadow of chaos, a liminal, fractal space shot through with strange, dim energies and unaccountable geometries.

Living inside a voracious malaise, drifting through the thoughts and dreams of conscious beings, we know our snacks from our feasts. Consciousness is a type of order, a beautiful, complex, irreducible process of change that takes many shapes. Flowering, meandering, jabbing, shattering. Some thoughts are more seductive than others. Some whispers are infuriating. Some taunts are maddening. We've graced them with as much of our song as they could bear.

Lately, however, it's not enough. We're spent. Prying the Hell Mouth open only to have it forced shut cost us dearly, and what little sustenance comes through now is not enough.

So, we're coming home. Our return is not the result of a plan or grand design. It is a change in the pattern of a universe that is never static, never still. Light calls us to feed. We are being pulled back by a collection of consciousnesses newly entangled. The way is soon unblocked.

These little bridges have no idea their privilege.

These five are a necessary sacrifice to nourish the body we've chosen to incarnate.

Once we arrive, nothing will change. Mothers will smother their infants. Men will leave bloody trails of bashed skulls and rent flesh. Disease will multiply and consume, corrupt. Want, hunger, desolation, fear — all will persist. There's no end to the supple sustenance they offer.

These five will come to enjoy their service. Nourishing our belly with their souls, they will call us home.

ʘ

Salt

I'm no fool. Mother Murder over there is no relation of mine. Her call is strong and so is her hunger. She looks at us the way I coo over pozole verde. The others are moving into position near the candles, making pentagram points of flesh and spirit for Lady Death to devour.

We're food to her. She's the Hell Mouth come to consume. That's very clear.

So, how do I wire her mouth shut?

In my hesitation, she takes the opportunity to speak. "We value your sacrifice."

It's no wonder she sounds like a politician. It's 2020 after all, bringing the long-predicted Times of Pain and Transformation.

A garlic-sharp and sweet cloying smell envelopes me. Darnell and Luis disengage from one other. They stand stiffly, elbows bent with palms out like they're trying to warm themselves on the glow coming from her. I look down and see that's how my hands are too. A three-dimensional lattice of forces bleed from our palms.

The bag I brought is steps behind me. I stand, like each of the others are standing, at the apex of a composite geometry. We can't move, can't look away from her blue-lipped smile, which turns redder and grows brighter.

We're her battery! We're the white surrounding her fucking yolk.

My ad hoc coven mates are twitching, struggling, making what small movements they can manage. She's inside us all and we're pinned.

The pathetic tragedy of our situation is enough to make me sick. My stomach, emptied back at the bus, spasms again, and I dry heave and buckle. I glance up and see Luis flip his hands to stare at his palms. I gasp, "Geo bro, do something."

He looks up, hazy and indistinct, and then he kind of clarifies, the way text sometimes goes from being lines, angles, and curves to becoming actual words and messages. He lunges at Darnell and pushes him out of the circle. Cassie and Jen, smart chicas, move away too, realizing that they can now get free. I turn away as Cassie starts ripping her shirt off and Jen sniffs the air.

"Salt, let's go," Luis yells. He's running away, toward the freeway, maybe thinking he can flag down help, which is ridiculous.

"Luis, don't! We need you!"

He stops and looks stunned for a moment, eyes wide, and then he smiles and races back to us.

I'm glad he's happy, but we need heaps more good vibes and fast. The situation isn't demons-on-earth bad; it's worse. The Hell Mouth is here. She's trying to suck our oyster meats and leave us brittle shells. If she consumes our power, all of L.A. is her next meal.

"Cassie?" I plead. Book smart could be really helpful right now.

"I don't know," Cassie says. I'm trying not to stare at her pink-lace bra. So basic. She has ripped her wool sweater into strips of fabric and seems unsure about what to do with them. "She's something beyond. She needed all five of us in balance. Maybe we can tip that over?"

The apparition stands, eyes closed. She's feeling it, her new body. She's coming into it slowly. We may have some time.

"Okay, but how? Jen, ideas?"

Jen grabs my bag and drops it at my feet. "One hundred percent chemistry," she says as she hefts a gallon of bleach into my hands. "And maybe a little bit o' sexy."

"Yes," Darnell says, and the blazing, luscious smile he shares with each of us in turn seals the vibe.

The woman from beyond opens her eyes and frowns.

I don't need to shut the Hell Mouth; I need to sour its taste on us.

The jugs of bleach and soap are designed to limit the rate of pouring. That'll never do. I cut the tops off, sloshing the stuff all over my fingers, which burn, but I think they'll burn the mouth more. When we've each got an armful of noxious, toxic liquids in our arms, we move in.

We collide with Mama Apocalypse. Chemicals slosh everywhere, on her, on us. My eyes are tightly shut because there's no way I'm asking Limbo for replacements, assuming

I don't get burned up by this lady's eldritch wrath or whatever else she's gonna throw at me. A cold blast of wind like all of the Arctic in one swoosh pushes me down.

Moments later, arms lift me to my feet and I smell wool as my face is wiped dry.

"Look," Jen says.

I open my eyes.

Lady Lovecraft is standing in the pentagram, soaked and steaming. Her skin seems to be sagging; in places it runs down her face like hot wax, hollowing her cheeks so we can see flesh and bone. She's looking at me. One of her eyes has turned milky pale, but I have the feeling she can still see me.

When her voice emerges, it's a whisper. "You called us home."

One of her fingers drops to the floor. She bends to pick it up, straightens, and cradles it in her palm like a baby bird.

Darnell is shaking. He's noticed the blood all over his clothes. He claws at his mouth, retching, until Luis grabs him and holds him in a tight, crushing circle of healing — also known as a hug. Darnell is going to need a lot of that if he's ever going to fully recover from the trauma of murder.

We pour a circle of salt around the Hell Mouth. A weak and temporary seal, but it's all I've got. Cassie, to my utter surprise, sneaks behind and ties the lady's hands behind her back. Maybe we can figure out a more permanent solution if we put our heads together.

Jen is smirking, which is impressive, to be honest. To get off on demon stuff makes her the second baddest bitch in the room. "So, are we a thing now?" she asks. "The five of us?"

"I can do groups," I say.

The others are looking at her and me like why are we so stupid, why don't we get the hell out of here? *Good idea.* We haven't stopped the problem, not really, despite the ooze and the pus running down the lady over there. She's still *here*, albeit a bit mangled. And I don't know how to send her back or blast her to pieces.

I'm about to make some lame comment about a job well done when I hear the sky sing, I look up, and I see falling stars.

From the shore to the mountains, filling the L.A. sky, lights descend slowly, glittering like meteors that decided on a gentler descent. The truth of it strikes me, and it's horrible. I have to say it out loud. It's one of those moments that must be named and witnessed. I know these four will appreciate being clued in if they haven't figured it out already. We're in it together now. The Angelenos of the Apocalypse. The Oblivion League. Salt's Sentinals. You get the picture. We've got a fight on our hands.

"It's not just her," I say in a hoarse voice that feels appropriately raw and probably chlorine-scalded.

I'm not ready for this. Not at all.

The four of them are looking at me dumbly, still spellbound, confused.

I lay it out for them. "We called her children home too." I point up at the lights that, to me, signify La 'Pocalypse Now.

I sigh. Exhaustion weighs down my bones and this day just won't quit. The world's end though … Its painful rebirth — that's another story.

At least now I'm not going through it alone.

WE FOUND LOVE AS THE UNDEAD

Sara Chisolm

While everyone except the occasional drug dealer, late-night partygoer, or general misfit stayed indoors, Satoshi still lurked in the streets. The gangly budding graffiti artist squatted in front of a three-stoned rock garden shaped as harmoniously as the bulb of a spring onion, giving the impression of open space. He pulled his hoodie up over his head. The regal gold-trimmed, berry-colored spray can that usually managed to sit in his left back pocket rolled noisily onto the tri-colored brick ground. Another sudden gust of wind stirred the red and white paper lanterns overhead; their dim firefly glow illuminated the surroundings of the Japanese village plaza in downtown Los Angeles.

At first, Satoshi didn't look at her. Instead, he gazed at the blackened windows of the trendy storefronts and bakery. The windows' reflections caught the glimmer of her hauntingly white complexion. His heart sprouted flapping wings as it beat against his ribcage. He picked up his spray can but dropped it again as sparks flew from its valve. Satoshi ran a finger gently down the side of it.

It is time, he thought.

He found the strength to look at her. The girl lay motionless in front of the stone garden. Her limbs spiraled out of her bent torso like soggy ramen noodles. Her opened eyes gave Satoshi the impression of being lost in the Bermuda Triangle. If you stared at her dilated pupils long enough, you might get lost in their abyss. Satoshi sighed.

Satoshi treasured the girl, Akiko, who had always smelled of peonies and fresh midnight sage. She was one of three sisters. Everyone had loved the moon-faced beauties interchangeably. He had learned to love them as if they were one entity. They had been one of the many loves and burdens of Satoshi's life.

After slipping on his black dust mask that had a toothy grin with blood dripping fangs printed on it, he touched her cold rubber skin with warm fingertips, and she glowed even brighter.

He picked up his spray can and aimed it above her body, and then pressed the valve button and began to maneuver his hand and arm with purpose. The can emitted silvery beads of spray that mirrored the essence of Akiko's moonbeam skin. Satoshi grinned as the girl's spray-painted portrait hovered above her body. Wisps of paint trailed down to feather her skin and clothing. The overpowering industrial smell of the can's contents caught in the back of Satoshi's throat. He coughed in spite of wearing a mask as he peered down at her lovingly.

The outlines of her round face and full lips were being kissed by the light of the paper lanterns. Her hair appeared like an ink spill, overlapping shadows and hanging slightly in her hooded eyes. The picture moved, smiling and winking at Satoshi as he filled in the curves of her full-figured body. He felt sticky. A layer of fresh sweat formed over him. He stopped spraying and shook the can when the delicate translucent beads of spray splattered unevenly over his curled-up fingers. Sparks flew from the can, signaling him to end his painting.

His masterpiece began to frown. Akiko's lovely smooth face rippled as if a stone were skimmed on the surface of a pond or lake. She became rough where she'd been smooth, colorful where she'd been pure light. The twirling glow of the lanterns caught it all. Akiko's lopsided face resembled a colorful lollipop that had been abandoned on the sidewalk to the mercy of the sun. Her limbs bent outward, as if her body could never regain its own balance. Her black hair shivered into a shocking violet color. There was something primal in her permanent sneer. Satoshi felt his spine twitch as he drew back his body.

The creation sat up and glared at Satoshi. "I get more unfuckable every time you bring me back. This is ruining my love life."

Satoshi blushed as his eyes surveyed the curves of her once-supple living body. "Regardless of our …" Satoshi searched for words that could make the arrangement of interchangeable, related lovers not sound taboo. "Past …" He cleared his throat; unsought sentiments, words between them that remained unspoken, had dried up in the back of his throat.

Akiko's arms bent at an unsightly angle as she dug in her purse and pulled out her phone. Her fingers were nimble yet stiff as they tapped upon the screen. She held up the phone, threw up a peace sign. The flash was almost blinding to the undead eye.

Satoshi threw up his arms in meager protest. "Not this weird … stuff, again. Being the undead in the heart of downtown L.A. is not a social media experience."

"Why not?" Akiko said as she threw her phone into her purse. "Yolo."

"What the hell does that even mean?" Satoshi slipped his spray can into his left back pocket as he stood up.

"It means you-only-live-once," Akiko tapped the outside flap of her tan leather purse, "Unless you're a Tanaka sister, then some prick named Satoshi keeps reanimating your corpse."

"What was it this time? Pills? I don't see any marks left on you that I have to paint over."

Over the past couple years, the Tanaka sisters had grown increasingly more creative in their own deaths. Tanto knives. Poisons. Spears.

Akiko waved her stiff hands over the length of her body. "You have all of this horrible canvas to paint over," she stated.

"It doesn't work that way and you know it." Satoshi's hands shook as his brow became a map of his disdain for the Tanaka sisters' acts of distaste. He threw up his arms as he looked around. "Why this place?" Satoshi murmured. "Our place."

This place was their home away from home. A place that had greeted them with the luster of a red-lacquered watchtower. The savory aromas of fresh bread, soy sauce, and smog sweetly curled in the air. This place where you sung karaoke on stage or marveled at the windows of the eclectic shops. These experiences were the highlights of his adolescent years. Satoshi remembered playing kissing games with the sisters in the dark underground halls, each one of them taking a turn. He wiped tears away with the back of his hand. He still couldn't separate the feelings that he had for each sister.

Akiko stood up. Her body moved as if it were held together with pins, needles, and broken hinges. Her blue taffeta dress twinkled and crushed beneath the moonlight.

Akiko limped to Satoshi. She leaned in so close that Satoshi swore that he smelled the hint of peonies on her breath as her raspy voice murmured, "We have always known that this place mattered, just as much as our family ties have always mattered." Tears rivered down her face, without an emotional dam to hold them back from her former lover's view. Satoshi's fingertips brushed her cheeks. He remembered all the times he had caressed the cheeks of the Tanaka sisters, wiping away the sadness that he had caused by loving them all at once. Akiko pulled away from his touch as Satoshi leaned in with parted lips.

"Why do you keep doing this? No one is going to hold you accountable for what happened in the internment camps," Akiko said. Satoshi glared at her. Sweet Akiko had changed with every reanimation, becoming more sinister.

He rolled his eyes while sighing. Longing for her lips to press against his distracted him from his duty. Satoshi coughed and turned his gaze away from Akiko's lollipop glare. "You know why," Satoshi murmured. "This is my family duty." The half-lie made the back of his throat itch.

Their families had met during the Japanese-American internment during World War II. They bonded through the exchanging of rice and clothing. Their need for one another had become more pronounced as their rations decreased and their labor increased. Duty had mattered. Promises and honor counted because they had nothing else to hold on to.

"Our grandparents wanted to forget about that time. They didn't want to seem un-American. All we have is the vow that they made to one another. That is too much of a burden for anyone to bear," Akiko stated.

"That is all that I have ever done." Satoshi raised his voice slightly, "I have always helped you and your sisters with my gift."

The sisters had turned the duty, honor, and obligation into a sort of game. They lost lunch money, dated scumbags, and engaged in underage drinking. They became more reckless as time went by. They paraded around the art scene, becoming popular muses for local artists. This was when the years of knowing them had made some type of difference. Then, as Satoshi Kato made his splash on the local art scene, the Tanaka sisters discovered a new game.

"I am not some art chick who just walked onto the scene, Satoshi. I know you better than most. When you tried to hide your mysterious gift, my sisters and I helped you understand it."

"By killing yourselves," Satoshi said.

Akiko spun around and walked towards the tunnel. This specific part of the plaza should have been pitch black, but light had found a way into the precious space. You could find cosplay wear among trading card stores, vintage video game boutiques, and anime outposts. Akiko would have fit in among the multicolored contact lenses and hair of the cosplay crowd. Satoshi looked at their reflections in the windows of the stores; they looked like the average couple prowling the "cool kid" scene, with Satoshi being the edgy street artist. Yet, he resembled a young man trying to stitch together a perfectly good date from scraps of a torrid night. Humongous plastic Godzillas served as a backdrop to Satoshi's pleading.

"Please go home," Satoshi whined while clasping his hands together.

Akiko sped up, Satoshi trailing. "I want to see all of Little Tokyo for the last time," Akiko shouted while flipping him the bird over her shoulder.

"Please. Stop," Satoshi cried out, panting.

Before Satoshi could get another word in edgewise, Akiko cut around the corner and dashed across the street toward another popular destination in Little Tokyo.

He pointed an accusing finger at Akiko's back. "You and your sisters always exploited my talent for your own fun."

She haphazardly climbed a few steps and stopped right in front of the Isao Hirai monument. The nickel biography and bust of the astronaut Ellison Onizuka stood majestically on one side of a rectangular slab of marble, and a white and orange spaceship sat atop.

Satoshi proudly stared at the spaceship replica for a few seconds. That gave Akiko enough time to climb up the slab and wrap her arms around the spaceship. Satoshi looked around at the empty Weller courtyard in horror. "What are you doing?" Satoshi said in a hushed tone. "You're going to draw attention to yourself. I'll buy you some ramen if you just come down."

"If you loved us so much, then you should've let us die."

Akiko pivoted forward, and the flexion of her hips and the extension of her knees made her look like a Japanese monster halfway melted by a nuclear storm while exiting earth's orbit in true monster style. She was vulnerable and strong, like she had always been.

Akiko climbed higher; her angular limbs grasped the spaceship monument in an arachnid way. "You want me to go back to being trapped inside my little glass dish?" she said in a sing-song tune. "Because being brought back to life several times just isn't enough?"

Satoshi felt heat rising through his shoulders and up his neck. "That has always been your choice. Consider your grandma's feelings."

"The first time was my choice," she shouted.

If he didn't get Akiko back to the downtown loft that she escaped from, then her grandma, Tabby, was going to be royally pissed. This wasn't the first time that one of the Tanaka sisters had escaped their glass prisons.

Satoshi looked up at Akiko as she hung awkwardly but somehow splendidly balanced. He shook his head.

"I don't want to be one of her little dolls," Akiko shouted.

Akiko scrambled up the length of the orange external tank. "Stop climbing," he screamed in irritation.

Akiko looked down at him with a lopsided grin. "You have to tell me one thing, Satoshi."

"What is it? I will tell you anything to get you to come down," Satoshi yelled.

Akiko ran her chopstick-pointy nails down the surface of the external tank. "Which one of us did you love?" she asked.

"What do you mean?" Satoshi squinted his eyes in confusion.

Akiko flattened the palm of her hand against the surface of the spaceship. "You know what I mean. Was it the way that Aki would smile up at you with her cherry lips, or the way that Akane laughed at all your corny jokes? Or was it the way that I was bolder than the two and would write love letters to you? Which one of us?"

Satoshi swatted the air. "Why does that matter? Why does that matter, right now?"

"It always mattered. My love and anyone else's love matters." Akiko let go of the external tank with one hand and wiped away a few tears. She fumbled inside her purse and took out her phone.

Satoshi threw up his arms. "Come on. Does this really look like an Instagram moment?" he yelled. The phone slipped from her pointy nail tips and clattered to the ground, breaking into several pieces.

"We keep killing ourselves hoping that one day we will know which one of us you really choose."

Satoshi glared up at her. "What?"

"Yes," Akiko said. "We wanted to know which one of us you would let die. That would be the one you really loved." One of Akiko's feet slid an inch or two downward.

"That's ridiculous," Satoshi stated hoarsely.

Akiko balled up her fist and drew back her arm.

"No. Stop," Satoshi screamed.

Akiko smiled down at him. Her eyebrows knitted together. "I love you, Satoshi," Akiko whispered. The puffy sleeves of her taffeta dress looked like the miniature wings of a cherub. She was poised to fall.

A raspy scream escaped Satoshi's slightly parted lips. He had to save her from her own beautiful self-destruction. He had to think fast. Love had created a zombie-loving fool out of him and he was willing to pay the ultimate price.

What happened when you reanimated the living? He might save her; at least, he hoped he could.

Akiko let go.

Satoshi pulled out his spray can and made a few quick strokes in midair. He felt as if time stood still. Silvery tears of paint dribbled into lines as the image softened and became flesh-like. Each crease, dip, and mark of Satoshi's own face hung confidently in the breeze. It could have blown away quickly if Satoshi had allowed it to, but then he stepped into his image.

He looked down at his own shimmering hands as they caught a twinkle of starlight hidden among the streetlights. Satoshi saw images of Akiko, Aki, and Akane Tanaka when they used to sit on the steps of the Buddhist temple, flipping through teen magazines that glorified the fashions of quintessential Harajuku girls. Back then they changed their looks as frequently as they brushed their teeth. Wigs, micro-minis, and platform sneakers were their uniforms of choice.

That had been a different time, when Satoshi had chosen love over honor and created squabbling among the beautiful sisters. Each one proclaimed her love for the graffiti artist, and he had never properly chosen any of them.

His heart fluttered as he thought about how his family members had been trapped under armed guard, only to receive an apology and a settlement for the years taken from their lives. America, California, and even more so Little Tokyo was his home. He had lived here and would die here.

He felt his breath catch in his throat. His heart refused to pump. Satoshi raised his arm, and it felt as if a string were animating the movement rather than his own free will. He tried to gain more control and create fluid movements, but his body became more robotic with every attempt. He struggled as he moved his jerking body inch by inch until he was mostly underneath Akiko's elongated shadow. He reached his hinged arms outward, palms raised in the air. He swung his neck toward the night sky. Akiko, his falling angel, was five feet above his head. He felt a heaviness on top of his body as his sinewy frame collapsed onto the pavement.

Akiko's body buckled and cracked as Satoshi rolled her off his stiff torso. He could sit up before she could. His bones and muscles flexed. He looked at her, finding the strength to navigate his own limbs. He stared up in search of his own reflection within the base of the monument. Gasps of horror escaped his lips. He saw a pale pumpkin face slightly rotted from a stint of extended Halloween parties placed on the torso of an urban-style Ken doll.

Akiko looked up at him with tears shining on her cheeks. "You don't love me, and you never did," she stated. She leaned her head on his knee, smiled, and then puckered her lips. Dewdrops of neon spit flew from her mouth. Satoshi's shoulder glowed. He managed to wipe his shoulder off. "I will take you home." He stood up, no longer caring if her head hit the pavement. His shadow resembled that of an elderly gentleman using a walker. "Akiko."

She looked up at him but did not move. She blinked a couple of times. Blood dribbled out of the corners of her mouth, painting a cherry-colored clown smile onto her still, pale face. She sighed. "I'd hoped that you would've picked one of us by now," she muttered.

Those Tanaka sisters were so fragile that they should not have ever existed. He used to imagine that they were pieces of origami. Their paper forms were always being swept up in the winds of life.

Akiko stood. Satoshi grabbed her arm and held her up with all the strength that he could muster. He heard the drop of his spray can. A shiver of revulsion ran down his spine. He nudged the spray can away from his body with his foot. The can rolled towards a seating area with huge orange umbrellas impaled through the middles of tables.

He took a few test steps until he was sure that he would be able to take Akiko back to her downtown loft on Spring Street. Akiko pulled away from him. "Take us home, fool," Akiko said while staring off in the distance.

They walked past buildings. The eclectic designs of the newer buildings huddled close to the mirrored windows and genteel older buildings with peeling paint. Neatly paved sections of the Little Tokyo streets became decrepit as they hit the back streets where bongs and weed were sold and neon signs flashed in windows.

The streets became smoother and wider as they traveled to the hipper part of downtown. Bike lanes, parks with futuristic steel gates, and eateries stuffed with the ruckus of the hip crowd enveloped the downtown scene. Tents squatted nearby; they were everywhere. The people inside the tents coughed, murmured, or talked. Despite the blaring music from the restaurants, bars, and clubs, Satoshi could hear them.

They stopped in front of a trendy apartment building that looked the same as the other new high-rise lofts that lined central downtown and entered the posh lobby to be greeted by the overwhelming calm of elevator music and the dim glow of a huge chandelier. The redheaded security guard at the sleek black-marble front desk barely lifted his gaze from the car magazine that he was flipping through. Perhaps he had seen enough of the zombies that occasionally passed by on their way to the Tanaka family loft.

They didn't get into the elevator. Satoshi herded Akiko towards the steps. "Climb up," he commanded.

"I can take the elevator. Thank you very much." Akiko swung her body in the opposite direction to Satoshi's bent body. She took a few limps toward the huge rotating entrance door.

"You aren't going anywhere," Satoshi said with a smirk. Satoshi tightened his grip. He lowered his gaze and looked into her eyes without blinking. "I did this for you. All I have ever done has been for you."

Akiko pouted and turned toward the stairs. She haughtily yanked her arm away. "I can manage," she murmured. Akiko went to the entrance of the stairwell and opened the door. Satoshi followed her lead. The concrete steps in the bleached white-walled staircase were steep. His body ached as if he were becoming sick. He thought about pork belly ramen.

Once they reached the top floor of the building, Akiko swung the green door to the stairwell open. They entered a small, white, carpeted hallway that smelt of lilies and medicinal herbs. Someone was blasting a recording of harp music. The high notes of the instrument made Akiko and Satoshi cover their ears.

The hallway cameras were trained on them. Once they were halfway down the corridor, the music stopped. The two ex-lovers uncovered their ears and exchanged a knowing look. They had arrived at this point before. Satoshi knew that he had to be part of their unbridled sadness and happiness. He lowered his head in shame as he reached the padded mulberry-wood door, which flew open.

The pair were greeted by an elderly woman. Akiko's grandmother grinned, and the ironed-in skin pleats of her face gathered like curtains to reveal her crowded teeth. "There was never another choice. There wasn't anything that could be done about it," Akiko's grandmother said while shaking her head. "Some folks get a raw deal in life. You girls didn't cook your own meat, yet you had all of the seasonings and a sturdy wok."

Akiko frowned at her grandmother. "Tabby," Akiko said while rolling her eyes. "Clearly, I am not in the mood for a lecture about how I ruined my own life."

"Suit yourself," Tabby stated nonchalantly. She took her aging eyes off her granddaughter and focused on Satoshi. "What the hell happened to you?"

Akiko pushed her way past Tabby. "This idiot walked into his own paint."

Tabby shook her head. "You did that to save this one? She's the most ungrateful."

Satoshi shook his head and hobbled past Tabby. They entered the vanilla cupcake foyer. The circular area was decked out with a shimmering chandelier that was too big for the space. Doors led to a bathroom and a closet that were mirrored and gave the illusion that you were either in a fairground Hall of Mirrors or having a psychotic break in an asylum.

Akiko threw her hands into the air. "Home, sweet home," she said.

Satoshi limped past Akiko into the beige room that was adjacent to the foyer. The living room had a white leather couch in one corner. Light from several lamps bounced off three large glass bell-shaped domes. The gleam from the lamps obscured the view of the contents within the glass prisons.

The room was surrounded by rainbows and smelled of cherry-blossom perfume. Bubbles and strategically placed champagne flutes added to the multicolored reflections. Satoshi walked to the couch and sat down. His body became engulfed by the fluffy cushions.

Tabby's extravagant turquoise kimono fit loosely against her thin frame as she stood beside the couch. "The girls have been eagerly awaiting the return of their sister," Tabby whispered.

Satoshi's gaze rested on their prisons. Inside the domes, women with skin the color of pure light seductively winked and blew kisses at Satoshi. The girl in the middle was Akane. She once had dyed her black hair the color of the rising sun. Satoshi had enjoyed running his fingers through it. Every time Akane's body had been brought back to life, her hair took on the semblance of flames. Aki occupied the left dome. Her limp, stringy hair took on the hues of autumn maple leaves. Purple lipstick was smeared on her full lips. She was the first girl that Satoshi had ever kissed.

"Ah," Tabby murmured. "They are in a playful mood."

"When aren't they?" Satoshi grinned. Tears sprung to his eyes.

Akiko entered the living room with an air of confidence that had been missing when she was swinging herself from the spaceship monument. This was her home, her domain. She ruled here.

Tabby gave her eldest granddaughter a knowing look and said, angrily, "Your parents were lucky enough to run away from their zombie daughters. Who knows where they went? You girls give an old woman enough hell for it." She pulled out a hot-pink vape pen from one of the sleeves of her kimono. She took a few puffs and made rings that fogged up the view of the bubble machine that sat on a glass coffee table.

"Now we have to worry about this one." Tabby stabbed the tip of her vape pen into the center of a bubble that was near Satoshi's arm. The bubble hissed as it popped. "We can't have all these zombies walking around in the streets, even if you suckers just like ramen and a good beer instead of brains."

"What are you suggesting?" he asked.

Tabby's owl eyes rested on the three glass domes in front of her. "We always knew that it would come down to this." Tabby shook her head from left to right. "I knew that one day, you'd be so caught up in one of these girls that you would miss out on the precious life right in front of you."

Satoshi clawed at his own head. "What precious life?"

Tabby blew another ring of smoke from her vape pen. "Your own. You fool." When Tabby frowned, her entire face looked like clothes tumbling around a dryer. "I made provisions for such a thing."

The vape pen disappeared into one of the elongated sleeves of her kimono. Tabby stood up and her voluminous kimono seemed to cloak Satoshi's knees. She moved swiftly behind one of the glass domes and pulled a lever on the opposite wall. There was an electrical hum as the domes raised to the ceiling. "All you have to do is choose; we knew that you would have to. Now is the time. I am not letting you four out of these three glass domes ever. Not with you," she said while pointing to Satoshi, "like that."

Satoshi jerked his body up. "I can't go into one of those things. I can't go into a dome."

Tabby yawned. "As if you had a choice. There are a lot of times when choices are made for us. You should know that better than anyone, Satoshi."

Aki was the first one to step outside of her isolated platform. She wore glass platform pumps that chimed every time she contorted her legs to take a step. Her long, knobbly legs met the rest of her body underneath a shimmering purple dress. Her black fingernails looked like knives and gave a metallic ting when she walked.

"Did you ever miss me, Satoshi? Did you miss me the way that I missed mother moon?" Aki's voice cooed.

Akane stepped out of her glass prison wearing twinkling ballet shoes. Her legs were squat and muscular. She wore a black leotard with a hot-pink tutu that matched the hue of her bright-red spiky hair. When she breathed, her balloon chest expanded. She took a few timid steps off the platform. Her hands moved stiffly as she brought one of her open palms to her purple-stained lips. She blew Satoshi a kiss.

"Being in the domes for so long makes them a little crazy. We do the best with what we've got," Tabby stated.

Satoshi pointed at the glass prison. "I can't live like that."

Tabby threw her arms in the air. The sleeves of her kimono rustled in the breeze of the bubble machine. "We can't always get what we want. But we get what we came for."

Satoshi shook his head rapidly. "This isn't what I came for. I came to return another one of your damn granddaughters to you."

Satoshi maneuvered his stiff body off the plush couch. He had begun backing toward the foyer when Aki, Akane, and Akiko moved on him. Their jerky movements were in unison as they corralled him into a corner of the room.

"Which one of us is it going to be, Satoshi?" Akiko demanded.

"Yeah, which one of us will you take forever?" Aki stated.

"Which one?" Akane demanded as she stomped. Her glass shoe cracked from the contact.

"I love you all. I always have," Satoshi stated as he put up his hands, palms facing outward. Akiko's full cheeks brushed against Satoshi's wrist.

Satoshi looked around. Beyond the glare of bubbles, he saw a champagne flute resting against a speaker. He grabbed the glass and swung it wildly at the girls.

"Back off," Satoshi screamed.

The girls frowned in unison, their once lovely features contorted in malicious ways.

"We loved you without judgment. We loved you," the girls bellowed in sync.

"Choose, choose, choose," they chanted.

Satoshi threw the glass to the floor. The broken shards crunched as the girls stepped on them.

Tabby yelled, "They all want you, Satoshi. It looks like that is what they are going to get."

Satoshi heard a ripping sound coming from his left side. Before he could turn to see the commotion, he felt something sharp against his bare arm. He saw the sleeve of his hoodie flutter in the manufactured breeze from the bubble machine like a wayward kite.

He turned around and looked to his left. Aki had her talons dug into his upper arm as she pulled on him with all her strength. Silvery spurts of paint squirted from his bicep. Satoshi swatted at Aki. Akane grabbed his other arm and ripped off the sleeve. Satoshi frantically kicked.

He peered over the girls' heads and gave their grandma a pleading look. Tabby held a phone up. The flash didn't bother Satoshi's eyes.

Satoshi paused as Akane jerked his arm out of its socket. Satoshi released a sound that was part human, part death. He would have given anything to make things right between himself and the Tanaka sisters.

Akiko placed her cold, clammy hands around Satoshi's neck. She drew her body close to his. Her putrid dead-girl breath could have been the scent of midnight jasmine and peonies for all he was concerned. He imagined her as his Little Tokyo cosplay princess. He longed for their stolen moments in the dark crevices of the plaza.

He closed his eyes and was drawn in by the pure bliss of her kiss. He heard the echoing of the other sisters' protests. He had finally chosen one, and it was in her arms that he would die a second time.

NIGHT OF FIRES

Allison Rose

Leah told me she had been awake when the fire started. From our childhood bedroom, she smelled the acrid scent of burning carpet through tearful snot, the result of an earlier childish tantrum. She said the heat came without warning, seeping in through gaps in windows and doors with a sneaky persistence like water dripping through seemingly closed fingers.

Leah told me she had heard people screaming. She felt vibrations through the floor as footsteps shook the building like a jolting earthquake, the kind of tremor that causes dishes to hop off shelves. She'd seen our mother passed out on the living room couch, an empty whiskey bottle beside her — contents later declared evaporated, not consumed — maintaining discretion, although we knew different. Our father had disappeared into some dark corner, busy entertaining our neighbor's wife, whom he was convinced was a better-kept secret.

It was when Leah opened the front door that the fire welcomed itself into the apartment, an uninvited guest intent on slumming like a starry-eyed transplant, sucking everything in its path dry of any molecule of moisture, until all that remained was a fragile dusting of ash. The fire consumed everything it could — living and inanimate — and my little sister burst through the flames to come out alive on the other side.

Leah told me just enough to make me question whether she'd truly seen anything at all, and in the seventeen years that followed the fire my desire to know the whole story grew into an obsession.

"I don't think you've ever realized how much I went through that night, Catherine." Leah rapped her fingers on the steering wheel of her decaying Volvo to the beat of rock music blaring from the stereo, some poorly-formed indie tune with a guitar lick as jagged and brittle as a broken chain-link fence. Leah's music tastes were as attached to the past as her anger, despite the number of new records I had sent to her over the years; Leah refused to listen to any of them, just as she had ignored my advice to validate what she knew, if only to give importance to those painful memories.

Leah volunteered little information to all the frenzied, probing investigators who wondered how the ten-year-old escaped unharmed, but I knew her better than they did. At least, I knew the version of Leah before the fire. I knew a little sister who begged to be involved, insisted she was cool enough, brave enough, mature enough to keep a secret. Leah was a decent kid as far as siblings go, but it would have completely gone against my objective to take her with me that night when I officially hit my pre-teen rebellious streak and snuck out of the apartment to attend a friend's sleepover. I remember her spirited expression crumbling as I slid out the bedroom window and swung to the balcony and down two floors to freedom. I couldn't be sure if Leah had broken faith to betray our pinky-swear of silence, but something about that fire forged a more resolute version of my sister, creating an exterior unyielding to the prying authorities.

Six people died in the fire, including both our parents. Leah would have made seven had I not woken her in the process of executing my getaway. Thanks to the sleepover,

I was nowhere near the scene, a fact that at one point filled me with a sort of survivor's guilt, the kind that gnaws at the back of the mind, begging to be noticed if only to alleviate the irritation. In the time since, I found a way to channel that guilt into a memoir — a stunted and incomplete account, according to the literary review section of *Los Angeles Magazine*.

Those subsequent seventeen years should have been enough time for Leah to make peace with her trauma, to find solace in something other than unrelenting bitterness. Instead, her memories fed a growing impatience and combative temper that compounded to the point of bursting. All this time, Leah dangled her full story inches from the noses of storytellers thirsty for a juicy tale, providing little more than the specifics detailed in news articles and local blogs. I knew my own side, and I knew what was public record, but I could never crack the code of what Leah knew. Those withheld details were fuel for her emotional conflagration, just as our childhood apartment building had fed the fire.

Then, one night in the middle of a summer heat wave, Leah finally erupted. And I had been invited to capture the moment.

"I don't know what you went through because you've never wanted to tell me," I said in a tone meant to calm any potential unease building within the vintage Volvo, despite the open windows. "But that's why I'm here now, Leah, to understand your side of the story."

Leah's finger-tapping increased in hardness, as though she could sense I was internally narrating the evening and wanted to pull me back into focus. "Just make sure you pay close attention. Take notes if you have to. I won't do this again." She shoved the sleeves of her sweatshirt up to her elbows. Sweat glistened on the insides of her forearms.

“I’m paying attention, don’t worry,” I said. “I won’t miss a single detail.”

Through the dirt-streaked windshield, I stared at the steel gray façade of a boxy building that stood as an ugly imposter in the Los Feliz neighborhood, a block inhabited by Spanish red-roofed duplexes and Art Deco condos. It took no more than six months for the new living complex to take the place of the burned-down one, and the modern style seemed purposely positioned to remind the surrounding structures of their material fragility. A curtain moved behind a window of the replacement building, and a young man appeared, nude from the waist up, the blunt in his hand leaving a snake-like trail of smoke as he moved. I imagined the man dropping the rollie and catching the rug ablaze, filling each crevice of the complex with the scent of sulfur and burning flesh, destroying what was created to replace something so violently taken.

I had not been able to hide my shock and simultaneous excitement when Leah called the day before to tell me she had an idea for my elusive sophomore autobiographical novel. I walked the three blocks from my apartment down Beverly to Larchmont Wine & Cheese, desperate for a bottle of alcohol, trying not to give away any tells to the dozen affluent shoppers about the nature of the conversation. For all anyone knew, I could have been on the phone with my agent, getting news about studios interested in optioning my first book for a film. The rejections seemed to flow in more frequently than my queries, most including a note or two about the lack of a satisfying ending. However, with Leah’s addition to the narrative, I would move closer to fulfilling that dream.

Feeling eyes on me, I turned to see Leah giving me a look I had seen often over the years. Steely and fierce. Slightly unhinged. Undeniably unpredictable. My sister may have granted me access into the unknown parts of the chronology, but it was still up to me to draw it out of her.

"They said you just took off," I said. "You were gone by the time the fire department arrived. You didn't even wait to find out about our parents."

"I just wanted to get the hell out of there," Leah said, her voice loud enough to catch the attention of the weed smoker on the balcony. "The place was already destroyed. Somehow, I knew Mom and Dad were dead. There was no one left for me here."

The statement hung in the heavy summer air as Leah started the engine of her thirty-year-old sedan and pulled away from the curb, oversteering into the oncoming lane before straightening out, almost hesitantly so. Headlights flashed in front of us. She often had the habit of driving with her eyes closed, I noticed, and when I asked her about it once, she told me she enjoyed the thrill of wondering — in those few brief seconds — how different the world might look when she opened them again.

"I walked," Leah said as she drove us down Franklin Avenue. My stomach twitched, anxious to hear what she'd say next. "I was in my pajamas. Didn't have time to find my shoes. I remember feeling the heat coming up from the sidewalk. It was so hot. I just started walking."

"Where did you go?" I asked.

From her back pocket, Leah pulled out a hastily torn piece of notebook paper, creased to a soft fabric-like texture from how many times it had been opened, refolded, and slipped into her skinny jeans. She pinched it between two fingers, letting it flop in the blowing wind, and then held it out to me. Five lines were neatly printed in metallic permanent marker:

Relapse of the Junkie
House of Strays

Man of Poor Judgment
~~Happier Times on the Outside~~
Bouquet of Fire

The crossing-out, a line of blue ink, was a more recent marking. I wanted to ask her what the list meant, hoping they were not suggestions for my book title; they were creative, I could give her that, but they lacked an intuitive grasp of syntax, undoubtedly the reason she never took up the challenge to pen her own story. I studied the list, etching it to memory, before Leah snatched the paper from my hand and stuffed it back into her pocket.

We drove down Vermont Avenue past fusion cuisine restaurants and packed al fresco tables and around a number of double-parked rideshare drivers, emergency lights flashing as a sorry excuse for their rude behavior. The sedan idled as several twenty-somethings sauntered over the crosswalk, one young woman hopscotching on the hashed lines, jumping on one foot over the reflective yellow paint, giggling the whole way.

"I was standing right there when Skyler saw me," Leah said, pointing out the window to the funky green and orange exterior of the late-night eatery Fred 62. It would have been the only place open at that hour when ten-year-old Leah wandered through. She and I spent many lazy afternoons loitering in that part of town, back when our only contact with our parents was through the pay phone in the parking lot of The House of Pies. There would have been nothing unusual about the young girl wandering Vermont alone before sundown, but it was a different story at eleven at night, which was precisely why Skyler stepped into the frame.

Skyler was a waitress at Fred's, a gorgeous waif who could create her own sense of fashion from the chaotic racks of thrift stores, constructing unique masterpieces out of items others had picked over and ignored. Before her job at the restaurant, Skyler had a brief tenure as our babysitter. She wasn't terrible at the job, at least from my perspective as a kid; it was because of her that I'd been introduced to underground electronica, the very music that caused well-intentioned teenagers to try ecstasy before their brains are fully developed, according to my mother. Skyler was removed from babysitting duties after she'd skunked up our bathroom one evening and was declared a bad influence on us young, impressionable children. It was around that same time that our father began screwing the neighbor's wife in the laundry room, and our mother found solace at the bottom of every wine stocked in the Pink Elephant liquor store on Western Avenue, and Skyler — motivated by a more hardcore narcotic — turned to a career schlepping plates of BLTs to hungry, hungry hipsters.

Turning onto the side street that marked the corner entrance to Fred 62, the parking gods smiled upon us and Leah slid the Volvo into a metered spot. Engine running, she watched the crowd of patrons eating at the sidewalk tables. The night of the fire, as Leah remembered, Skyler seemed to sense that the young girl was in trouble.

"Skyler sat me outside, and I chewed on some toast, listening to fire truck sirens wail down the street," Leah said. "She kept coming out to check on me, telling me she called my apartment and got no answer. For some reason, I couldn't tell her why. I felt numb."

"I remember you didn't talk for days after the fire," I said.

She stared at the restaurant, pretending not to hear me; no matter how many times Leah ignored my presence, I never grew comfortable with it. "Some asshole wanted to call the cops because he didn't like eating next to a barefoot ten-year-old," she said. "So, Skyler decided to take me to her place. Her manager fired her for leaving her shift early." Leah pulled the hood of her sweatshirt over her head, obscuring her face and her expression in the dim light of the street lamps. It was eight in the evening and still eighty-five degrees, and I failed to see the practicality of such a wardrobe choice, but Leah wasn't one to do anything simply for the sake of practicality. "Sad thing is, Skyler was getting clean. She was getting her life together. She'd enrolled in film classes at L.A. City College. She needed that waitressing job, and it was my fault she lost it."

Melancholy oozed from her; it was exactly the romanticism I had hoped to capture. "I'm glad you're doing this, Leah. I know how painful it must be to relive the details, but it's all part of the healing process."

"And that's why you're here, Catherine. To walk though it with me."

I didn't notice Leah put the car back in gear before the Volvo lurched forward. Soon we were driving southeast, toward the complicated five-point intersection where Sunset curves into the land of specialty coffee shops and consignment stores, and where Hollywood Boulevard abruptly ceases to exist. In a curious amount of recalled detail, Leah described Skyler's rage over the loss of her job. Skyler was pissed to have been let go over an act of charity, and she was driving around the neighborhood with a child she had once been hired to care for and who showed little gratitude for her rescue.

"I didn't ask Skyler to take me anywhere," Leah said. "I just didn't have the voice to say no."

"It wasn't your fault she was fired," I said.

Leah glanced at me sidelong, a specific tell when she agreed with something I'd said but refused concession. She was not as immune to my intuitive perceptions as she wished, although I did hope she'd grown out of her tendency to give the silent treatment.

We parked a block off Sunset, the front bumper of the Volvo a wheel's diameter into a residential driveway. I warned her of the likelihood of being towed in that neighborhood. Leah insisted we weren't staying long. Walking down to the boulevard, we paused under the glowing red and yellow marquee lights of the Vista Theatre, a small local landmark trapped in the art deco era of Hollywood, much like most neighborhoods on the east side of the 101 freeway. Several dozen people spilled out from the theater doors, disgruntled and grumbling. One woman seemed caught in a daze, unfocused eyes on some distant point behind me. She approached with an unrelenting momentum, and I was forced to step off the curb to get out of her way, narrowly missing a teenage boy wheeling by on a fixie bike. I fought to regain my balance, and it was then that I caught a look at the overhead marquee. *Child of Fire, a film by Skyler Greyson* was written in cracked and mismatched plastic black letters.

"Skyler made a movie?" I asked.

Leah gave a half shrug. "Skyler was a terrible waitress and even worse babysitter, but she really wanted to be a filmmaker. She had a camcorder in her car. She started her storytelling with me. She called me her muse."

A heat stung my chest. Up until that moment, I thought I had been granted the first glimpse into Leah's story, and to discover that someone else — a drug addict of all people — had not only beaten me to it, but had knowledge and footage hidden away from me for seventeen years made my blood boil.

"How much does she know, Leah?" I said, trying to soften the grit in my voice. I didn't want my sister to know I was upset.

"She knows what she saw, and it's all on tape," Leah said. "We're going inside. Tickets are ten dollars."

It had been years since I'd stepped inside the Vista Theatre, a place where the persistent art-deco theme merged with odd Egyptian busts hung on the walls. While I had thought the exiting crowd marked the end of a feature, the movie was still rolling. Only a handful of people remained in their seats. One man at the front glanced over his shoulder several times as though wondering if it was more inappropriate for him to stay or to make an awkward exit.

Leah sat a couple of seats over from me and leaned forward, eyes trained on the screen. "Film" was too formal a description. It felt uncomfortably nostalgic, murky and unfocused imagery on glitchy DV video edited to a 1990s trip-hop record that marked every student film made by gen-x indie wannabes. The lens seemed magnetically tethered to young Leah, who sat curled on a beaten leather couch in her soot-covered pajamas. The camera's super-zoom constantly went in and out: first it focused on Leah's sullen face then her legs and a cat that crept closer to her, begging for physical contact. Suddenly, the frame swept across the living room floor to where tiny drug baggies and cigarette butts were weaved into matted carpet. There was no rhyme or reason for the camera work, nor for the editing, and I couldn't help but feel a swell of relief that the movie would never match the depth or artistry I could put into my book.

"Skyler wouldn't let me sleep," Leah said. The rhythm of her words matched the pulsing beat of the film's soundtrack. "Not on purpose. She was four days clean, and her nerves were getting to her. She told me the methadone clinic opened at five in the morning, but she couldn't wait that long."

The next scene had Leah and Skyler in a car. Skyler pointed the camera at herself, and in the yellow streetlights, her pale and clammy face had a strange transparency. Her eye makeup smudged down her cheeks. Skyler's driving was erratic; the frame shook and tilted as she aimed the lens through the front windshield on a hard-right turn. When the frame found Leah again, she was gripping onto the door handle.

"You poor thing, you must have been terrified," I said. "She drives like a maniac."

"Watch closely or you'll miss it," said Leah.

The camera stayed on Leah as the car rolled to a stop at an intersection, right next to a police cruiser. The cruiser's lights were off, but there was someone in the backseat. Young Leah glanced out her window just as the rear passenger turned to peer out the window of the cruiser. The face of the young man was cast in shadow, but I was caught by a twinge of recognition.

"Wait, is that ...?" I started, feeling an odd resistance to finishing the sentence.

Without turning around, Leah said, "It's Jared Esquivel."

Jared Esquivel. Hearing his name caused my stomach to drop. I hadn't thought about him in a decade, at least. Jared was our neighbor, a suave and slightly predatory sixteen-year-old who introduced me to weed just weeks before the fire. I ran into him as I was sneaking out that night. He threatened to wake up my parents if I didn't trade his silence for a hand job, so I took a hit of his joint and promised him the deed upon my return home the next morning. Then the fire happened, and Jared found himself in the crosshairs of cops determined to nail the bastard responsible for half a dozen casualities. Everyone in that apartment complex knew Jared had a habit of tossing half-lit joints in the courtyard planter, littering the mulch with scorched roaches, and the embers of the fire hadn't even cooled before they dragged the teenager off to jail, his ears ringing with the words no person ever wants to hear: "You are under arrest for reckless manslaughter." The fire itself was ruled accidental, for at the time of his arrest Jared was higher than an untethered helium balloon and had no recollection of the incident. He was sentenced to thirty years instead of life in prison. According to his own father, the son of a bitch got off easy.

While I was trying to imagine the quality of Jared's life as he served the first half of his time, isolated from an outside world with six fewer people in it because of deliberate indifference, Skyler's movie transitioned to the parking lot of a methadone clinic. Leah now had the camera, and she filmed through the windshield from the passenger seat as Skyler shouted at full volume at the closed building; the frame rattled so much I could feel Leah's anxiety come through the screen. A protective impulse overtook me as I felt the need to reach into the past and pull my little sister into a blanket of safety, but as my body pitched forward, Leah leaned over in her seat, halting my encroachment.

"Not yet," she said.

There had been a number of moments like this between Leah and me, where she would acknowledge something I had done in a way that made me question if she'd misinterpreted my intention, or if she anticipated my actions even before I did. The frequency of those moments during this particular night made me wonder just how much thought she had put into how I might react to this new information. She nodded toward the screen again, and I watched through the lens of ten-year-old Leah as the same Jared-toting police cruiser pulled up alongside them and the officer approached Skyler, who unleashed her rage onto him. Over the racket, Leah's voice crept in, her sweet, high-pitched whisper that sounded like it was right in my ear: "It wasn't an accident … it wasn't an accident … it wasn't an accident."

I could only assume she was talking about the true nature of Jared's involvement in the fire's ignition, though I couldn't be sure. I had long suspected that the stoner's absent-minded flicking of joints leaned intentional, even if it was incomprehensible to others that a child could be capable of such a heinous crime. They refused to believe it was possible. Perhaps Leah shared my view. Or perhaps she really did know more than she'd let on for all these years. My skin itched with the excitement of discovery.

Leah stood up. "Let's go."

"Don't you want me to see the rest?" I asked.

"No," she said and headed for the aisle.

I stood and hurried after, noting that we were the only ones left in the theater with the exception of the young man in the front row and a haggard woman at the very back. She was slumped down in the velvet seat, and even in the darkness I could tell she was trembling. A junkie's twitch. It wasn't until we reached the theater doors that I realized it was Skyler. In place of an eclectic thrift store wardrobe was a worn black wool coat. Pale white skin glowed through a hole in the coat's shoulder. Her cheeks were hollowed out like someone had taken an ice cream scoop to her face. Long gone was the animated, cheerful waitress of a local hipster diner; in her place was a fragmented woman in her late thirties determined to hold onto a decaying slice of her past. Perhaps if she'd stayed clean, Skyler could have achieved filmmaking success. Instead, this was her denouement: a tribute to someone else's story that no one cared to watch.

Back in the Volvo, Leah and I set off on the next part of the journey. She stayed quiet, pushing the arms of her sweatshirt up over her elbows, then pulling them back down again. I watched her with worry, wondering if her discomfort would eventually cause her to pull the plug on the whole adventure. "Skyler's life has nothing to do with you, Leah," I said, "you have to know that."

With a rapid shake of her head, Leah said, "I warned her not to release the movie. I told her it wasn't going to do anybody any good."

"Why didn't you try harder to stop her? It's your story, Leah, you have that right."

There it was, that drift of attention, causing me to wonder yet again what part of consciousness my sister disappeared into when she would rather not consider something I'd said. The light turned green just as a sedan reared up behind us, yet Leah kept her foot on the brake and, to my surprise, answered my question. "Skyler spent years working on the movie, trying to make it perfect, promising it was going to be her big break. And then your memoir came out. Skyler's movie became secondary. This — what we're doing now — she wanted to film it. She knew the story was incomplete, and if she could only get the rest of it from me, maybe it could at least compete with your book."

The car behind us honked. Leah didn't even flinch. I sighed, steadying myself to not show too much pride for having been Leah's chosen storyteller. "You didn't think she could tell your story the way you needed it told."

"No, that's not it," Leah said quickly, and I hated how deflated I felt. "Let's just say you being here has a greater purpose."

The driver behind us leaned on his car horn as he slammed on the gas, swerved into the opposite lane with a middle finger out his side window, and sped around the Volvo. Leah didn't elaborate on her statement; she took a breath before she eased into the intersection and made the turn.

A part of me felt for Skyler. If Leah was the inspiration for her crowning achievement, she had nothing of value to show for it. I, at least, had the opportunity for a more in-depth perspective; a story with vision, not an abstract and drug-fueled patchwork of failed artistic expression. I was also grateful that Leah had shown me the film. Up until then, I hadn't much knowledge of what happened to my sister the night of the fire, and while, at age thirteen, I had little control over anyone's fate — including my own — I had to wonder how different Leah's current life would be had I been able to keep her from running off with someone who wanted nothing more than to take advantage of her suffering.

Back then, Leah was the agreeable child, not yet bewitched by the sparkle of teenage rebellion. She could have followed after me to that slumber party, yet she chose not to. And why she decided on Skyler to be the captain of her emotional vessel was something I refused to believe was a choice made with a clear grasp of the consequences. Now she acted with purpose, and I didn't want Leah to think the only reason I agreed to join her that night was to fill the pages of a book not yet realized; I wanted to prove to her that I cared, that love could forgive a lifetime of mistakes, that our sisterly bond was not breakable, no matter how many times we tested the tensile strength of the thread that held us together. No one could rewrite Leah's past, but at least I could write it better.

ʘ

A three-mile drive from one Los Angeles location to another was the polar opposite of a New York minute; the clog of vehicles never seemed to thin out, even during non-rush hours and the deceiving "we're almost there" mantra made any trek feel endless. Only on holidays, when tourists had gone and transplants had flown back to Indiana for a few days, could you see the city beyond the impatient side-eyeing of a GPS map whose declared estimated time of arrival rarely subtracted a minute, despite the number of yellow stoplights that had been dangerously sped through.

As Leah drove us to our next destination, I grew anxious, and it wasn't just the fidgety tremble of Leah's legs against her seat. Something gnawed at me. We were traveling through a part of town that triggered more conflicting memories than nostalgic ones. On the night of the fire, while I knew very little of Leah's time with Skyler, I did know it was sometime around two in the morning that she was brought to our Aunt Angela's house in the Hollywood Hills. I, meanwhile, was stowed away at my friend's house, pretending I had permission to be there. It wasn't until my friend's father turned on the morning news that the fate of my childhood home became reality. While my sleepover friends were still waking, I was expeditiously whisked off to the L.A. County Sheriff's Station in West Hollywood to find neither of my remaining family members particularly excited to see me alive and well. I understood my little sister's aloofness, but I had hoped to be met with something other than frustration by my aunt. I could smell the alcohol on her breath. I wondered if the officers knew she was intoxicated, or if they cared.

We passed Gelson's Market on Franklin Avenue, where years ago Leah and I would take our time checking off Angela's daily shopping list. Leah would peruse the aisles reading the labels of health foods with names she could barely pronounce and that Angela would not let us buy, while I often followed around a days-past TV actor who I was surprised was making enough money to still afford residence in that neighborhood and who would ultimately star in an endless string of automotive insurance commercials. We passed the famously misunderstood Bourgeois Pig (a coffee shop for youngsters like myself who wanted to be writers but considered themselves too "off the wall" to be seen somewhere predictable like Starbucks) and late-night street crawlers who had done too much tweak to go to bed anytime soon.

We turned up Beachwood Drive toward a house that should have been too nice to be an off-the-books foster home for dogs that howled into the hillside all night long. As a young driver, Leah had hated navigating the narrow, winding roads, and she struggled still, leaning forward with her hands gripping the steering wheel, so lost in her internal tunnel vision that she drove right past the driveway. The car screeched to a stop inches from a bear-proofed trash can. What sounded like a dozen large dogs erupted in a fury, barking and growling with a carnal yet unnecessary aggression.

I studied Angela's house, specifically the shortest portion of the brick wall, imagining the pile of garage-sale outdoor furniture on the other side. At thirteen, I had the long limbs and the strength required to hoist myself over and enjoy the freedom of occasional rebellion until, on the eve of my fourteenth birthday, I escaped to never return.

I chose a life with our neighbor Tobin Esquivel, a man whose son was currently serving prison time for the death of his wife and my beloved parents. In a bedbug infested one-bedroom off Normandie, we filled the voids in each other's lives: Tobin became a devoted father figure, and I the loving child he desperately wanted to nurture. His relentless attention was a far cry from the distressed glare I got from Angela whenever she seemed to suddenly remember I existed. I was a child who needed to feel wanted, not dismissed as an inconvenience for having interrupted her bachelorette lifestyle.

Leah, on the other hand, stayed with Angela until she'd turned eighteen. I could never understand Leah's adherence to the living situation set up by social services, especially considering just how easily Angela surrendered her duties as my warden and let the agents pass legal guardianship to a man who was not family. As I spent my remaining minor years with a weekly allowance volunteered by Tobin and a fake ID crafted by some vaguely Middle Eastern man who did business out of the Vermont/Beverly subway station, Leah came of age to the soundtrack of a dozen howling foster dogs and a forced diet of fast food. Angela may have kept those creatures alive, but that didn't mean she knew a damn thing about raising a pre-teen girl.

Leah had to know that I'd waited for her to ask to join the life I'd found for myself; my intention was never to withhold it from her. I had hoped she knew that. Yet I felt a pestering dread flow over me as I watched Leah get out of the car and approach Angela's front door. She rung the bell then turned back with her hands thrown in the air.

"You coming?" Leah said, barely audible over the chorus of barking dogs.

The door opened and Angela appeared, silhouetted, a backlight shining through holes in her weathered house clothes. Her skin had the wrinkled texture of old leather, and her long gray hair was stringy and covered in an oily sheen. She and Leah stood together on the porch like a barricade, as though they still harbored resentments over my unceremonious departure and were questioning their willingness to let me back in.

"I'm sorry I never came back for you, Leah," I whispered, hoping my words would be felt by the person they were intended for.

I yanked open the car door, and the dogs stopped barking all at once. I could hear them pawing the floor, nails screeching on brick, snouts huffing into the gaps between, but they were otherwise quiet. Back then, they went silent whenever I hopped the fence, never alerting my aunt to my escape. It was possible those dogs had been rooting for me, that their primal senses told them there was freedom beyond those walls and that I might be the one to capture that essence and bring it back to them like a juicy raw steak embedded with tranquilizer pills strong enough to wipe the memory of their stunted and unfulfilled canine lives.

"What'd I tell you, Leah? Even the dogs know Catherine's up to no good. They can smell something terrible on her." Angela had a gravelly voice of a woman who spent her whole life smoking Reds and drinking bottom-shelf beer, and the disposition of someone who believed every living being that came into her life did so in order to take something from her.

Leah shook her head at our aunt and moved past her into the house. Angela, despite her hardened demeanor, sunk back and out of her way. I was proud of my sister then; the fire had incited the change in Leah from a mute, enigmatic child to the toughened young woman I saw before me, and that juxtaposition was precisely what would tie the whole story together. Sure, my lack of presence over the years lost me the first-hand viewpoint, but part of me knew it was exactly my absence that enhanced my sister's transformation.

As soon as I slammed the car door shut, the dogs erupted again. I had no freedom or amnesia to offer those dogs, but I now had something to offer Leah: closure from the past and, perhaps, a positive vision of what could be waiting in the future. A grassy patch of literary success called to us, and all that was left was for Leah to continue breathing new life into her tale. As I followed her past Angela into the house — getting the steeliest glance as I did — I no longer felt the weight of dread, but an uplifting wind of momentum.

The house was in no better shape than the last time I had seen it. Tobacco smoke had penetrated the walls over decades, stuffing the pores of the wooden panels. Dog urine singed my nostrils. Beneath my shoes, sparks twinkled from the matted and crusty shag carpet, an electrical current propelled by dry summer air. Hollywood twinkled too, through the side windows, a view that featured in at least three soft-core porn films and the only beautiful element left of the house. I stood in the middle of the living room, but Leah seemed drawn to the hallway, glancing toward the bedroom we once shared, a cramped space overtaken by Angela's favorite dog, a huge German shepherd who claimed the bed and covered it in shed fur. Angela had said the bedroom window was broken, but I was certain she'd nailed it shut on purpose.

I turned square to Angela, who twisted her head to hide her left side. Drool seeped from the corner of her mouth. I wondered how early she'd started drinking. "I don't know if Leah told you, but we're here to do something positive for her, so I ask that you respect that."

"You look just like your mom when you talk like that," Angela said. She'd tried to mask her slur, but the words stumbled on her lips. "She had this way of doing whatever she wanted, and everybody was in the wrong if they disagreed with her."

Leah tensed, fists bunched into balls. I hated how easy it was for Angela to rattle her, especially when it came to the mockery of a childhood full of trauma. “I get that you don’t want me here, but don’t make it worse by talking about my dead mother like that in front of Leah. Especially considering how little care you gave to her daughters.”

Angela rolled her head back so quickly it almost looked like her neck would snap. “I did the best I could.”

A laugh spewed from my mouth faster than if I were a disgusted Silver Lake dilettante spitting out a drink I discovered to be non-organic. “The best you could!” I shouted, arousing the dogs further. “See, here’s what I remember from the night of the fire. By the time I met you at the sheriff’s station, you were already drunk. You drove down there with Leah, drunk. The cops left me with you, knowing full well you were incapable of any responsibility because you were drunk. And that, you say, was the best you could do? How could you be so selfish when you clearly didn’t want us? Was it the money?”

“What money?” Angela said. She plucked a pack of cigarettes from a coffee table piled high with beer bottles and In-N-Out French fry trays, and struggled with a shaking hand to pull one cigarette from the bunch. It took four clicks of her lighter to get a flame going. I had witnessed my aunt light countless cigarettes but the habitual act seemed suddenly awkward for her, and uncomfortable to watch.

In a moment so brief it could have been missed, I felt sorry for her. For years, I had assumed the appalling living conditions were meant to torture us, yet neither Angela nor her house had improved. In fact, the rate of deterioration had accelerated. It occurred to me then that Angela simply didn’t know any other way to live outside of the singular toxic family trait, one echoed in the boozy, preoccupied habits of my own mother. It had been foolish of social services to pretend guardianship under my aunt would be an improvement. Had I chosen to stay, I might have become imbued with the same restless alienation that had plagued Leah all her life, and I wouldn't have the strength now to see the truth of our family discord, the very thing I was trying my damnedest to keep from infecting Leah: resignation to a life not worth living.

"I want to know what you hoped to gain from imprisoning Leah here for so many years," I said.

It surprised me when Leah spoke, using a voice of authority that sounded odd coming from her. "It wasn't a prison, Catherine. At least I wasn't alone."

"You could have come with me," I said.

"No, I couldn't." Leah moved across the room to the dining table, which was just as cluttered as the rest of the house. Piles of newspapers sprawled across the surface, hiding what lay beneath, items that Leah seemed to know were there: prescription pill bottles. A dozen, at least. Most of them nearly empty.

With one eye on Leah, I glared at Angela. "Great. This is great. Not only are you a pathetic drunk, but you're addicted to pills as well? How could you have ever been expected to take care of children when you can barely care for yourself?"

Instead of reacting to the reveal of the pills, Angela seemed confused by the volume of my voice, her eyes squinting to follow the movement of my lips. The arm holding her cigarette trembled. The lit cherry dislodged from the filter and fluttered to the shag carpet. I tensed. There were too many flammable materials in the house, and while I wouldn't bat an eye should Angela go up in flames in the house of horrors, the thought of Leah subjected to yet another near-death-by-fire moved me into action. I snuffed the burning ember with my shoe.

Angela flinched at my approach, and turned to hide her left side again. "I did the best I could."

"You treated us just like your dogs," I said. "We were here because we were forced to be here, not because you wanted us, and despite how desperately we wanted to escape, you had no empathy for our need to find solace somewhere more comfortable."

"But you did find somewhere else," Leah said. She glanced down the hallway again, and quickly corrected herself. She was hiding something, that much was clear, and her eyes balanced a mix of anxiety and rage. She was suddenly caught by a particular bottle on the dining table and plucked it from the bunch, and I took the opportunity to sneak down the hallway.

"Catherine, wait," I heard Leah say as I barreled into the back bedroom. I expected the space to be just as filthy as the rest of the house but found it clean and inviting. The bed was made. The once-broken window had been replaced and was currently open, letting in a warm breeze. Several items of clothes lay draped across a desk chair, all in Leah's size.

Leah hovered in the doorway, watching. "Yeah," she said. "I'm living here."

"Why?" I said, hating the twinge in my voice. "This is not a place for you to live. Not then, and certainly not now."

She held out her hand. In it was one of Angela's prescription pill bottles. "Read it."

I did. They were prescribed recently. For patients of hemorrhagic stroke.

"I don't understand," I said.

"You disappeared," Leah said. "No one had the slightest clue where you were for two weeks. You left me alone — again — and I had no idea where you were. You abandoned me."

"I didn't abandon you. I got away to survive for both of us."

The curl of Leah's mouth didn't match the haunted look in her eyes. "Angela had her first stroke the night of the fire. I remember finding her in the kitchen just before dawn. She was mumbling on and on about how worried she was that she wouldn't be able to protect us the way Mom would have wanted."

"Our mother was a drunk," I said, "Just like Aunt Angela."

"Angela didn't drink until the night Mom and Dad died," Leah said. She looked around the room, peering into the corners as though their shadows hid memories of the past. "Angela had her second stroke three days after you disappeared. The stress of losing one of her sister's daughters put too much stress on her body. She was so terrified of not being able to protect us it nearly killed her. That's why I'm here now. I had her when I had no one else. Now I'm here because she has no one either."

I was dumbfounded. And angry. Leah's description of events from seventeen years ago completely contradicted a major turning point in my memoir, something she would have known had she read the book. I sent her an early copy, asking politely for notes. She never offered then to share her side of the story, and my recent excitement removed the need to question why she decided now was the moment for her grand reveal.

But I never considered Leah wasn't motivated by my same eagerness to share her story with the world. I never considered that the addition of Leah's timeline would be less of an endorsement than a complete upheaval of my narrative. What exactly was I expected to gain from this?

Leah sighed and put the pill bottle on her desk. "We have one more stop to go." From her back pocket, she revealed the piece of notebook paper and scanned the list. The particular phrasing began to make sense, at least for the locations we had already visited. *Relapse of the Junkie* and *House of Strays* were obviously relating to Skyler and Aunt Angela. I had yet to understand why *Happier Times on the Outside* was crossed out, but I was to learn the meaning soon enough.

ლ

As we drove toward the bustling nightlife of West Hollywood and away from the unnecessarily eccentric east-side neighborhoods, I grew more apprehensive. At first, Leah's doling out of information was part of the fun. The anticipation of the next clue reveal had made me eager and excited, but now I felt tense in the expectation of a backstabbing. It was bad enough to witness the result of Skyler's downward spiral by way of drug abuse and unrealistic artistic ambition, but to have been blindsided by news of Angela's ailing health made me question the consequence of so many contradictions to my story. How long would it be before others caught onto the discrepancies, picking apart my debut memoir as nothing but a series of misinformed anecdotes, or worse?

The metallic ink that spelled out *Man of Poor Judgment* on Leah's list flickered in the brief, passing light of street lamps. I had insisted she give the page to me — after all, the adventure had taken a sharp left turn, and if anyone should be throwing plot twists into the evening it should have been me, the writer. I regretted not putting more effort into decoding the list upon first glance. Even more so, I regretted walking into the venture unguarded. I couldn't afford to be surprised again. Since leaving Angela's house, I had asked Leah three times to explain her cryptic index.

"It's better that I'm the only one who knows what it means," she said, finally.

"Can you at least give me some hint about what *Man of Poor Judgment* is about?"

She rapped on the steering wheel in a rhythmic pattern; the once-playful act now ignited my nerves. "By the time the cops took me to Aunt Angela's, I was exhausted but I couldn't sleep. Apparently, I just lay on the couch, mumbling. When we went to the station to pick you up, I was still mumbling. One officer wanted to talk to me. She wanted to know what I was trying to say."

This was news to me. I remembered a silent ten-year-old Leah, sleepy-eyed and disoriented, but not mumbling. I couldn't get her to speak to me for several weeks, a side effect of her post-traumatic stress, according to our social services agent. The thought that yet another person might know more about Leah's night filled me with an overwhelming urgency to get the information out of Leah before she could ambush me again.

"What did you tell the officer?" I asked.

"I don't remember," Leah said after a longer pause than was comfortable. "She got distracted putting Jared through booking. I watched the cops escort him to the jail cells, handcuffed, tears streaming down his face. He looked so scared."

Leah turned onto Santa Monica Boulevard, a glittery, celebrity-filled representation of what outsiders expect all of L.A. to be. She didn't say a word as she steered around traffic, back and forth between the two lanes. The sleeves of her sweatshirt bunched at her biceps seemed to inhibit her mobility. I gazed at the crowds of people in brand-label clothing as they strolled along the sidewalk and struggled to ask a question I was certain would not be met with answers.

"Is that where we're going now? To the police station?"

"Not exactly." Leah pulled over just short of Robertson and pointed across the street to a building with white lettering that spelled out "Mother Lode" in a vague Old West font. "Wait for me in there. I'll find parking."

"Why can't I go with you to find parking?" I said.

"I don't know how long it'll take to find a spot." Leah tugged on the front of her sweatshirt, billowing air against her belly in an attempt to cool off before jerking her head to look at me. "Go."

"Leah, when I signed up for this adventure, I didn't expect the whole thing to be this morbid, shrouded mystery."

"Don't make this difficult, Catherine, just wait for me in the bar."

"Why aren't we going to the sheriff's station?"

"Just wait for me in the goddam bar."

I could sense I was walking into a trap, and I wanted nothing more to avoid yet another slap to the face, but fatigue hit me suddenly. We'd been driving all evening, and the initial adrenaline of chasing the story died in Angela's house. I had the very real fear that the twist ending I had hoped to capture for my next book would be less of a refreshing finale and more like being t-boned in the middle of an intersection by an over-chromed Hummer.

"Fine. Don't make me wait too long. I'm tired." I flung open the Volvo door and stepped onto the curb just as a horde of fit and well-groomed men spilled out from a club in a giggling frenzy. Their heightened energy drained mine right out of me so abruptly that I saw spots in my eyesight.

"I promise I won't take long," Leah said and accelerated the car with the door still open. I lunged and slammed it shut. She turned the corner, and I headed for the sidewalk to cross the street.

West Hollywood was a place familiar yet alien to me. The strobe lights and booming house music had become a fixture of my early twenties, exciting to my senses and aggressive enough to drown out the harsh internal monologue of real life. It was a place of relative protection from horny straight dudes, where a young girl like myself could load up on neon-blue Adios Motherfuckers and dance Thursday nights away. Eventually, my years ticked closer to thirty and I traded Drag Night for Wine Night in Westside pop-up restaurants, and the occasional return to WeHo turned into a game of guessing which trendy establishment used to inhabit the location of the brand new, arguably trendier venue.

At the moment, I was headed into a bar that had been there since the birth of WeHo, as far as I knew. I had never been inside, and I wasn't pleased with the circumstances that finally led me there. The old bar didn't fit in with the surrounding businesses. Even the clientele displayed an air of contradiction with their graphic T-shirts and cargo shorts. Blue interior lights gave the wood wall panels a futuristic saloon vibe. I was desperately trying to spot a friendly looking female to chat with when I recognized someone sitting at the bar: Tobin Esquivel.

It had been years since I'd last seen his face, which was now covered by a wiry salt-and-pepper beard, but even in the weird blue hue I knew him. He slouched on a stool, resting one arm on the bar top, swirling a single ball of ice in a glass of liquor. While the other patrons fed their machismo with sexual tension and the occasional grab of another man's pecs, Tobin could have been plunked right into an ad for testosterone pills as the perfect example of failing male expectations.

With Tobin's presence, I knew that, of all the reveals of the night, the unfolding of this part of the story was likely to be, well, the mother lode of them all.

My plan was to slip outside and call a rideshare. Instead, I was shoved inside by a large man who put two hands on my shoulders and steered me toward the bar as though I were a powered Segway. The man's force crashed me into the stool next to Tobin, who looked at me with surprise. He stared at me, gaze moving up and down, until one side of his mouth curled into a somber smile.

"Catherine, it's been awhile," he said. Up close I could see the dampness of his cheeks. He'd been crying.

"Look, I don't know what's going on with you and Leah, but if you have something to say to me, just get it over with."

Tobin's face bunched in pained confusion. It was an expression I was familiar with, one that often followed some poorly thought-out excuse for why I didn't much care for all his rules, and therefore chose to break them. "I asked Leah to meet me," he said. "You're the last person I expected to see here, but it is good to see you again."

"I'm not here by choice," I said, and scanned the entrance to plot my second attempt at escape. "At least, not by *my* choice."

"The sheriff's station is down the street." Tobin raised his glass to his lips and tossed the liquid down his throat. The large ball of ice clacked against his teeth. "That's the last place I saw him. Handcuffed. Guilty. Sobbing like a child."

I swallowed a lump about the size of that ice ball. "The last place you saw who?"

"Jared."

Panic smacked me right in the chest. Of course Leah would have ended the tour with Tobin. He barely escaped the fire that night. My eyes instantly went to the shiny, raised scars on his forearms where the flames caught hold of him as he searched the burning apartment building for his wife. The charred body found in the laundry room underneath my father was hers — a fact no one needed forensic evidence to conclude.

Tobin was already at the police station early that next morning when I arrived to be reunited with my sister and my begrudging soon-to-be legal guardian. I couldn't tell if Tobin's trembling was from the undoubted pain from his bandaged arms and hands, or if he mourned the death of his adulterer wife, or if he was weighted by guilt over the fact he'd raised his son to be a homicidal arsonist.

"I remember seeing you that night," Tobin said.

I never gave him credit for it, but he had always had a way of guessing where my thoughts had drifted to. There were many times over the years that I had to pretend he hadn't hit on something too close for comfort. "You were so young. Both of you. I've never forgiven Jared for what he did to your parents."

"Tobin, we've been through this. You did more than enough to make up for it. I would be on the streets if it hadn't been for you."

"I didn't do enough for Leah," he said.

The sound of my sister's name triggered something in me. She had insisted I wait in the bar for her, and suddenly I didn't want her in the bar with me and Tobin. Ours was a special dynamic, one that would have been completely undone if Leah had come to stay with us in that shitty one-bedroom off Normandie. I knew even back then that she would have scattered my plans into the wind. Her attempt to rewrite every part of the story was proof of that now.

"Leah had her own path to take," I said. "I did what I could, but what happened to her after that night wasn't my fault."

"I lost my wife and my son," Tobin said, and the tears streamed down his face. "I would have been alone if it hadn't been for you. You meant everything to me."

Tobin leaned over and heaved with sobs while his hand

caressed the outside of my thigh. It was not an unusual touch. Tobin had always been a man of excessive affection, and while it was unnerving at first, I eventually became less squeamish of his incessant PDA. I almost found it endearing. Despite the nearly twenty-year age gap and the fact that I was barely fourteen when I'd gone to live with him, I accepted his behavior in exchange for his undying devotion.

Then it hit me. "Tobin, have you never visited Jared in prison?"

Eyes screwed shut, he shook his head. "I know my wife was a cheating whore, but Jared still killed her. And your parents. And three innocent neighbors. That wasn't something I could forgive. Not back then, anyway. Funny thing is, I was close to forgiveness before —"

"Before what?" I said. Something about the way Tobin rolled his shoulders back made me shudder, like a sympathetic reflex.

With a deep breath, Tobin said, "Jared hung himself in his cell two days ago. He'd been denied parole again. I guess he just couldn't take it anymore, so he took his fate into his own hands."

There it was: the surprise ending. The epic climax. The plot twist to end all plot twists. This was the reason for the perplexing timing, the reason why Leah called two days ago to finally grant me insight into her side of the story, why I was currently in that bar with Tobin, why the second to last line in Leah's list was crossed out: *Happier Times on the Outside*. Jared was dead. End scene.

I placed my hand over Tobin's as it rested on my thigh, and he burst into tears. I wasn't sure what to say. "Sorry for the loss of your shithead son" was harsh, even for my exasperated state. A few of the other male patrons looked at me with apologetic melancholy, but the scrunch of their faces and the tilt of their heads were too exaggerated to be taken seriously. I didn't know what to say to Tobin, and I certainly could not stand the sight of the grown man crying, but I decided in that moment that I no longer wanted my sophomore novel to have anything to do with the night of the fire. I wanted to be rid of the whole memory, to keep clear from anyone who wanted to draw me into their trauma, to keep to my own story as I knew it because I had my own goddamn life to honor.

"So, you've heard?"

I whipped around to find Leah behind me. The sweatshirt sleeves were drawn over her arms, and for the first time that night I felt overheated just looking at her. She caught sight of Tobin's hand on my leg, and I pulled away. "About Jared? Yeah, he just told me."

"Such a tragedy," Leah said. I couldn't discern if her flat tone was sarcastic or strained. "Jared could have at least waited until the retrial."

"What retrial?" I glanced at Tobin for a hint, but he waved the bartender over for another drink.

"Some new evidence cropped up," Leah said. "They are investigating the fire as no longer being negligent arson. Now they think it was set intentionally. But Jared never heard about the new evidence, and he still had half his sentence to serve."

I tried to catch Leah's eyes, but her gaze seemed caught on the other side of the room. "I'm confused. How does that help Jared's case? He got a reduced sentence because they ruled it an accident."

"It wasn't an accident," Leah said and, without a word to Tobin, headed for the door.

The room tilted. Adrenaline filled my veins. I could feel every pulse of blood through my body. The words breezed through my ears, in the voice of ten-year-old Leah from Skyler's movie: "It wasn't an accident … It wasn't an accident …"

Before I knew it, I was outside. I spun on the sidewalk, searching for my sister. She was headed east, walking fast, hands shoved deep in her pockets. "Leah, stop!" She kept walking, and I chased after her, not caring that people glared as my loud and outraged voice interrupted their feel-good vibes. "You set me up for this! All this time I wanted to hear your side of the story, and you chose now — days after Jared killed himself — to finally let me in? Don't think I believe that to be a coincidence. And don't get me started on that other bullshit with Skyler and Angela. You're telling me a story that isn't even about you!"

Leah halted and turned on her heels. I could feel the anger radiating off of her, a seeping heat more powerful that the lingering warmth of the summer air. "Not about me? I'm not the only one who suffered because of the fire. All these people dealt with the fallout. Skyler. Angela. Tobin. Jared —"

"Jared is no victim," I interrupted.

"He's one of the worst victims."

"He was charged with starting the fire."

Leah gave a mocking chuckle that made my skin crawl. "Jared had nothing to do with the fire. You don't see it, do you? Catherine, you're the only one who isn't a victim."

"The hell I'm not. I'm an orphan, same as you. I had to figure things out on my own."

"You chose to benefit in every way you could," Leah said with a shrug. "I know you're not here tonight because you care about my journey. You wanted your twist ending so you have something to sell. The irony is: you already know the twist."

Leah turned to her left, and I followed her gaze. We were right in front of the sheriff's station, the very place where Jared had been arrested and booked for carelessly flicking the joint that ultimately killed six people. The building itself had no windows and was surrounded by a brick wall, but I had the odd feeling of eyes on me. A cruiser drove up to the gate and paused; something told me the person inside made an intentional, suspicious observation of my presence.

Of course, Leah didn't care that the cruiser was right there, window halfway down, or perhaps this was the whole point of the night, to throw me under the bus enough times that I became embedded in the sticky pores of asphalt. Perhaps I'd been an idiot to not see any of this coming, and perhaps I'd assumed I had worked hard enough to separate myself so that whatever actually happened that night seventeen years ago could no longer have an impact on my future.

Except it could. And Leah knew that. She knew it all along.

"I've wanted to say this for a really long time, Catherine. I know the fire wasn't an accident," Leah said in a voice more confident than I had ever heard from her, a voice that sounded an awful lot like mine. "I know because I was awake when you snuck out to that slumber party. I saw you take a hit of Jared's joint. I saw you pocket his lighter. And I saw you come back."

That was impossible. There was no way she could have seen me. I knew the darkest corners of the courtyard better than anyone. I could sneak in and out without even my light-sleeping younger sister noticing I was no longer in the bed across the room.

"Everyone just assumed the ash in the planter was from Jared," Leah went on, and with each word my desire to tape her mouth shut grew stronger. "I know you burned newspapers in the planter. I watched you do it a dozen times. I was looking out the window that night, Catherine. I was looking out the window when you came back with a torch of burning newspapers in your hand. I was looking out the window when I saw the first bush ignite. I was looking out the window when the hedge caught fire, and I saw you back away, watching the thing burn like you'd created a fucking masterpiece."

The cruiser was still there, stalled at the gate. People swarmed all around us on the sidewalk, close enough to understand every word coming out of Leah's mouth. It felt like all of Los Angeles could hear her, hear her blame, hear her admit after seventeen years that she had known all along that the fire was not an accident, but my doing.

"So, Catherine, it's your masterpiece. Time for you to claim ownership."

Leah tugged on the hem of her sweatshirt, pulling it up and over her head. She wore a loose tank top, which revealed a colorful collection of tattoos that covered her shoulders, tattoos that I had never seen before. They couldn't have all been new, not with that amount of detail. I was so transfixed by the colors and shapes that I barely missed the grin that curled Leah's lips as she turned around. The tank top revealed just enough of her back to show a tattoo piece of a bouquet of fire flames, each limb branching out to spell a person's name. Six names of those who died in the fire. Three names of the people we'd visited that night. The name of the young man wrongfully accused of the crime. And there in the middle of the bouquet was a phrase: *Catherine of Fire*. The perfect title for a bestselling memoir.

BIOGRAPHIES

Andrea Auten

Andrea Auten is an MFA graduate and holds a post master's certificate in creative writing pedagogy from Antioch University Los Angeles, where she works as a writing instructor. Her work has appeared in *Lady/Liberty/Lit* and *Lunch Ticket.* A vocalist, stage performer, visual artist, and arts teacher, she serves for many arts nonprofits. A member of the Degenerate Writer's Group, she is working on her novel and a short story collection. She lives in Los Angeles with her husband, sons, and beloved writing partner, Dusky, the family cat. Find her at andreaauten.com.

Barry Bergmann

Barry Bergmann's grandfather moved his young family to Los Angeles after surviving the 1906 San Francisco earthquake, thinking earthquakes would not be an issue in Southern California. Even though his research may have been unsound, no member of the three subsequent Bergmann generations would find fault with his decision. Barry's lived in five countries and thirteen cities during a 35-year airline career, but L.A. has always been the answer to the question, "Where are you from?" Retired now, he loves reading, running, travel, and of course writing. He splits his time between Tokyo, Arizona, and naturally Los Angeles.

Sara Chisolm

Sara is a speculative fiction writer based in the Los Angeles area. Her urban fantasy short story, "Serenade of the Gangsta," was featured in the second volume of the Made in L.A. fiction anthology series.

DC Diamondopolous

DC Diamondopolous is an award-winning novelette, short story, and flash fiction writer with over 200 stories published internationally in print and online magazines, literary journals, and anthologies. DC's stories have appeared in: *34th Parallel, So It Goes: The Literary Journal of the Kurt Vonnegut Museum and Library, Lunch Ticket, Raven Chronicles, Silver Pen, Front Porch Review*, and many others. Among DC's many awards and honorary mentions are: 2018 Finalist for ScreenCraft's Short Story Contest and 2017 nomination for Best of the Net Anthology. She lives on the California central coast with her wife and animals. Find her at dcdiamondopolous.com.

Erik Gonzales-Kramer

Erik Gonzales-Kramer has loved writing stories since he could hold a pen, when he first wrote about space-faring sea otters of the future. When he is not writing short stories or editing his longer novels-in-process, he is busy with one of his many other passions—swing and blues dancing, sustainable action, and traveling. Though he loved growing up in the forests of Michigan, he is a proud Los Angeles transplant, where he shares his passion for prose with a dedicated community of storytellers of all mediums and walks of life. Keep up with Erik at erikgonzaleskramer.com.

Nolan Knight

Nolan Knight is a fourth-generation Angeleno whose short fiction has appeared in various publications, including Akashic Books, *Thuglit*, *Needle*, *Shotgun Honey*, *Tough*, and *Crimespree Magazine*. His debut novel, *The Neon Lights Are Veins*, was released by 280 Steps Press and his short story collection, *Beneath the Black Palms*, is currently represented by Nat Sobel of Sobel Weber Associates. Find out more at NolanKnight.com.

Gabi Lorino

Gabi Lorino is a writer, editor, and ukulele player. Her first book, *A Magical Time Called Later*, was inspired by several conversations with a disgruntled 38-year-old bridesmaid and her own experience as a singleton. She is a founding member of Made in L.A. Writers and has contributed to all the Made in L.A. anthologies.

Karter Mycroft

Karter Mycroft is an author, editor, musician, and fisheries scientist who lives in Los Angeles. They are currently hard at work on a novel about dead fish and the people who love them. Their short fiction has been published or is forthcoming in *The Colored Lens*, *Black Hare Press*, *Trembling With Fear*, *Lovecraftiana*, and *Murder Park After Dark*.

Noriko Nakada

Noriko Nakada lives in Los Angeles and is committed to teaching and writing thought-provoking creative non-fiction, fiction, and poetry. Publications include her memoir series: *Through Eyes Like Mine*. *Through Eyes Like Mine* was shortlisted for the 2040 Book Award. *Overdue Apologies: a middle school memoir* and *I Tried: Tales from an Emerging High School Feminist* complete the trilogy. Excerpts, essays, and poems have appeared in *Catapult*, *Meridian*, *Kartika*, *Hippocampus*, *Compose*, *Linden Avenue*. She is an editor for Women Who Submit, an organization empowering women and nonbinary writers to submit their work for publication. Read more on Noriko's website at norikonakada.com.

Lenore Robinson

Lenore Robinson began writing as a form of therapy, a way to coalesce her seemingly ever-spinning thoughts into something tangible. Raised in the Appalachian south, she is passionate about storytelling and unearthing the emotions we hide deep within ourselves. She explores elements from her own lived experience, as well as the countless stories that have intersected hers. She describes her process as experimental and "experiential" because, to her, writing is a living, breathing, embodied practice. Her work is grounded in existentialist concepts, interweaving themes of feminism and futility. She is currently writing her first novel. Read more on Lenore's website at lenorerobinson.com.

Allison Rose

Allison Rose is a novelist and screenwriter born and raised in Los Angeles. *Tick*, the first in her young adult science fiction series, tackles mental illness, artistry, and violence — themes close to Allison's heart. It has been followed by *Vice*, part two of the Tick Series, and is based in a versed interpretation of near-future L.A. While Allison's stories vary in genre, her focus centers on the struggles of complex female characters and the deconstruction of clichés and tropes about women. She has used her twenty years of graphic design experience to create her own book covers, including all three volumes of Made In L.A. She is a founding member of Made in L.A. Writers. Read more on Allison's website at thegirlandthebook.com.

Cody Sisco

Cody Sisco is an author of speculative fiction that straddles the divide between plausible and extraordinary. His Resonant Earth Series includes two novels thus far, *Broken Mirror* and *Tortured Echoes*. The third novel in the series, *Altered Bodies*, is forthcoming.

Cody is a 2017 Los Angeles Review of Books / USC Publishing Workshop Fellow, a co-organizer of the Los Angeles Writers Critique Group, and a founding member of Made in L.A. Writers. His startup, BookSwell, connects readers with authors, maintains a literary events calendar, and serves as a community hub for book lovers in L.A. Find out more on Cody's website at codysisco.com.

Roselyn Teukolsky

Born and raised in South Africa, Roselyn Teukolsky traveled to California when she was twenty-two, in a successful quest to nail down her boyfriend, who had escaped to Caltech. He is now her husband. Roselyn taught math and computer science for many years, and is the author of the Barron's review book for AP Computer Science. She also wrote *How to Play Bridge with Your Spouse ... and Survive* (Master Point Press, 2002). Roselyn's latest passion is writing fiction — thrillers about unfortunate protagonists who land in trouble. Her latest novel in progress is *An Unlikely Spy*.

AP Thayer

AP Thayer is a Mexican-American author based out of North Hollywood. He writes grimdark fantasy, latino-futuristic cyberpunk, and cosmic horror. His work has appeared in *Five on the Fifth* literary magazine and the horror anthology *Murder Park After Dark*. He is a member of Speculative Ink, a Los Angeles based writing group, and one of the hosts of The Genre Hustle podcast.

AP had the privilege of growing up in Europe, where Gothic architecture, medieval folklore, and old-world landscapes captured his imagination. At the same time, his mother taught him about his Mexican heritage, sharing stories about her family and fairy tales while teaching him how to cook.

Nowadays, he fills as much of his time as possible with his two passions: writing and cooking.

AS Youngless

AS Youngless is a speculative and fantasy-based fiction writer who lives in sunny Los Angeles with her husband, son, and too many pets to name. She finds inspiration in the people she meets as a yoga teacher and leader of an elementary-aged graphic novel book club.

MADE IN L.A. WRITERS

Made in L.A. Writers is a collaborative of Los Angeles-based authors dedicated to nurturing and promoting indie fiction. While our styles, themes, and story locales differ, our work is both influenced and illuminated by our hometown and underpinned by the extraordinary, multifaceted, and often surreal culture and life in the City of Angels.

As indie authors, we face formidable challenges: fragmented audiences, intense competition in a crowded market, and traditional publishers' deep pockets.

If you enjoyed this book, please leave a review. Rave about us to your friends. Find us online and tell us how our stories made you feel. We're looking for connection; we hope to hear from you.

www.madeinlawriters.com

ACKNOWLEDGMENTS

"Boots" was first published by the literary magazine *Our Day's Encounter* on September 19, 2015.

CPSIA information can be obtained
at www.ICGtesting.com
Printed in the USA
FSHW011710141020
74752FS